P9-CFL-017

HE WANTED TO KISS HER

Jake decided to try it.

When he leaned his head down to her, Eleanor's mouth dropped open. "It's okay," he teased, "I don't bite."

Eleanor scooted back on the seat, away from him. "I don't think we should do this."

Jake followed her. "Do what?"

She looked up again and he took advantage of her open mouth and kissed her. When his lips met hers, sparks shot through his body. She was so soft, so sweet.

She didn't respond immediately, so he increased the pressure slightly, encouraging her to participate with him.

She pulled her mouth away. "Jake . . ."

"Don't talk. Kiss me," he ordered, taking her mouth in his again.

This time she gave. A little. Enough to make him want more. "That's it," he encouraged. "Kiss me."

Eleanor moaned into his mouth and he felt her hands go up to his shoulders, pulling him closer.

"I want you, Eleanor."

She eased her mouth away from his and looked up at him with clear eyes. "I want you, too."

He grinned. "So, what are we going to do about it?"

"Nothing," Eleanor stated simply.

Reviews of Angela Benson's **BANDS OF GOLD**

BANDS OF GOLD is a love story that touches all the hidden corners of the heart. Ms. Benson's unforgettable characters, refreshing sense of humor and unexpected plot twists makes her debut novel a resounding success. Readers won't be able to turn the pages fast enough. Christina's and [Jackson] Duncan's story is one romance readers won't want to miss. Four stars.

—Romantic Times

BANDS OF GOLD is a well-written, fun to read romance novel between two professionals. Christina is a great character and Jackson provides a sensitivity not often seen in a hunk. Angela Benson treats the big woman with a tender understanding. Four and one-half stars.

—Affaire de Coeur

Set in Atlanta and Boston, this intense love story makes the reader laugh, cry and cheer. Written in a beautifully simplistic style, there's nothing simple about **BANDS OF GOLD.** The plot is convoluted, the characters memorable, and the complexities of their relationships thoroughly explored. A multi-cultural romance with universal appeal.

—The Paperback Forum

Ms. Benson makes her debut with a well-written, passionate tale about choices. Secrets untold, a hint of mystery, and the romance of the secondary characters will hook you from the very first page.

—Rendezvous

Angela has woven a story about families, values, and mystery. She brings us a heartwarming story of learning to trust, learning to love, and commitment. Angela has burst onto the publishing world with a wonderful book about accomplished African-American heroes and heroines. You will need the tissues with this read!

—Genie Romance Reviews

Reviews of Angela Benson's **FOR ALL TIME**

Beloved Arabesque author Angela Benson (*Bands Of Gold*) follows up her successful debut with *FOR ALL TIME*. Readers meet Joshua and Gloria Martin, well on their way to achieving the American dream, until Josh suddenly loses his job. While the couple assures each other that it's a temporary setback, time goes on, and the strain of a shattered dream begins to pull at the fabric of their marriage . . . The truly talented Angela Benson deftly illustrates the joys and trials of a couple fighting to remain in love.

—Kensington Publishing

I recommend all women read [**FOR ALL TIME**]; it's more than a romance—it's a story about values and commitment . . . A story magnificently written with style and polish.

—Rendezvous

FOR ALL TIME is a tremendously realistic relationship novel that shows what can happen to a family when a spouse loses his job and [also shows] that trust is as important in a relationship as love . . . Five stars.

—Affaire de Coeur

FOR ALL TIME is a fascinating story of a couple who struggle to keep their marriage together . . . Angela Benson expertly combines a cast of well-drawn characters with a talent for storytelling to give us an emotionally gripping book . . .

—Genie Romance Reviews

FOR ALL TIME will touch every woman's heart with its pathos and passion as Ms. Benson takes a heart-rending look at the stark realities of marriage after the honeymoon is over. It's one of the best romances of the season . . . Four stars.

—Romantic Times

Most readers will be able to identify with one of the characters/situations . . . with **FOR ALL TIME,** Angela Benson has proven that she has a voice to be heard in the African-American romance genre.

—Storyline Treasures

Ms. Benson is a quality author of genuine relationship tales . . . **FOR ALL TIME** is a book for all seasons as it brilliantly portrays the plight of a job loss on a middle-class family. The characters are real and allow the audience entry into their mind, soul and angst.

—The Paperback Forum

A good story . . .

—The Atlanta Journal-Constitution

ROMANCES ABOUT AFRICAN-AMERICANS!
YOU'LL FALL IN LOVE
WITH ARABESQUE BOOKS FROM PINNACLE

SERENADE   (0024, $4.99)
by Sandra Kitt
Alexandra Morrow was too young and naive when she first
fell in love with musician, Parker Harrison—and vowed
never to be so vulnerable again. Now Parker is back and
although she tries to resist him, he strolls back into her life
as smoothly as the jazz rhapsodies for which he is known.
Though not the dreamy innocent she was before, Alexandra finds her defenses quickly crumbling and her mind,
body and soul slowly opening up to her one and only love,
who shows her that dreams do come true.

FOREVER YOURS   (0025, $4.99)
by Francis Ray
Victoria Chandler must find a husband quickly or her
grandparents will call in the loans that support her chain
of lingerie boutiques. She arranges a mock marriage to
tall, dark and handsome ranch owner Kane Taggart. The
marriage will only last one year, and her business will be
secure, and Kane will be able to walk away with no strings
attached. The only problem is that Kane has other plans
for Victoria. He'll cast a spell that will make her his forever
after.

A SWEET REFRAIN   (0041, $4.99)
by Margie Walker
Fifteen years before, jazz musician Nathaniel Padell walked
out on Jenine to seek fame and fortune in New York City.
But now the handsome widower is back with a baby girl in
tow. Jenine is still irresistibly attracted to Nat and enchanted
by his daughter. Yet even as love is rekindled, an unexpected
danger threatens Nat's child. Now, Jenine must fight for Nat
before someone stops the music forever!

*Available wherever paperbacks are sold, or order direct from the
Publisher. Send cover price plus 50¢ per copy for mailing and
handling to Penguin USA, P.O. Box 999, c/o Dept. 17109,
Bergenfield, NJ 07621. Residents of New York and Tennessee
must include sales tax. DO NOT SEND CASH.*

Between The Lines

Angela Benson

PINNACLE BOOKS
KENSINGTON PUBLISHING CORP.

PINNACLE BOOKS are published by

Kensington Publishing Corp.
850 Third Avenue
New York, NY 10022

Copyright © 1996 by Angela D. Benson

All rights reserved. No part of this book may be reproduced
in any form or by any means without the prior written consent
of the Publisher, excepting brief quotes used in reviews.

If you purchased this book without a cover, you should be
aware that this book is stolen property. It was reported as "un-
sold and destroyed" to the Publisher and neither the Author
nor the Publisher has received any payment for this "stripped
book."

The Arabesque logo Reg. U.S. Pat. & TM Off. Arabesque is
a trademark of Kensington Publishing Corp.

First Printing: May, 1996

Printed in the United States of America
10 9 8 7 6 5 4 3 2 1

Acknowledgments

Special thanks to Tom Kerlin and Marie Hardin at the *Clayton News/Daily* in Jonesboro, Georgia, and Bill White at the *Opelika-Auburn Daily News* in Opelika, Alabama, for teaching me everything I know about the newspaper publishing business. I couldn't have written this book without you.

Prologue

"Reconsidering our plan?" Mathias Sanders asked his lifelong friend Randolph Mason. The fifty-five-year-old men had lost track of each other after high school, but they'd found each other twenty years later at a publishing convention. By then, Mathias had moved to Lamar, Alabama, a small town about two hours from Atlanta and owned the *Lamar Weekly News,* while Randolph had been on his way to becoming the chairman and CEO of New York-based Mason Publishing, now the largest black-owned publishing company in the country. The cement of their renewed friendship was common tragedy. Randolph and his then fifteen-year-old son, Jake, had been alone since his wife, Tammy, had succumbed to cancer some seven years earlier. Mathias and his then eleven-year-old daughter, Eleanor, had lost their Barbara suddenly to an aneurysm less than a year before.

"Not really," Randolph said, studying a recent photo of twenty-eight-year-old Eleanor. With her hair pulled back in a stern bun and her blouse buttoned to her neck, the girl defined "prim miss." But the expressive, brown eyes set in her beautiful mocha-complexioned face hinted at passion. "We aren't forcing them to do anything, Mat. We're only providing them an opportunity."

Mathias lifted a finger for the bartender to bring him another drink. "An opportunity," he repeated, then looked at Jake's photo on the bar next to Eleanor's. Thirty-two-year-old Jake had his father's strong chin, his big, alert, brown eyes, and his coarse, jet black hair. And from the stories Randolph had told over the years, Mathias knew Jake also had his father's integrity and strength. "Somehow I don't think that's how they're going to view it when they find out."

Randolph popped a couple of peanuts into his mouth. "*If*, my friend, *if* they find out. Let's think positively here."

Mathias raised his glass and took a swallow of his tonic water. He didn't drink alcohol. He never had. "Okay, I'm thinking positively. Eleanor *is* going to kill me *if* she finds out what I've done."

"You haven't *done* anything, Mat. And all we're planning is a business deal."

Mathias gave a "humph." "Yeah, business *and* personal."

Randolph ran a strong, lean finger around the top of the bowl of peanuts. He and Mathias had often discussed bringing their children together, but they hadn't thought they would be interested in each other. Until now. "We have to do this, Mat. For their sake as much as ours."

One

Jake Mason rocked his right leg from side to side impatiently as he sat in the expansive living room of the Sanders home wondering how he had allowed his father to convince him to come to Lamar, Alabama, of all places. He'd seen enough of Lamar already to know there was a good chance he'd die of boredom before the three months he'd given himself to do this job were up.

He checked his Cartier watch for the fifth time. Four-thirty. Mr. Sanders was supposed to meet him at four. Where was he? Was punctuality something small-towners lacked? Jake hoped not, because he knew his eyes would be on the clock for the entire time he was here.

Jake stood, pushed his hands into the pockets of his suit pants, and began to pace. The cluster of picture frames atop the baby grand piano in the corner of the room near a set of French doors caught his attention. He strode over to the piano and scanned the photos. Most of them were of Sanders's daughter, Eleanor. Jake knew this because Mr. Sanders had given Randolph many of these same photos.

He took his hands out of his pockets and picked up the frame holding what he thought was Eleanor's most recent photograph. The bun that was apparently her favorite hairstyle made her face look stern and older than her years. But it was the buttoned-up blouse with the collar tight around her neck that made her look mousy. All she needed were the stereotypical wire-rimmed glasses. Jake placed the picture back on the piano, grateful that Eleanor held no appeal for him. A romantic entanglement with Sanders's daughter was the last thing he needed.

The sound of splashing water caused Jake to look toward the French doors. A pool, he thought. So small-towners *did* believe in swimming. Thank God for that. He could use a swim now himself. It was hot in Alabama in the summertime.

He walked to the French doors and peeked through the white lace curtains. There was a pool, all right. An Olympic-size in-ground pool that made his mouth water.

The splashing continued but Jake didn't see anyone. He opened the door and started in the direction of the sound. Maybe Mr. Sanders had gotten so engrossed in swimming that he'd forgotten their meeting. Jake could understand that.

By the time Jake reached the pool, the splashing had stopped and a figure that he immediately knew wasn't Mr. Sanders stood drying her legs with a fluffy white towel. Damn, what a pair of buns on that honey, he thought. She stood bent over from the waist with her back, rather her buns, to him, all chocolate and glistening from the water.

Jake's eyes traveled her body, starting with the full hips covered with a thin strip of white cloth that gave new meaning to the word *thong*. He'd heard of thong bikinis, hell, he'd seem them, but this honey wore a one-piece suit in white that had less material than a lot of jockstraps he'd seen. His eyes continued their trip down her long legs and he couldn't help but wonder how it would feel to have those legs wrapped around him. His lips curved in a smile. Maybe Lamar, Alabama, wouldn't be so bad after all.

If Jake could have formed a rational thought, he would have made his presence known with an introduction, but he couldn't so he continued watching the beauty. When she stood to her full height, he was surprised that she wasn't very tall, five-four at most. With those Tina Turner legs, he wouldn't have been surprised if she'd been six feet tall.

Turn around, honey, he pleaded silently. He had to see her face. Everything else was exactly as he liked it. Though he didn't consider himself a hair man, there was something about the wet mane plastered against her shoulders that made him want to shout.

Turn around, he pleaded again. He felt his breathing quicken when she started walking away from him. He opened his mouth to call after her but he heard someone call his name. He closed his mouth and squeezed his eyes shut. *Damn Mr. Sanders's timing.*

Jake made his way back through the French doors, dismayed he'd missed meeting what was probably the most exciting woman in this one-horse town.

"Jake, my boy," Mr. Sanders began. He walked over and grabbed Jake's hand, pumping it for a few seconds before saying, "Damn," and pulling Jake into his arms for a bearhug.

"I can't believe this is our first meeting," Mr. Sanders continued. "I feel like I've known you forever."

Jake couldn't help but smile at the greeting. The older man's enthusiasm was contagious. "I feel the same way, Mr. Sanders. Dad has talked so much about you and your daughter that I feel I know you, too."

Mr. Sanders smiled and Jake knew then that the fifty-five-year-old man had probably been hell with the women in his younger days. Jake knew all too well how women responded to the sincere smile of a good-looking man, and he had no doubt Mr. Sanders had been an attractive young man. He still was. He was tall, Jake's height, about six feet. He had the same salt-and-pepper hair Randolph sported and the same muscular build, but there the similarities ended. There was an openness in Mathias Sanders's face that Jake had never seen in his father's.

"Have a seat, my boy," Mr. Sanders said as he walked to the eight-foot upholstered couch that stretched in front of the idle brick fireplace. "How do you like our town so far?"

Jake's thoughts went immediately to the woman who had been in the pool. He liked *her,* but he couldn't tell Mr. Sanders that. "It's certainly *not* New York."

Mathias Sanders laughed, a rich full laugh that caused the wrinkles around his eyes and mouth to become more pronounced. "You're right about that, but give us a chance. Lamar is not such a bad place."

It didn't really matter to Jake if Lamar was a bad place or not. This assignment was exactly what he needed to prove his capabilities to his father and to himself. And he was going to do it. Big Time. And his father would be so impressed, he'd beg Jake to take a lead role in Mason Publishing.

Jake only wanted to do the job he'd been assigned and get out of this town and on with his life. He also wanted to find out who the woman was at the pool, but he didn't have the nerve to ask. "About the paper, Mr. Sanders—" Jake began, but Mathias interrupted him.

"Not tonight, Jake. Tonight is family time. We'll have plenty of time to do business later. Now tell me some more about yourself and what you've been doing. Maybe you can add to what your father has already told me."

Jake settled back against the pillows on the sofa, giving up on his plans for a business discussion tonight. He told Mr. Sanders about his recent trip to Asia, leaving out most of the exciting things he'd done and the exotic women he'd met.

"You're a lucky young man, Jake. You should be glad your father encouraged your travels. A man needs broad horizons. So does a woman. I wish I could get my Eleanor to see that." Mathias laughed, but this time the wrinkles around his eyes didn't get involved.

Eleanor. How quickly Jake had forgotten about her, while thoughts of the beauty by the pool refused to leave his mind. "Eleanor doesn't like to travel?"

Mr. Sanders shook his head. "I sent her off to

college in Georgia, but she came right back home. Never wanted to go anywhere."

Jake detected a bit of sorrow in Mr. Sanders's voice and he wondered what caused it. "Like they say, different strokes for different folks."

Mr. Sanders laughed as Jake had hoped he would. "Maybe you're right, Jake. Eleanor is different, all right."

Jake agreed with him, but he had a feeling it would be rude to say so.

"Have you seen her around here?"

Jake shook his head and his thoughts returned to the beauty by the pool. That certainly hadn't been Eleanor. There was no comparison between the beauty and the mousy-looking woman in the photographs. Maybe the beauty was her best friend. Some beautiful women surrounded themselves with less attractive friends to make themselves look better. He hoped the beauty he'd seen wasn't that shallow. Not that it would matter to him if she was. He was only here for three months and she could make the three months seem a lot shorter if—

"Don't you think so, Jake?" Mr. Sanders was saying.

Jake shifted his attention to Mr. Sanders and nodded. He didn't have any idea what the older man was talking about.

Eleanor wanted to scream. She should have said something, but she'd been too mortified to do much more than slink back to her cottage beyond the pool.

The nerve of that man. Just who the hell did Jake Mason think he was? Oh yes, she knew who he was.

Even though she'd only gotten a quick glimpse of
him as she'd toweled her legs, his face burned itself
on the pages of her mind. How could she forget it?
The man looked better in person than he had in
the photos her father had shown her, and she hadn't
even thought that was possible.

Jake Mason was one fine brother. Too fine, if you
asked her. His tailored suit only enhanced his broad
shoulders and slim hips. She could tell that much
even though he'd been over a pool's length away
from her. And that leer that masked itself as a smile
across his mahogany-colored face was enough to
make lesser women weak in the knees. It wasn't fair
that a man could be so attractive.

And he had to know it. It took a man very secure
in his looks to stare at a woman the way Jake had
stared at her. Either that or he was crazy. And she
didn't think Jake Mason was crazy. No, Jake Mason
was used to staring at women, and unless she was
way off base, she was sure women usually returned
his stare with one suitably welcoming.

Well, she wasn't one of those bimbos and she
wasn't going to act like one of them. She was a
woman. A liberated woman. And she hadn't appreciated Jake's appraisal. She wasn't a piece of meat to
be ogled at by some man like a dog would ogle a
juicy bone. The man had been practically smacking
his lips as he'd stared at her upturned bottom. She
could have died when she'd looked through her legs
and glimpsed him staring at her. If wishes came true,
the ground would have opened up and swallowed
her right there. Better yet, it would have opened up
and swallowed Jake.

She tightened the towel she had wrapped around herself and quickened her steps. She needed the security and safety of her home now. Knowing she was fully out of his sight, she broke into a run for the last fifty feet to her door.

She dropped the towel on the hardwood floor of her living room as soon as she entered the front door. By the time she reached the marble tile of her bathroom, she'd discarded the suit as well. She turned on the water in the shower, adjusted the shower head, and stepped in. Leaning back against the tiled walls, she let the water massage her body. The soothing warmth was a welcome balm to her muscles, but it did nothing for her attitude. No, it'd take more than warm water to restore her good spirits. Nothing short of getting Jake Mason out of Lamar would do that.

Fifteen minutes later, Eleanor stepped out of the shower refreshed, but still peeved. She toweled off with another of the fluffy white towels she'd bought in nearby Welles, loving the sensuous feel of the soft cloth against her naked skin.

Dry, Eleanor tossed the towel aside and reached for the perfumed lotion she always used. After seating herself at the bathroom vanity, she massaged the lotion into her skin. The soothing sensation felt sinfully good.

Finished, she got up and reached for the robe she kept hanging on the bathroom door. She removed it from its hook, but she didn't put it on. Rather she walked from the bathroom to her bedroom and threw the robe across the treadmill that held most of the clothes she had *not* worn that week.

Eleanor loved being naked. She often thought

that if it wouldn't kill her father, she'd join a nudist colony. Since she knew that act would indeed kill him, her only alternative was to turn her home into a mini-nudist camp. It was why she kept her blinds closed and her drapes drawn at all times.

Thoughts of Jake Mason entered her mind again. She was tempted to call Carl Winters, her childhood friend and the paper's top investigative reporter, and ask if he'd gotten the results from the background search she'd ordered on Jake Mason, Randolph Mason, and Mason Publishing, but she didn't do it. She knew Carl would probably hang up on her anyway. She'd been bugging him about results since she'd given him the assignment a couple of days ago. The last time she'd spoken with him, he'd told her not to call him again.

Who was Carl to tell her when to call? she asked herself. She was paying for his services. She could do whatever she wanted. She reached for the phone on her black lacquer nightstand. It rang before she could pick it up.

"Hello," she said, hoping the call was from Carl.

"Hey, girl," her friend Megan began. "Do you want to go over to Welles tonight? Victoria's Secret is having a sale."

Eleanor sighed, glad to hear from her friend, but disappointed the call wasn't from Carl. She really needed the information on Jake. She'd hoped to act on it at dinner that night. "I can't tonight. I'm having dinner with Dad and a business associate."

"That fine brother you've been talking about?" Megan asked. Eleanor found the enthusiasm in her friend's voice disgusting. "How about I come over and have dinner with ya'll?"

Eleanor rolled her eyes. Sometimes it amazed her that Megan was her best friend. "Not tonight. Tonight's all business."

"But I want to meet him."

Eleanor flinched at the whine in her friend's voice. She and Megan were both only children, but she hoped her own behavior wasn't as spoiled as Megan's. "You'll get to meet him. I promise. But not tonight."

"Are you interested in him? Is that why you don't want me to meet him? I thought you said you weren't interested in him."

Goodness, Eleanor thought, how had she allowed herself to get into a discussion about men with Megan on a night when she didn't have four hours to waste? "I'm not interested in him, Megan. We're discussing business tonight. I don't think this is the right time for you to make your move."

The silence made Eleanor think Megan was considering the truth in those words.

"When will you introduce us? You know there aren't many good men here in Lamar. If you're not interested, then I definitely am."

Eleanor glanced at the nightstand, at the miniature grandfather clock that had been her mother's. "It's getting late, Megan. If I don't hang up, I'm going to be late for dinner."

"Well, you tell that brother about me now. I want his appetite whetted before he meets me."

Eleanor rolled her eyes again. When Megan was between men, which she always was, she got a bit

desperate. She'd been that way since she and her
mother had moved to Lamar and the two girls had
become fast friends. The other eighth-grade kids
had called them "the odd couple" and the name
had stuck. The beautiful Megan and the smart
Eleanor. Nobody could figure out what they had in
common, but everybody knew they were best
friends. An odd couple, but an inseparable one.
"I've gotta go, Megan. Let's go shopping tomorrow.
I'll tell you all about Jake then."

That seemed to appease Megan because she hung
up without much protest. Eleanor jumped up and
went into her closet to find something suitable to
wear. Since she'd already given Mr. Mason an eyeful,
she wanted to be sure her dress for dinner bespoke
of the woman she truly was.

She settled on a navy Carole Little suit and a bone
blouse with a baby doll collar. The ensemble would
cover her from neck to mid-calf, revealing nothing
of her shape and in no way hinting at the navy
French-cut silk panties and matching lace bra she'd
have on underneath. Satisfied she'd picked the perfect outfit, she strode to the kitchen for a bite to eat
before dinner. When she arrived at her father's
house tonight, she didn't want hunger to distract
her. Her task tonight was to grill Mr. Mason and find
out the *real* reason for his and his father's sudden
interest in the *Lamar Daily News*.

Jake placed the last of his underwear in the chest
in the Sanders guest room, still amazed at how
quickly Mathias, as he had instructed Jake to call

him, had convinced him to move into his home though Jake had been determined to stay in a hotel or find a rental unit. Mathias was almost as bad as Jake's father. Neither man understood the meaning of "no" and both pushed until they got their way.

"A young man should enjoy himself, see the world, experience life," his father had told the young adult Jake when he'd expressed an interest in working for Mason Publishing. "You don't have to work, Jake."

Jake had tried to explain that he knew he didn't *have* to work; he *wanted* to. But Randolph hadn't listened. And over the years Jake had found it easier to go along with his father's wishes. He'd learned early that a man with money could always find things to do with his time—and his money.

Over the years Jake had engaged in one venture after another, and though he'd made a great deal of money, he'd never found his niche, a spot where he could stay and flourish. Sometimes he blamed his father for his rolling-stone-like relationship with work. But he knew much of the responsibility lay squarely at his feet. He could have dug in his heels at any time, but he hadn't.

He shook his head, forcing the negative thoughts away. He'd been surprised and honored when his father had asked him to work this deal with the *Lamar Daily*. Not because it was a big deal, but because this was the first time his father had *asked* for his help. He'd work this deal, all right. He'd come up with a proposal so fantastic his father would regret waiting so long to give Jake a place in the family business. Yes, with this deal Jake would prove to himself and his father how capable he really was.

Jake turned back the homemade quilt on the generations-old four-poster bed and stretched out to pass the time until dinner. He hadn't planned to live in the Sanders home, but it appeared that was exactly what he was going to do. The room, furnished with a desk, nightstand, and armoire, or chifferobe, as Mathias had called it, that matched the bed and chest, was comfortable, which was all Jake needed.

Well, he also needed privacy, but maybe that could be arranged. He wouldn't even consider bringing a woman to the Sanders home. Hopefully, the beauty at the pool had her own place with enough privacy for their pursuits. He still didn't have any idea who she was, but he guessed she was one of Eleanor's friends. Hopefully, he could get Eleanor to introduce him.

Eleanor entered the patio doors of her father's house promptly at six. Though she would deny it, she was anxious about meeting Jake. She wondered what he would think of her appearance tonight. Well, it really didn't matter as long as he realized that the Eleanor he was going to do business with was this Eleanor and not the Eleanor he'd seen by the pool.

"Eleanor, you're finally here," her father said when he walked into the living room with Jake trailing behind him.

"You make it sound like I'm late, Dad. It's only

six," she answered her father and smiled in Jake's direction. Her eyes drank in the sight he made in the tan Armani suit that molded to his form like a woman to her lover. Casting those thoughts aside, she extended her hand. "Welcome to Lamar, Mr. Mason."

She noticed the twinkle in Jake's eyes. Was he thinking about their earlier meeting? Or did he know where her thoughts had been? She sincerely hoped not.

"Mr. Mason's my father, I'm Jake," he said in a deep baritone voice flavored with a hint of New York accent. He took her hand in both of his and squeezed it softly before letting it go.

Eleanor felt the tingle from her hand up her arm and down her body all the way to the toes of both her feet. Heavens, she had to get control of herself. It was just as she'd figured. Jake Mason was a womanizer. He probably expected her to swoon at his feet. She flashed what she hoped was a haughty smile that only partially turned up the corners of her mouth. "Jake it is then."

Mathias clapped Jake on the back and said to him and Eleanor, "Why don't we have a before-dinner drink?"

While Mathias prepared their drinks, Eleanor and Jake seated themselves. Unfortunately for Eleanor, she and Jake both chose the couch. She wondered if he did it on purpose. Did he know how flustered he made her? Was he thinking about their earlier meeting?

"So you're interested in our paper, Jake. For the

life of me, I don't see what Mason Publishing wants with a small-town paper like ours."

Jake allowed his gaze to travel from the bun atop her head, to the string of pearls that lay around the prim collar of her blouse, to the navy pumps on her feet before focusing on the lipstick-less lips that had mouthed the accusation. And it had been an accusation. He was sure of it. "I asked my father the same thing, Eleanor. His interest surprised me as well."

Eleanor bristled. It was one thing for her to wonder about Jake's intentions for her paper, it was a whole other thing for him to suggest that the *Lamar Daily* wasn't worth his time. She leaned toward him and spoke softly, but clearly. "Well, I know you don't see it and that's why I want you to know right up front that I'm going to fight you all the way on this. Your dad may have used his friendship with my father to persuade him that this was a good deal for us, but I don't believe it for a minute."

Mathias brought their drinks before Jake could comment, which was probably good since Jake hadn't formed a comment. Well, he mused, it seemed there was more to Little Eleanor than he'd first thought. She might dress like a mouse, but she definitely had a mouth on her.

"Are you two getting to know each other?" Mathias asked with obvious hope that they were.

The saccharine-filled smile that Eleanor gave her father almost made Jake laugh.

"Of course, Dad. I think Jake and I are coming to an understanding. Aren't we, Jake?"

Jake took a swallow of his drink, which turned out

to be sparkling water, before answering. When he did, he spoke to Mathias. "Eleanor was telling me what to expect during my stay here in Lamar."

Mathias took a seat in the wing chair next to the couch. "I'm sure Eleanor will help you get settled. Even though you won't be here very long, we'll make you as comfortable and as welcome as we know how. Won't we, Eleanor?"

Eleanor lifted her glass to her lips and gave her smile again. "He can count on it, Dad."

Jake coughed to cover up the laughter that bubbled up in his throat.

"I was thinking that maybe we could have a party to introduce Jake around."

Eleanor coughed then and Jake knew she was choking on the idea of giving a party for him. "Now, Dad, maybe Jake's not interested in that. He'll probably be going home every weekend anyway."

Jake smiled what he hoped was a good imitation of Eleanor's fake smile. "On the contrary, I'm here for the duration." Her eyes widened and he added, "At least until our business transaction is complete. Your dad has even offered me his guest room. It seems I'm going to be a member of the family."

Two

Jake watched the corners of Eleanor's lips droop and that fake smile slip from her face. She was good, though. She recovered so quickly that if she hadn't already made her feelings clear, he'd question whether he'd really seen the change in her expression.

She smiled in the direction of her father, then said to Jake, "He forced you, didn't he?" Before Jake could answer, she turned to her father. "Dad, I'm sure Jake was only being nice. I'll help him look for a place tomorrow."

"No, you won't, Eleanor," Mathias said. "Jake is staying here and that's that. I won't hear of my best friend's son staying in some run-down apartment."

Eleanor placed her glass on the cocktail table in front of her. "The Ferguson house is empty. I'll see about renting that for Jake."

Mathias shook his head. "That doesn't make sense. Jake can stay here. Besides, I get lonely in this big house all by myself."

Jake saw Eleanor roll her eyes toward the ceiling. He wanted to laugh. He had the feeling Mathias often used his "loneliness" as a ploy to get his way.

"Right, Dad, but let's think about Jake."

Jake watched the conversation ping-pong between Eleanor and her father. It irritated him that they were discussing him as if he weren't present. Even though he agreed with Eleanor that he'd much prefer to stay somewhere else, for some perverse reason, he couldn't let her have her way. "I kind of like the idea of living near someone I know," he offered. "And since I know only you and Mathias, I think here is great." He took a long swallow of his drink. "Unless you know of a place near where you live?"

Eleanor shot him a look that said she knew he was toying with her. He acknowledged her with a smile.

"Well," Mathias began, "you get to live near both of us. Eleanor lives in the cottage out beyond the pool."

Jake couldn't let the opening pass. He glanced over at Eleanor. "Still living at home," he said, then shrugged his shoulders in disdain. "I guess it's cheaper." He delighted at the ire that flashed in her big, brown eyes, knowing his tone left no doubt to what his real thoughts were about a twenty-eight-year-old woman still living at home.

"It's not the money," Mathias said. "It's the pool."

Jake pulled his eyes from Eleanor's pinched face and looked at Mathias. Thoughts of the pool brought thoughts of the beauty he'd seen. He wasn't too sure now that Eleanor would introduce him to her friend. He might have to fend for himself. "So, she's a swimmer?"

Mathias gave a "humph." "More like a fish. She and Megan make sure that pool gets more than enough use."

Megan. That must have been who she was. "That must have been Megan I saw in the pool when I arrived earlier."

The sound of Eleanor's choking brought Jake's eyes back to her.

"What's wrong with you, Eleanor?" Mathias asked, leaning toward her.

She patted her hand against her chest and shook her head. "I'm fine, Dad, something went down the wrong way."

Mathias looked at her for a few long seconds as if he wasn't sure he could believe her. Jake saw his concern and felt a bit envious of the relationship between this father and daughter.

"All right, then," Mathias said, "but be careful. Why are you drinking so fast anyway?"

Eleanor's eyes widened at her father's question and she glared in Jake's direction. He knew she would give her dad an earful because of that comment. He also knew she'd wait until he was gone.

"So," Jake asked Eleanor, "was that your friend Megan I saw earlier in the pool?"

"Right, Jake." Eleanor thought he was being sarcastic.

"Maybe you could introduce us sometime."

She studied his face. Was this man kidding or did he really not know that she was the woman at the pool? "You're serious, aren't you?"

The question in his eyes was immediate.

Eleanor felt as though she'd been punched in the stomach. He really didn't recognize her. And after the way he'd stared at her. Lusted after her. He didn't even know who she was. The cad didn't even recognize her. Though she hated to admit it, she was hurt.

"Megan was here today?" Mathias asked. "Why didn't you invite her to dinner?"

Eleanor slowly moved her head from side to side. By the way her father was carrying on, you'd think Jake was a visiting relative instead of a business associate planning to gobble up their newspaper. Where was the man's head these days? "I didn't think it was appropriate to invite Megan to a business dinner, Dad." There was no mistaking the censure in her voice.

Mathias stood and pointed at the two younger people as if they were disobedient children. "You two are too much alike. All you think about is business. Well, this is more than business and you had better face it. Randolph and I have been friends for years and no business deal is going to stop that. Now come on, let's eat dinner."

It was the longest dinner Eleanor had ever endured. And the most infuriating. Her father obviously thought Jake's presence ranked right up there with the Second Coming. He hung on to every word the man said. And Jake Mason said a lot. About nothing. The amount she'd learned about Mason Publishing's intents for their paper could be held in a thimble. The man was closemouthed. Yes, closemouthed and smart. He was weaseling himself into her father's confidence just as his father, Randolph, had done. Her father was being set up like the fatted calf. She had to help him because he was too blinded by the Mason men to even know he needed help. She shook her head in dismay.

"Something wrong, Eleanor?" Jake asked.

Eleanor directed her gaze to him. Had he been watching her? Had he finally realized she was the woman in the pool? She flashed him a smile. "No, everything's great, Jake. Just great."

Jake sat back in his chair. He'd actually enjoyed the dinner and he'd had to refine his opinion of Miss Eleanor. Although she was a bit homely, she did have spirit. And he liked that. He liked her. And he liked baiting her.

"So when do you think we should have the party, Eleanor?" Mathias asked. "We want Jake to feel welcome."

Eleanor cut a glare in Jake's direction, before turning to her father. "I don't know, Dad. We're going to be awfully busy."

Mathias waved his hands in dismissal. "You're always busy. What about Megan? She could plan it for you, couldn't she?"

Eleanor knew Megan would love that. "What about Ms. Delaney? She could do it."

Mathias shook his head at her reference to his one-day-a-week housekeeper. "No, Megan is the right person. I still can't believe you didn't invite her to dinner."

Eleanor didn't want to get back on that again. "Okay, Dad," she said, "I'll ask her." She looked at Jake. "She wants to meet you anyway."

"She wants to meet me? Why?"

Eleanor looked away from him and played with the dessert pudding Ms. Delaney had prepared.

Never would she tell him she'd showed Megan his picture. The man was conceited enough as it was. "Well, Dad talks about you all the time." When she saw the smug, masculine, too-good-looking-for-words expression cross his face, she couldn't help but add, "Megan doesn't think anybody could be all that Dad has made you out to be."

"Eleanor," Mathias warned. "What's wrong with you tonight? Jake's our guest."

Jake laughed. "That's all right, Mathias," Jake said. "I'm beginning to think of Eleanor as the bratty little sister I never had."

Eleanor opened her mouth for a retort, but nothing came out.

Mathias stared at Eleanor and chuckled. "You've done the impossible, Jake. You've made Eleanor speechless."

Eleanor slammed the door to her cottage and kicked off her shoes. Jake Mason, hah. The man was a joke. A *big* joke. She just hoped the last laugh wasn't on her and her father. She slipped off her jacket, blouse, and skirt and threw them on the floor with the clothes she had pulled off earlier in the day, then trekked to her kitchen for a drink. Something strong. She pulled out a two-liter bottle of RC Cola and lifted it to her lips, welcoming the burning sensation in her throat. She took only a few swallows before dropping the bottle from her lips. "Oooh, that was so good," she said aloud, then placed the bottle back in the refrigerator and trooped to her bedroom.

She pulled off her bra and panties, hung them on the treadmill, then plopped down on the side of her bed and picked up the phone. Her eyes caught the time on the clock. Eleven-thirty. My how time flies when you're having fun, she thought dryly. She pushed aside any consideration for the time and punched in the seven numbers.

"Hello," Carl answered. She was glad he didn't sound as though he'd been asleep.

"Hi, Carl," she said, "this is Eleanor."

"I know who it is, Eleanor. The question is do you know what time it is?"

Eleanor turned away from the clock, propped her feet up on the bed and leaned back against the headboard. "It's time you gave me some information on Jake Mason and Mason Publishing, that's what time it is."

Eleanor held her breath. She didn't think she could stand it if Carl told her to call back in the morning. When he released a resigned sigh, she knew she'd hit paydirt.

"The report'll be on your desk in the morning. Can't you wait until then?"

Eleanor didn't answer and Carl didn't repeat his question. Eleanor knew the loser would speak first.

"Okay, Eleanor, what do you want to know?"

She smiled. "Everything. Start at the beginning and tell me all."

Carl told her about the beginnings of Mason Publishing, the company started by Randolph Mason and his wife, Tammy. He told her about their happy marriage, the birth of their son, and the struggle they had had to start their business. When he told

her how Tammy Mason had died of cancer the year
Jake Mason was eight years old, tears formed in her
eyes.

Tears for the little boy Jake who'd lost his mother
and tears for herself and the mother she'd lost. The
tears streamed down her cheeks and fell on her naked breasts as Carl told the story of a driven Randolph Mason, a man determined to make something
of his life for himself and his son. The tears began
to dry as Carl told her about the ruthless takeovers
Randolph Mason had executed during his tenure as
CEO of Mason Publishing. The man didn't seem to
have a heart, at least not when it came to business.

"What about the son? What about Jake? What's
he been doing?" She wished for the hundredth time
this week she'd paid more attention to her father's
news of Jake over the years. But no, she'd been too
focused on his good looks and her silly dreams and
fantasies of a knight in shining armor to remember
a word her father had said.

"Your typical rich man's son. Travels. Dibbles and
dabbles in various business concerns. He must have
the golden touch, because he's made a good
amount of money without very much effort."

Eleanor pondered that information. Not that it
surprised her. Jake had the typical Playboy profile—
good looks, lots of money, and plenty of time. "Why
did his father send him here?" she asked aloud,
though the question was really to herself.

"That, I don't know," Carl answered. "This is the
first project Jake has done for Mason Publishing.
Maybe his father thought it was time he assumed
some responsibility in the family business."

Eleanor wiggled her toes and stood up to stretch, the phone cradled between her ear and her naked shoulder. "Has he had any experience at all in the publishing industry?"

Eleanor imagined Carl tapping his pencil to his forehead in impatience. "Nothing formal. Though I doubt he could be Randolph Mason's son and not know something about the business."

"I'm not too sure about that. What did he study in college?"

Carl was quiet.

"He did go to college, didn't he?"

"He went," Carl answered.

Eleanor knew he was holding back some information and she wondered why. "What is it, Carl? I know there's more."

"He graduated from Yale."

Yale. She was impressed. "What was his major?"

"Drama."

Eleanor howled. Drama. So, Jake Mason had entertained thoughts of becoming an actor. Must have been his good looks. And he must have found out looks weren't enough.

"Did he ever do any acting?"

"Not professionally. It seems his real interest was his track career."

"He ran track?"

"Almost made the Olympic team. He was good."

"I bet," Eleanor said. He probably had lots of practice running from one woman to another.

Eleanor asked Carl a few more questions before ending the conversation. She could hardly wait to read his report in the morning. After she hung up, she pirouetted around the room. So, Jake Mason was a would-be actor and athlete. She laughed out loud at the thought. She knew now he'd never take her newspaper. He wasn't even in her league.

Mathias opened the door to his den, looking over his shoulder as he did so. He didn't see anyone, so he rushed into the room, quickly closed the door, and practically ran to his desk. After he sat down, he pulled off his glasses and wiped his eyes with his forefinger and thumb, grateful he'd made it through tonight's dinner. Once again he wondered if he and Randolph were doing the right thing. He picked up the phone and punched in Randolph's New York number.

"I've been waiting for your call," Randolph said when he answered after the first ring. "How'd it go?"

"I'm not too sure, Randy," Mathias began. "Eleanor didn't seem to like Jake much. She was downright mean to him during dinner. Not like herself at all."

Randolph leaned back in his chair. He was pleased. Of course Eleanor resented Jake's presence and what he was trying to do. He wondered why Mathias didn't understand that. But then he knew why. Mathias still saw Eleanor as his little girl, not as a woman. He suspected that was the reason for Eleanor's conservative nature. But Randolph had a gut feeling that below that conservative exterior was a woman who could warm his son's heart and his bed. She couldn't be Barbara and Mathias's daughter without inheriting some of their passion. Randolph and Mathias had shared enough over the years for Randolph to know that Mathias and Barbara had shared a loving and passionate union that rivaled his marriage with Tammy. In his opinion, a man couldn't ask for more. "How did Jake respond to her?"

Mathias liked Jake. Had liked him before he met him, and meeting him had only confirmed his feelings. Jake was a good man. Good enough for his Eleanor. But not if Eleanor didn't want him. "You've got a great boy there, Randy. I guess I would say he tolerated Eleanor."

"Tolerated her? What exactly did the boy do?"

Mathias gave a half-smile at Randy's reference to his son as a boy. He knew that was exactly how Randolph saw Jake. As a little boy. A little boy who needed his father's direction and guidance. But the Jake that Mathias had met wasn't a little boy. He was a man.

Mathias wondered again how different the boy would have been had someone other than Randolph been his father. Not that Randolph hadn't done the best he could. Mathias knew he had. But Randolph was such a strong man. Maybe too strong for a son who loved him as much as Mathias was sure Jake loved him.

"I mean Jake handled himself well. He didn't let Eleanor put him on the defensive." Mathias sighed. "And she was trying to put him on the defensive. No doubt about it."

She's exactly what Jake needs, Randolph thought. Someone to push him and make him stand up for

what he believes in. That and someone to love him
as his mother had loved Randolph. Randolph firmly
believed that the love of a good woman made a difference in a man. Made a man a man. He knew
that's what loving Tammy had done for him. And
he wanted that for his son. "Well, keep me posted.
Are your plans all set for tomorrow?"

Mathias and Randolph went over their plans one
by one, making sure they hadn't missed anything.
When they were finished, Mathias hung up and sat
in his den for a long while wondering over the rightness of what they were doing. When he started getting sleepy, he picked up his glasses and left the den
to get ready for bed.

Three

Eleanor arrived at the newspaper office early the next morning. She wanted to make sure she was there before Mr. Jake Mason arrived. It made her angry even to think about it.

She picked up the *Welles Daily*, the *New York Times*, and the *Wall Street Journal* from the mat in front of the building, unlocked the door, and headed for her office. Her mind screamed when she saw the additional desk in her already cramped space. A desk for Jake.

She dropped down in her desk chair, threw the papers and her briefcase on her desk, and propped her feet up. She could almost strangle her father. How could he even consider merging their paper with Mason Publishing?

She remembered her mother bringing her to the paper for lunch with her father when she'd been a child of about seven. She'd loved coming here where her daddy worked. He always made her feel like a princess. He was the king, her mom was the queen, and she was the princess.

Sadness settled around her heart. "I miss you so much, Mom," she said softly.

Eleanor still remembered the first day she'd come

to the newspaper office without her mother. Mrs.
Lewis, the woman her father hired to care for her,
had brought her. But it wasn't the same. Her father
must have understood because he'd allowed her to
stay with him until he was ready to go home. And
that became the pattern for their lives.

Every day after school Mrs. Lewis would pick
Eleanor up and drive her to the newspaper office.
She'd do her homework while her father and his
staff worked on the next week's edition of the paper.
When she was finished, her father would give her
some small task to do around the paper. "This is
our business," he'd say. "You need to learn it."

And that was the beginning of her love affair with
the *Lamar Daily*. Throughout high school, she continued coming to the newspaper after school. And
her assignments progressed from the trivial to sub-
stantive reporting.

When her father changed from a weekly paper to
a daily paper during her junior year in high school,
she'd even had her own column, "Lamar High
Live." Because her high school didn't have a newspaper, her father gave classes to interested students
about running a paper. Not just the journalism end,
but the business end. Her father always said you
needed to know your business. His encouragement
led her to study journalism in college and then to
go for her MBA.

She'd been back in Lamar at the paper about six
years now and she enjoyed every minute of it. She'd
missed her father and the paper while she was away.
And she'd come back full of ideas. When her father
had settled on just being the publisher and made

her managing editor two years ago, she felt she'd gotten her head. There was so much she could do, so much she wanted to do. At the top of her list was starting a monthly magazine targeted at African-American families. She'd already added a weekly insert to the *Lamar Daily* to test the concept, but that was only the beginning.

Eleanor wanted a magazine with national distribution, but they didn't have the capital to start it now. Neither she nor her father had considered outside funding. He'd taught her early on that, when people put in their money, they wanted some control. And she and her father both prided themselves on being able to make decisions for the paper without having to deal with bureaucratic red tape. There were only the two of them to consider.

Until now. That's what she didn't understand. Why would her father bring in Randolph Mason and all the red tape of Mason Publishing? The planned merger seemed to go against everything he'd taught her. She shook her head. She could only conclude that Randolph Mason had somehow tricked her father into believing a deal with him would be different. But she didn't buy it for a moment.

She smiled as she got up and put fresh water in the coffeemaker. Too bad Randolph hadn't sent in the big guns. He probably thought it wasn't necessary when dealing with a couple of hicks like her and her father. Well, she'd show Mr. Mason precisely what he was up against. She'd make the older Mason regret he'd ever sent his drama-trained, track-running son to manage this deal.

She went back to her desk and picked up the

Welles Daily, flipping quickly through its pages. Finding no news of interest to her or the residents of Lamar, she closed that paper and picked up the *Times.* She did the same with the *Wall Street Journal* before turning around in her chair and flicking on her computer to check the wire for any late-breaking stories.

"Morning, Maxie," she heard her father say to the newsroom secretary, who must have arrived in the last fifteen minutes.

"Morning, Mathias," Maxine Walters said. Maxine was an attractive, almond-skinned, slightly graying woman about her father's age and she'd had a crush on him for as long as Eleanor could remember. She didn't understand why her father didn't know it. Everybody else did. No one called Maxine Walters anything other than Maxine or Ms. Walters. No one except Mathias Sanders.

"This here is Jake Mason. He's going to be with us for the summer. He and Eleanor will be sharing an office."

"Nice to meet you, Ms. Walters," came Jake's smooth voice. The man was a born charmer.

"Eleanor in her office?" her father asked, cutting off any conversation that may have started between Jake and Maxine.

By the time she heard Maxine say "Yes," her father and Jake were walking through Eleanor's office door. She stood and greeted them.

"How come you left so early this morning?" her father asked. "I'd planned on the three of us having breakfast then driving in together."

Eleanor had guessed that was his plan and she'd

deliberately set out to circumvent it. The smirk on Jake's face told her he knew that.

"There were some things I needed to do this morning," she lied. She knew and her father knew she was rarely in the office this early. Maxine was usually the first one in, and Maxine usually made the coffee.

"Anything I can help you with?" Jake asked solicitously.

She turned and glared at him. "Thanks, Jake," she said sweetly. "But I don't think you can help." The unspoken words, *with anything*, hung in the air.

"Well," her father interrupted, "I'll leave Jake to you, Eleanor. Show him around the newsroom, the press room, you know the drill." He looked at his watch. "I'll meet you two for lunch at, say, one o'clock."

"But Dad—"

"That's fine, Mathias," Jake interrupted. "Eleanor will probably need a break from me by that time. I have a million and one questions."

"I'll bet," Eleanor muttered under her breath.

"Good," her father said, backing out of the office. "I'll see you two later."

Eleanor stared after him. She and her father had to talk. She was not going to baby-sit Jake Mason, drama graduate and track star. She had *real* work to do and none of it included teaching Jake about the newspaper business.

"This my desk over here?" Jake asked, forcing Eleanor's attention to him.

"No, it belongs to Bill Clinton," she answered, rolling her eyes.

Jake dropped his briefcase on the desk. "You'd better stop rolling your eyes like that before they get hung in that position."

Eleanor rested her hands on her hips. "Why are you really here, Jake?"

He sat down in his chair and leaned back with his hands behind his head. "You already know. The *Lamar Daily* is merging with Mason Publishing. I'll decide how to position it with the rest of our holdings."

Eleanor rested against the corner of her desk and crossed her arms. "We don't need you to position us, Mr. Mason. We already have a position and plans for our growth. We don't need you or your father's money."

Jake dropped his hands from behind his head and leaned forward. "That's not what your father said."

"That's not what your father conned my father into agreeing to, you mean."

"That's not what I meant at all. Your father doesn't seem to be the kind of man who can be easily conned." He shrugged his shoulders. "But then I've only known him a day."

He'd backed her into a corner. To maintain her position, she'd have to agree that her father was a pushover where Randolph Mason was concerned. She wasn't ready to do that yet. She stared at Jake for a couple of long seconds before getting up and heading for the door. "Come on, if you want the tour." She left the office without looking back.

"Megan's on the line for you, Eleanor," came Maxine's voice over the intercom just as Jake and

Eleanor returned to the newsroom after Eleanor's halfhearted tour. Jake wondered why Eleanor cringed at the words.

"What's the matter?" he asked. "I thought Megan was a friend of yours." Plus, Jake wanted an introduction to her in the worst way.

Eleanor's gaze met his. "Tour's over." She turned and marched back to her office, closing the door behind her.

Jake watched through the window in the wall separating Eleanor's office from the rest of the newsroom as she picked up the phone. She saw him and turned her back to him. He smiled, then proceeded to enter the office and plop down in his chair. She turned and gave him a look he was sure cast aspersions on his parentage. He grinned. Obviously, she'd forgotten he was sharing her office.

"Maxine has to stop announcing my calls over the intercom like that," Jake overheard her whisper.

He shook his head. So that's why she'd cringed. She didn't like her business broadcast over the intercom system. He didn't see what harm it did, but obviously it irritated her.

Jake didn't bother to pretend he wasn't listening to her call. It seemed her friend Megan was leaving town for a while. Damn! He hoped she wasn't going to be gone for long. He wanted to meet her.

"See you in a couple of weeks," Eleanor said, then hung up the phone and turned to Jake. "Common courtesy says you don't listen in on other people's conversations."

Jake shrugged. "There are no secrets in a newsroom. Even *I* know that."

Eleanor pointed to the green metal desks scattered about the room outside her office. "There's no privacy out there. This is *my* office. There *is* privacy in here. And if we're going to get along, you'd better understand that."

Jake reached across her desk and picked up her copy of the *Times*. "I'll try."

"You'd be wise to do better than try. I'm not afraid of you, Jake Mason. Or of your high-powered father and his Mason Publishing."

Jake lowered the paper so he could see her. He would have grinned but she was so wound up, he didn't think she'd appreciate it. "What are you so bent out of shape about? Ease up some, Eleanor. We're going to be cramped in this office for a long time. Let's try to be friends."

"Friends?" Eleanor said the word as if it were a curse. "You must be joking. We can't be friends. You're the worst kind of enemy."

Before Jake could respond, a wiry, copper-complexioned brother in gray dress slacks, a white button-down shirt, and a black tie stuck his head in the office door. "Eleanor, they want you down in advertising. Seems there's some problem with the ads for today's edition."

Eleanor jumped out of her chair and rushed past the man and in the direction of the advertising manager's office. Jake watched her strut off, and as he did, he wondered why she was so uptight.

"Don't let her get to you," the man said. "She's all right. You'll get used to her."

"And how long will that take?"

The man smiled. "A while." He extended his hand. "I'm Carl Winters. You must be Jake Mason."

Jake shook the hand. "Nice to meet you, Carl."

"Has Eleanor introduced you to everybody yet?"

Jake shook his head. "We went on a tour, but not many people were around when we started."

"Come on, then, I'll do it. And maybe even get you a cup of coffee."

Jake got up and clapped Carl on the back. "I'm glad I met you, Carl. Eleanor had me wondering if that Southern hospitality I'd heard so much about was a myth."

Eleanor was grateful when the waitress removed their lunch dishes. She was ready to leave this restaurant and Jake's company. And her father's. The man was completely taken in by the smooth-talking Jake. It was so unlike her father.

"It sure is hot here," Jake said. By his tone, you'd think he'd made some brilliant discovery.

Her father pushed back from the table. "Why don't you and Eleanor go for a swim? She goes at lunch most days." Mathias winked at Jake when Eleanor gasped. "She didn't know I knew."

"It's not like I was trying to hide something from you," Eleanor countered. "There has been no reason to discuss it."

"That's not important now, Eleanor," her father said in dismissal with a wave of his hand. "Why don't you take Jake here and the two of you hit the pool for a while?"

"Maybe another day. I usually swim instead of

lunch, not after." She glanced at Jake. "I'm sure Jake doesn't want to go swimming on a full stomach."

Jake didn't give her father time to respond. "She's right, Mathias. We should've gone before lunch or instead of it. But it's a good idea. Maybe we'll do it tomorrow."

Yeah, right, Eleanor thought. And tomorrow Hell will freeze over. "Maybe."

"Good, good," Mathias said. "Now how did things go this morning?"

Eleanor listened while Jake told of her tour and the introductions made by Carl. She waited for him to comment on her lack of courtesy, but he didn't and she wondered why. As if he'd read her thoughts, Jake turned to her and smiled.

Heaven help her, that smile made her insides quiver. The man was a practiced flirt. He wasn't her type at all. And heaven knows, she wasn't his. She'd have to keep her traitorous emotions in check. She was *not* going to be one of Jake Mason's small-town conquests. Megan could have him.

"Mathias Sanders, there you are."

It was Mrs. Thompson. The elderly woman cornered her father at every opportunity trying to get free publicity for one of her projects or another.

"Good afternoon, Mrs. Thompson," her father said, standing up and reaching for the older woman's age-spotted hand. "It's good to see you. Won't you join us?"

Eleanor hoped Mrs. Thompson had other plans. Lunch with her and Jake would be more than she could stomach.

"No, no," the gray-haired woman said. "I'm meeting my bridge club. I stopped to tell you how much we appreciated the story you ran on our Bridge Club Tournament. Those were some good pictures, too. Too bad you didn't get any of me."

Eleanor picked up her napkin to hide her smile. Mrs. Thompson never changed. She glanced at Jake and saw he didn't bother to hide his smile.

"Well, you know we couldn't run photos of everyone. We do our best." Her father gave her his biggest smile. Goodness, he was as bad as Jake. "Have you met my new partner, Jake Mason?"

"Your new partner," Mrs. Thompson said. "I thought this might be Eleanor's beau." She extended her hand to Jake. "Nice to meet you, Mr. Mason. Welcome to Lamar."

Jake stood up. "Thank you, Mrs. Thompson. It's a pleasure meeting you." His hundred-watt smile flashed and Mrs. Thompson blushed. A sixty-plus-year old woman blushed. Eleanor wanted to kick Jake.

"Are you married, Mr. Mason?" Mrs. Thompson asked.

Eleanor could have kicked Mrs. Thompson then.

Jake smiled. "Not yet. But then they don't have Southern belles like yourself where I'm from."

Eleanor watched as Mrs. Thompson batted her eyelids. Goodness, the older woman was flirting with Jake.

"Eleanor, dear," she said, addressing her for the first time, "this is a good one. You'd better keep an eye on him."

Jake smiled again and Eleanor wished she had the

nerve to slap that smile off his face. Thank goodness Mrs. Thompson floated over to her friends at a distant table before Eleanor could make a comment. Jake's laughter brought her attention to him.

"What's so funny?" she asked.

"Small towns," Jake answered with a huge, mocking grin on his face. "I think I'm going to like it here."

Eleanor knew he was having fun at her expense, but her father spoke before she could put him in his place.

"We like to think our town has a certain charm." He cut a glance at Eleanor. "How's the party planning going? We want Jake to meet the people of Lamar. Have you spoken to Megan about helping you plan it?"

No, she hadn't, and she was hoping her father would forget it. No such luck. "Megan's out of town. She won't be back for a couple of weeks."

"Well, damn. Where did she go and why did she have to go now?"

Eleanor glanced at Jake. "She had some personal business to take care of."

Mathias turned to Jake. "I guess this means we'll have to put off your party until she gets back. You don't mind, do you, son?"

"Not at all, Mathias. Eleanor is doing a great job of making me feel welcome."

"I'll bet," Mathias muttered.

Jake laughed. "Like I said before. She's the bratty little sister I never had."

Eleanor stood up, slapping her napkin on the table. "Since the two of you seem to like talking about me as if I'm not present, I'll leave and you can continue." She grabbed her purse from the back of the chair. "Besides, some of us have work to do."

Before Eleanor reached the door, she knew she had behaved badly. What was wrong with her? Why was she acting this way? It didn't take her long to figure out why.

Jake Mason.

Four

Eleanor wasn't surprised when her father entered her office, shut the door, and closed the blinds. She wondered where Jake was.

"What's wrong with you, Eleanor? Why are you so rude to Jake? And to me, for that matter?"

Eleanor placed the layout she was studying on her desk. "You don't have to say it. I know I've been out of line."

"That's an understatement," he said. The "young lady" at the end of the sentence sounded as loud as if he'd spoken the words.

"Why are you doing this, Dad? Why are you giving them control of our paper?"

Mathias released a heavy sigh before he sat in the chair at Jake's desk. "We've been over this before, Eleanor." He searched her face before continuing. "Randolph and I have talked about going into business together off and on over the years."

Eleanor leaned forward in her chair. She didn't like what she was hearing. "But why this, Dad?" she asked, her lips tight.

"Don't use that tone with me, young lady," he said in the inflection he'd used long ago, when she'd complained about wanting to stay up beyond her bedtime. "This is still my newspaper and don't you forget it."

Eleanor wanted to roll her eyes at her father's oft-used phrase, but she knew if she did, she'd get a lecture and her schedule for the afternoon would be shot. "I'm sorry, Dad, but I don't see why you want to merge the *Lamar Daily* with Mason Publishing."

Mathias stood up, put his hands in his pockets, and faced the window to the newsroom. Eleanor stood to her full height of five-four and pulled on her father's arm to turn him around. She hated having to look up to him. It was one of the things that helped keep her a child in his eyes. "Dad?"

"It'll be good for us, Eleanor. Think what it would mean if we were a part of Mason Publishing. Some of the changes you want to see around here could actually happen with the Mason Publishing money behind us. It's a great opportunity."

Eleanor knew he was right. It was a great opportunity. In fact, too great. "What do they get out of it?"

"What?"

"Mason Publishing? What do they get out of the deal? I see what we get, but what do they get?"

Alarm flashed in Mathias's eyes and he looked away again. "You know Randolph and I have been friends for years. He understands he won't get as much out of the deal as I will, but he thinks there's money to be made with the *Lamar Daily.*"

Eleanor wasn't so sure. The *Lamar Daily* hadn't made much money over the years. Maybe with some changes they could do better, but she didn't think they'd ever become rich. No, that kind of potential was not in their newspaper. The *Lamar Daily* was a good small-town paper, but that's all it was. "Randolph Mason didn't get rich buying small-town papers, Dad. And something tells me an astute businessman like him knows how to keep business and personal matters separate. There must be something in this deal for him."

"Don't look a gift horse in the mouth, Eleanor," Mathias warned, looking at her again. "You're getting what you wanted. You should be happy."

Eleanor knew there was no discussing this with her father. In Mathias's eyes, Randolph Mason could do no wrong. "I don't want this merger to happen, Dad. What if Mason Publishing starts telling us how to do our business? We've always counted ourselves lucky that we didn't have to cut through a lot of corporate red tape. Why do you want to subject us to it now?"

"This isn't *another* corporation. This is Mason Publishing. And Randolph Mason is my best friend. You worry too much."

She didn't think so, but there was no use telling him that now. "If he's not planning to make any changes in our business, what's Jake doing here?"

Mathias shook his head. "It's still a business deal, Eleanor. Randolph thinks this paper is the place for Jake to get involved in the business."

"But why now? Why us?"

"That was Randolph's call. Jake's overseeing this deal. He's here and you have to work with him in addition to sharing office space with him." She would have interrupted, but Mathias continued. "I know you don't like his sharing your office, but we don't have much space. And since he'll be working mostly with the two of us, it was either have him share your office or have him share mine." He smiled. "And since I'm the boss around here, you got the office mate."

"I still don't like it, Dad," she said, meaning more than sharing her office.

Mathias touched his daughter's cheek. "I know you don't, sweetheart. But you have to deal with it. You can work with Jake and me or you can work against us. Either way, this deal with Randolph is going through."

Jake chose that moment to make his appearance and Mathias dropped his hand from Eleanor's face. He gave her a final pleading look, then said, "I have an afternoon meeting with the mayor. I'll see you two tonight."

Jake watched Mathias leave and he knew instinctively words had passed between father and daughter. From the uneasy look in Eleanor's eyes, he guessed the conversation had not been a pleasant one. For some reason Jake couldn't name, he wanted to comfort her.

"So, what are we doing this afternoon?" he asked.

"About lunch—" she began slowly.

"Yes," he interrupted, "I enjoyed that tasty Southern cuisine." He hoped she understood why he couldn't let her finish. He didn't want her to apologize. He felt an apology would somehow take away from the tenuous and strange relationship they were forming. In fact, Jake enjoyed sparring with Eleanor. It thrilled him to see her all riled up. It was more than obvious she didn't want him in Lamar. And she had no intention of allowing him to make any changes in the way they ran the newspaper. But that didn't matter. Somehow he knew the two of them would work through their differences.

Eleanor stared at him a few seconds. "This afternoon we lay out tomorrow's paper and edit the editorials and columns."

Jake knew she didn't understand why he didn't want her apology but he was glad she accepted his gesture. He grinned. "Where do we start?"

At ten o'clock the next morning, Eleanor dropped down in her office chair, kicked off her low-heeled black pumps, and propped her stocking-clad feet on her desk, wishing it was time for her lunchtime swim. It had been a heck of a morning. Columnists. She couldn't live with 'em and she couldn't live without 'em. She'd spent the better part of the morning arguing with Tempest Tanner, their most temperamental *and* most popular columnist, about her treatment, or rather, mistreatment, of the recent demise of one of the Lamar's oldest residents. Eleanor shook her head. For some reason columnists couldn't comprehend slander and libel. Maybe it's because the newspaper would be liable and not the individual columnist.

Eleanor crossed her legs at the ankles, leaned back in her chair, and attempted to run her hand through her hair. The barrette that kept her black hair in a bun on top of her head stopped her fingers and she had to settle for rubbing her hands across her head. Some days she wished she could wear her hair down, but she knew wearing it up made her look more mature, more professional.

Eleanor lifted her wrist and checked the time on the Spelman watch she'd bought at the last class reunion. Two hours. Two hours and she could escape for a refreshing dip in her father's pool. Nothing relaxed her like a swim. She'd been on the swim team in high school and college. She'd been told she could have been a competitive swimmer, but she enjoyed swimming too much for that. If she allowed it to become a job, what would she do for relaxation?

And if she was lucky, she could go to the pool without Jake as she'd managed to do yesterday after work. He'd spent this morning with her father and she hoped their meetings would keep them occupied through lunch and her swim.

"Call for Eleanor from Horace," came Maxine's voice on the intercom.

Eleanor made a mental note to speak with Maxine again about the intercom, then picked up the phone.

"Oh, no," she said when she learned Horace Page was in the hospital with a broken hip. "Don't hesitate to call us if you need anything, Mrs. Page. My father and I will visit Horace today."

After a few more exchanges Eleanor hung up the phone. "What am I going to do?" she asked herself.

"About what?" was Jake's response.

So he was back. "Horace Page is in the hospital."

Jake sat on the corner of his desk. "Horace? That's the sports reporter, right?"

Eleanor nodded. "And the sports editor is in

Alaska on a four-week vacation. Who's going to cover sports while they're out?"

"There has to be somebody. You've got about twelve people on the news staff."

"Everybody's busy. We don't have anybody."

"Get a freelancer," Jake suggested.

"This isn't New York, Jake. The closest thing we can get to a freelancer is a sports reporter from the high school."

"Do that. How hard can the job be anyway? Even I've heard the old newspaper saying, *Sports is entertainment; not brain surgery.*"

She leaned a finger against her cheek and considered his words. "You've heard that, have you?"

Jake flashed his trademark grin. "Publishing's in my blood."

"It is, is it?" Eleanor said, an idea forming in her mind.

"Of course. Just like it's in yours."

Eleanor snapped her fingers. "You're right. And I've thought of the perfect solution."

"See, I knew you could do it. Are you going to go with one of the high school kids?"

Eleanor shook her head. "Actually I was thinking of someone a bit more mature."

"Who?"

"You."

"Me?"

"Yes, you. Didn't you say a high school kid could do it? Well, if publishing is in your blood, you can do it, too."

Jake stood. "Me? A sports reporter?"

Eleanor scooted around to her desk. "Don't

sound so surprised, Jake. I know you can do it. After all, everybody knows sports is entertainment, not brain surgery."

Jake's mouth dropped open, but no words came out.

"You can do it, can't you, Jake?" Eleanor baited, knowing Jake wouldn't be able to resist her challenge.

"What's my first assignment?" he asked, suitably insulted.

She scribbled the name of the school on a slip of paper and handed it to him. "Girls basketball at the high school. Take a photographer with you. Ben's available."

The Lamar High School gymnasium was very different from the gymnasiums Jake remembered from his high school days. The building was old, the bleachers were older, and the kids somehow seemed younger. Basketball in the summer was new to him, too, but Ben had explained that Lamar did things a little differently since the school system ran on a year-round schedule.

Ben led him to the press box, which was really the seat next to the scorekeeper, a little blue-haired woman, who smiled at Jake, but who couldn't seem to concentrate on much more than keeping track of the score.

Ben handed Jake a sheet that put names to the numbers on the jerseys and for the next hour Jake engrossed himself in girls' basketball. During time-outs and quarter breaks, Jake's eyes roamed the spectators that filled the gymnasium. They came in all shapes, sizes, and ages—children, parents, grandparents. It seemed the game was more than a high school game; it was a community event.

When the game was over, Ben introduced Jake to the school principal, the girls' coach, and other members of the Lamar High coaching staff. Jake was feeling like a member of the community when he left.

As he climbed into the sports van with Ben and headed back to the paper, he felt a sense of accomplishment. He didn't consider himself a reporter and he hadn't come to Lamar to be a reporter, but he'd been assigned a job and he'd done it. Well, he'd done part of it. He had enough notes for a story. Now, he had to write the story.

"You're all right, Jake," Ben said when they reached the office, then he ambled off in the direction of the darkroom.

"So are you, Ben," Jake said, but he knew Ben didn't hear him.

Jake walked into the newsroom, ready to work on his story. Eleanor met him at the door. "How'd it go?"

"It went," was all he said. "Now I have to get the story written. I want to make deadline." He stepped past Eleanor and strode to his desk.

Eleanor stared at him. "You're going to write the story *now?*"

Jake looked up from the computer screen. "If I can get this computer to work." He flicked a button, and when the screen didn't light up, he raised the terminal off the desk a little. "How old is this equipment anyway?"

"About fifteen years."

Jake lowered the computer. "Fifteen years? It's ancient."

Eleanor perched on the corner of her desk. "You're right, our equipment is ancient. But according to my father, Mason Publishing will infuse us with enough money to modernize."

"Is that what your father said?" he asked absently, still fiddling with the terminal.

Eleanor confirmed.

"And how much will this modernization cost Mason Publishing?"

Eleanor gave a figure and Jake whistled. "That's a lot."

Eleanor shrugged her shoulders. "To us, maybe. But certainly not to you. That sum is a drop in the bucket for Mason Publishing."

He stared up at her. "So you think we're going to be the gravy train for the *Lamar Daily?*"

"There's no way my father would consider this deal if Mason Publishing couldn't provide enough money to do the things we want to do around here."

Jake forgot about the terminal and his article and gave her his full attention. "What other things do you want to do?"

Eleanor moved to sit in her desk chair. "A new computer system is first. One of those pagination systems. That would make us more efficient as well as enhance the look of the paper. Next, we'd want funds to add a Sunday edition. I know we'd get the advertising support, but we need up-front capital to get started. Then, we want to start a magazine targeted at African-American families."

Jake smiled at her. "You don't want much, do you?"

"A paper is like a life. You have to dream big. That's what we're doing."

"So you don't think you'll get all the things you've named?"

Eleanor nodded. "I think we'll get the things I mentioned, but there are a dozen other things I'd like to see us do." She grinned. "I'm willing to go slowly. I don't want to break Mason Publishing."

Jake returned his attention to the computer. "I bet." He slapped the side of the computer terminal. "What's wrong with this thing?"

"Stop hitting it like that," Eleanor admonished. "Let me see." She walked to his desk and leaned over his shoulder. Ignoring the rich smell of his cologne, she hit the Control and Reset keys. The machine seemed to take forever to reboot. She leaned away from him as it did so.

"What did you do?" he asked, oblivious to the effect he was having on her.

"I rebooted the machine. You should be ready to go in a minute or so."

"I hope so."

She leaned over his shoulder again. "Okay." She pressed the Enter key twice. "There you go. It's ready."

Jake hit the Insert key and clicked a couple other keys, then turned around and smiled at her. She couldn't help but smile back. The man was gorgeous.

"Thanks, Eleanor. It's working. I'll have to remember to reboot when I'm having problems." He turned back around and started on his story.

Eleanor remained behind him for a few seconds. She didn't understand Jake Mason. She'd been sure he'd come here to destroy the paper she'd known her whole life, yet here he was as excited as one of the high school kids about the story he was writing. What was it with this man?

"Make sure to save," she said before she went back to her desk and flicked on her computer. She might as well use this time to edit tomorrow's stories. After about twenty minutes, she heard Jake.

"Dammit," he said.

"What's wrong now, Jake?"

She heard the click of a couple of keys and the machine started to reboot. "I've got it covered."

Eleanor went back to her work.

"Dammit, now I can't find my story."

She heard him hit the side of the terminal again. "What'd you do?" she asked, getting up and walking over to him.

He looked up at her. "The keyboard froze, but I rebooted like you did before. Now I can't find my story."

Eleanor hit the Retrieve function key to view the file listing. "What's the name of the file?"

"Name? I didn't get that far. The keyboard hung when I was about three-quarters done."

"Uh-oh."

"Oh, no, I don't like the sound of that."

Eleanor gave him her first real smile, then touched his shoulder. "It wasn't saved. You lost your story. I'm sorry."

"Damn. Now's a fine time for you to tell me." He slapped the computer terminal on its side again. "Stupid machine doesn't even have an auto-save feature."

Eleanor chuckled as she went back to her desk. "Don't blame the machine, Jake. It's old and it doesn't have a mind or any modern features. It only does what you tell it."

"What's that supposed to mean?" Jake said, his voice raised.

Eleanor knew when to retreat. "Nothing. Just don't forget to save this time."

"You can bet on it," he muttered, then hit the side of the terminal again.

Randolph picked up his phone on the first ring. He knew who was calling.

"So what's happening on the Jake and Eleanor front?" he asked as soon as Mathias came on the line.

Mathias chuckled. "Jake became a reporter today."

"A reporter? Jake?"

Mathias laughed again, then repeated the story of the hospitalized sports reporter.

Randolph joined him in laughter. "So how'd he do?"

"According to Eleanor, he lost his story twice in the computer. But he got it done."

Randolph filled with pride. It wasn't that he was surprised Jake could do it. He knew Jake could do anything he set his mind to do. No, Randolph was more surprised Jake had done it. And apparently had enjoyed doing it. "What did Eleanor think of that?"

"I think it may work in our favor, Randy. She's thinking about him in a whole new light. She only made three negative comments about him tonight at dinner and those were inconsequential. I think the way he handled that story has made her reexamine her first opinion of him."

"Good. Good. Maybe we're getting somewhere."

"Don't get too excited. We still have a long way to go."

"I know. I know. But this is a start in the right direction. What's next?"

"I've told Eleanor to throw a 'Welcome to Lamar' party for Jake. She's hesitant to do it, but I've cornered her into asking her friend Megan to help."

"Megan? The teenage hormone you used to talk about?"

Mathias laughed. "She's not a teenager anymore."

"Do you think that's wise, Mat? Having this Megan around Jake? What if Jake gets interested in her instead of Eleanor?"

"I don't think that'll happen. Jake isn't Megan's type."

Randolph harrumphed. "I've never met a woman who didn't think Jake was her type. What makes this Megan different?"

"Megan's a flirt, Randy. Personally, I think she's in love with one of my reporters. No, you leave this to me. Megan is the ingredient we need here. She'll flirt and Eleanor'll be jealous. You watch."

"You sound pretty confident for a man who only a few minutes ago told me not to get too excited."

"I know, I know. But you should see them together, Randy. They're going to be a great couple."

"I hope you're right, Mat. I hope you're right."

Five

Coffee with Carl had become a part of Jake's routine in the nearly two weeks he'd been in Lamar and this morning was no different. Initially, Carl had allied himself with Jake to protect him from Eleanor, but now Jake felt they'd formed a real friendship.

"How was the game yesterday?" Carl asked, sipping from his coffee mug, his legs propped on his credenza.

Jake rolled his chair across the padded floor and threw the day's edition on Carl's desk. "You'll have to read it in the paper."

Carl placed his cup on his desk and picked up the paper, opening it to the sports section. "Not bad for a rookie."

"A rookie? I'm a reporter of experience. I've gotten more bylines in the last two weeks than most new reporters get in a couple of months. Hell, I may even get a Pulitzer for that track story."

Carl laughed. "Don't wait on that Pulitzer, Jake. If anybody in Lamar gets a Pulitzer, it'll be me."

"Keep telling yourself that, friend," Jake joked, knowing Carl was right.

"Hey," Carl protested, "not you, too. I don't get

enough kudos around here as it is. I thought a big-city boy like yourself appreciated my worth."

Jake sobered. "I do and so do Mathias and Eleanor." Carl was the paper's most capable journalist. It was an odd day for the *Lamar Daily* when the headline story carried a byline that didn't belong to him. Jake wondered what kept a journalist of his obvious talent in Lamar. Carl would be hell at a larger paper and get a lot more exposure, too.

Carl grunted. "Mathias appreciates me, but I'm not too sure about Eleanor. Sometimes I think she still sees me as her geeky friend from school."

"I didn't know you and Eleanor were in school together," Jake commented. He'd thought he and Carl were about the same age. Now he wondered if Carl knew Megan and, if so, how well.

Carl nodded. "For twelve long years. For a while we were pretty close friends, but that was B.M."

"Excuse me?"

"Before Megan." Carl picked up his coffee mug again. "Eleanor and I were geeks together until Megan."

The hurt in Carl's tone surprised Jake. It seemed out of character for Carl to harbor ill feelings about something that had happened years ago. Jake wondered about it, but he couldn't miss the opportunity to learn more about the mysterious Megan. "What happened when Megan came along?"

"She and Eleanor became fast friends." Carl shook his head. "What an odd couple they were. That's what the kids called them, the Odd Couple."

"Megan was the slob?" Jake asked, thinking of the

Oscar character. He knew without asking that Eleanor had to be Felix.

"That's not why they called them the Odd Couple. It was because they were so different."

Jake could imagine. The beautiful, alluring Megan and the prim, unassuming Eleanor. Well, maybe unassuming wasn't correct. Eleanor had too much mouth to be considered unassuming. "The beautiful and the plain, I can see that."

"You got it right. Megan was gorgeous, even in eighth grade. Eleanor could be a looker, but she doesn't know it."

"So Megan is still gorgeous?"

Carl sneered. "So gorgeous she has her own fan club."

Jake nodded. From the little he'd heard about Megan, he could understand why the men of Lamar had formed a club for her. Obviously, Carl wasn't a member.

"Too bad she's the president," Carl added.

Jake laughed. "So Megan is a bit self-absorbed."

"More like a *lot* self-absorbed."

"You sound like you don't like her."

Carl stared at Jake a few seconds before speaking. "Nobody *doesn't* like Megan."

Jake wanted to follow up on that, but before he could, Carl pushed away from his desk and stood. "I've got to see Wanda in composition. I'll talk to you later."

Jake stared after Carl, wondering what he meant by his last statement about Megan. Eleanor found him that way.

"What's on your schedule for this morning?" she asked.

When Jake looked at her, Carl's words about Eleanor sounded in his ears—*Eleanor could be a looker, but she doesn't know it.* The words had escaped him when his friend first spoke them, but now they registered. For the first time since he'd been in Lamar, he assessed Eleanor—really assessed her, not as his father's best friend's daughter, not as a bratty younger sister, not as a business rival, but as a woman.

He studied the bun atop her head and wondered how she'd look with her hair down. He realized now that he didn't even know how long her hair was. It was a rich, dark brown and appeared to be very thick, though he couldn't really tell from the way she had it rolled up on her head.

"Is something wrong with my hair?" Eleanor asked, patting the bun to make sure it was in place.

Her question brought Jake's attention to her face. "No, nothing's wrong with your hair." But you have beautiful big, brown eyes, he added to himself.

"Then why were you staring?" she asked, clearly not believing his words. "I'll go check it out myself."

Jake couldn't help but watch the gentle sway of her hips as she walked away from him. He knew it wasn't a practiced walk, merely the walk of a woman comfortable in her body. For once he appreciated the distance from the newsroom to the bathrooms. Though Eleanor wore a skirt that fell to her knees, he could see she had strong, firm calves and trim ankles and that made him think her thighs would be strong and firm, too.

Disappointment settled around him when she entered the bathroom door and he could no longer see her. It was probably a good thing. Now was not the time for sexual thoughts about Eleanor. No, he had come to Lamar to do a job. Not to get involved with the daughter of his father's best friend.

He dropped down in his chair. He wished to hell Megan would hurry up and get back.

Eleanor leaned against the bathroom door, grateful for the protection it provided from Jake and the emotions he stirred in her. Why had he been staring at her? At first, she'd really thought something may have been wrong with her hair. But when he'd looked in her face, she'd known his thoughts had nothing to do with her coiffure. No, Jake Mason had been assessing her attributes as a female. And, heaven help her, she wasn't sure if she'd measured up to his standard of womanhood. At least, not dressed the way she was.

She walked to the mirror and stared at herself. She'd never before questioned her dress. She dressed for authority, not for allure, deliberately choosing the conservative outfits that some considered unfashionable. And that hadn't been a problem until now. Until Jake. Now she had thoughts of silk miniskirted suits in bold colors.

She'd been hurt when Jake hadn't recognized her as the woman at the pool and she secretly hoped that one day he'd laugh and tell her it was all a joke, that he'd known all along it was her. But that hadn't happened in the two weeks he'd been there and she

was pretty sure it wouldn't happen until he met
Megan.

At least, she hoped he'd make the connection after he met Megan. Surely, he'd know Megan wasn't
the woman by the pool. Heaven help her, she'd kill
him if he didn't figure out then that she was the
woman.

Hearing the bathroom door open, Eleanor quickly
stepped into an empty stall. What was she doing?
she asked herself. Why was she hiding out in the
bathroom trying to unravel the feelings Jake Mason
aroused in her? Once again, she wished the man
had never come to Lamar. This time, she acknowledged the paper wasn't the only thing she was
afraid Jake Mason would steal.

No, right now Eleanor was concerned about Jake
Mason stealing her heart.

Jake couldn't keep his eyes off Eleanor. He'd covertly observed her all afternoon. A couple of times
she'd caught him staring, but he'd averted his gaze
each time, and since she hadn't said anything, he
figured she hadn't thought much about it.

He'd learned a lot about Eleanor. First, she chewed
the end of her pen while she worked. Though he'd
seen pens with chewed ends here and there around
the newsroom, he'd never really thought about them.
Now he knew they were Eleanor's pens.

What surprised him more was how cute she looked
while she chewed. She'd put the pen in her mouth,
push it in and out a couple of times, then play with
the tip with her tongue before grasping it with her

full, unpainted lips. There was something erotic in her every motion. He was almost relieved when Mathias came by to talk with her.

"I need to steal Eleanor for a while, Jake," the older man said.

"Fine, sir," Jake said, with a grin. "I'll make the most of the privacy."

Eleanor grinned back and he noticed her whole face lit up with that grin. Why hadn't he noticed that before?

"Don't get too comfortable," she said. "I'll be back. Soon."

Eleanor followed her father to his office, glad to get away from Jake. She'd thought things would get better as the day went on, but they hadn't. He was still staring at her. Well, maybe not staring, more like observing. She'd been tempted to ask him if he liked what he saw, but she wasn't sure she wanted to know his answer.

"You seem to be dealing with Jake a lot better," her father said after she was seated in the burgundy leather visitor's chair in front of his massive oak desk.

She tried not to think how much easier it would've been to put Jake and his desk in this large office rather than her smaller one. "Well, you know what they say, 'Keep your friends close and your enemies closer.' "

Mathias sighed. "Jake is not the enemy, Eleanor. We're all on the same side."

"I hope you're right," she muttered.

"Of course, I'm right. Look how he pitched in with the sports reporting. He could have snubbed his nose at doing that menial reporting job that you gave him, but he didn't. He did what was best for the paper."

"Okay, Dad, I get your point," Eleanor said. She couldn't deny that Jake had done a good job. She'd been surprised by his enthusiasm for the project. And more than a little pleased. His actions made her wonder if she'd initially judged him too harshly. Jake Mason was proving hard to dislike.

"Now," her father said, interrupting her thoughts, "have you given any thought to the specifics you want from our merger with Mason Publishing?"

She wished she could say she didn't see any potential for good to come out of the venture, but that would be a lie. "Sure I've thought about it. If they're going to give us money, you bet I can spend it. But I want to make sure the money doesn't come with strings attached."

"Yes, yes, yes. You've made your position clear. Have you discussed any of your ideas with Jake?"

Eleanor shrugged her shoulders. "I've mentioned some projects I'd like to see funded."

"And what was his response?"

"He said something about a gravy train."

Mathias laughed. "So Jake thinks we want to milk Mason Publishing."

"As if we could actually do that. They probably have so much money they don't know what to do with it."

"I'm sure you're wrong there. Randolph is my friend, but as you've said before, he's also an astute businessman. The only guarantee we made was that the newspaper will remain in our control. They can't sell it or break it up without our agreement and everybody keeps their job. Including you and me. Other than that, everything's up for grabs."

"Everything?"

"Everything. That's why it's important you work with Jake on this. Randolph has given him a free hand with this deal."

"Why this deal, Dad?" Eleanor asked for the tenth time since she'd learned of the deal. Maybe this time she'd get a satisfactory answer. "Jake's not a newspaperman. That much is obvious."

Mathias sighed, leaned back in his chair, and twirled a pen in his hand. "Like any parent, Randolph wants Jake to take over for him someday. And he thinks this deal is the project to bring Jake in the fold."

"And you think Mr. Mason is going to support whatever Jake decides?"

Mathias nodded. "That's what I know."

Eleanor had figured as much. But there was one point on which she wasn't sure. "And are you going to support me?"

"You know how much I love you, Eleanor, and I want to see you happy."

Eleanor knew her father's hedging wasn't a good sign. "I know that, but it doesn't answer my question."

Mathias dropped his pen on the desk and leaned toward her, concern in his eyes. "Are you happy, Eleanor? Really happy?"

"Of course, I'm happy, Dad. Do you think I'm not?"

He searched her face for any sign that she wasn't

telling the truth. "I worry about you sometimes. Trapped in a small town, with this small paper. You're a young woman. You should experience life beyond Lamar."

Eleanor felt a tightening in her chest. "I am experiencing life. As you always say, 'If it didn't happen in Lamar, it didn't happen.' "

The old newspaper saying her father used so much didn't make him smile this time.

"You know what I'm talking about, Eleanor. Sometimes I think I did you a disservice by encouraging you to spend so much time here."

Eleanor got up from her chair, walked around her father's desk, and hugged him. "That's not true. You were and still are the best dad a girl could have. I love you, Dad."

"I know you do, sweetheart. I know you do."

Eleanor took comfort in her father's embrace, but she realized he hadn't answered her question. She'd let it go for now, but soon she would demand an answer.

Eleanor began dropping off her clothes as soon as she walked through the door of her cottage. By the time she reached her bedroom, she was nude and her phone was ringing. She picked it up on the second ring.

"So how is handsome doing?"

Eleanor welcomed the cheery sound of Megan's voice. She reclined on the bed and prepared for a long conversation. "When did you get back?"

"Who said I was back?"

Eleanor laughed. "You're too cheap to call long distance."

"Ahh, you know me too well. So, how is the fine brother from New York doing?"

"Thriving. He's enjoying the sights and sounds of Lamar."

"I bet he is. The man is probably bored out of his mind. But I'm sure I'll be able to fix that. *If* you ever get around to introducing me, that is."

Eleanor knew her friend was right. It was time Jake met Megan. She couldn't wait to see his expression when he learned she wasn't the woman at the pool. "Well, you won't have to wait long. Dad wants you to plan a 'Welcome to Lamar' party for Jake."

"All right," Megan whooped. "Be sure to give Mr. S. a big kiss for me. If he was a little younger, I'd have my eye on him."

Eleanor chuckled. "Don't even think about it, Megan. If Maxine hasn't gotten his attention in all these years, you don't stand a chance. Besides, I don't think you're stepmother material. Though it would be fun to call you Mom."

"Don't even joke about something like that, Eleanor. You calling me Mom. It gives me chills. You still haven't told me about handsome. You haven't decided that you want him, have you?"

"Of course not," Eleanor answered a bit too quickly.

"You're sure?"

"Yes, I'm sure. He's not my type."

"Your type is a whole other conversation, Eleanor. I don't think you know what your type is. Now before you get your panties all twisted because of that statement, tell me what Jake's been up to."

Eleanor's flaring temper quickly faded. "He's our interim sports reporter."

"What? You're kidding! New York Jake is covering local sports? You *are* going to bore the man to death."

Eleanor chuckled again. "Believe it or not, he's enjoying it and he's good at it."

"I bet it hurt you to say that."

Megan was right, but Eleanor was not about to tell her. "And he's become good friends with Carl."

"Now I *know* the man is leaving town soon. Carl would bore a dead person. I don't believe you, Eleanor. Why are you putting him around all the dull people? If it wasn't so late, I'd come over there and introduce myself to him tonight."

"How did you know he was staying here?"

"Earth to Eleanor. This is Lamar, remember? There's no such thing as a secret. Especially secrets about a man as attractive as Jake. Everybody's talking about him."

"You stopped by the beauty shop today, didn't you?"

Megan laughed. "You know I had to get my weekly do and catch up on the gossip."

"I don't see how Betty gets anybody's hair done as much as she talks."

"Don't knock it. Betty has all the news."

"You're telling me," Eleanor said. Everybody in Lamar knew what a gossip Betty was.

Megan proceeded to tell Eleanor the latest news from the Betty hotline.

"Hey, why don't you have lunch with me tomorrow?" Eleanor suggested after all the gossip was discussed. "Drop by the office a little before noon and I'll introduce you to Jake."

"It's about time you invited me, girl. I was planning to show up on my own if you hadn't."

"I sorta figured that."

"Be sure to invite Jake to lunch with us."

"Don't worry. I'll invite him. I may even invite Carl."

Megan snorted. "Don't even think about it. The brother needs to get away from Carl. I'm telling you Carl is the dullest man I ever met. He was dull in high school and he's even duller now, if that's possible."

"You've never liked Carl, have you, Megan?"

"He's too much of a Goody Two-shoes. Even when we were kids, he was always judging me. Who's he to judge me?"

Eleanor laughed. "You're just upset because Carl is the only man in Lamar you don't have wrapped around your little finger."

"Like I'd even be interested in Carl. Please. I want a real man, not a boy."

Eleanor felt again that Megan protested a little too much when Carl's name was mentioned. She was almost sure Megan had a crush on him, though she'd never been able to get her to admit it. "If you say so, Megan. But I still may invite him to lunch with us."

"Hey, that might be a good idea. You can talk to Carl while I get to know Jake a little better. Better yet, why don't you go to lunch with Carl and leave Jake with me. I'll take good care of him."

"I bet you would," Eleanor said, ignoring the flame of jealousy that flared up in the middle of her stomach.

Six

Jake couldn't get Carl's words out of his head. *Eleanor could be beautiful, Eleanor could be beautiful.* He was about to agree with him. From where Jake sat, Eleanor needed to loosen up on the dress. The woman gave new meaning to the word *conservative.* She could also do something with her hair. He wanted to see it in a style other than that old maid's bun she wore every day.

Not that he didn't know what she was doing. He did. Eleanor was the corporate woman to the T. Her professional image was one of no-nonsense work.

He shrugged. Maybe it was because she worked for her father. He noticed she had a difficult time with the older members of the staff. They still wanted to treat her like a teenager. He knew her getup was part of her barrier against that, though he didn't think it was working.

"Here comes trouble." Carl leaned his head in Jake's office. "Megan has hit the floor."

Jake stood and walked to the door. "How do you know?"

"Don't you feel the rumbling in the foundation?"

"What are you talking about?"

Carl folded his arms across his chest and leaned

back on the desk nearest Jake and Eleanor's office. "Don't you hear all that chatter in the hallway? It's Megan time."

Jake kept his expression clear, but he felt the excitement bubble up in him. He was finally going to meet the woman by the pool. Anxious, he straightened his tie.

Carl shook in head in disgust. "Not you, too."

"What?"

"Megan's already got you under her spell and you haven't even met her." Still shaking his head, he continued, "I thought you were different. I knew I was the only sane male in Lamar. Now I wonder if I'm the only sane male in the country."

"Are you sure about that, friend?"

Carl dropped his arms and straightened. "Of course I'm sure," he answered with what Jake thought was a mite much enthusiasm.

"If you say so."

"Yes, I do say so."

Jake clapped Carl on the back. "Don't get all upset. So you don't like Megan. In a way I'm glad. It leaves the field clear for me. If you were interested, we'd have to duke it out for her."

Carl snorted. "You must be kidding. I'd never fight over Megan. Though that's the kind of stunt that would get her attention."

"Let's be glad it won't come to that. You're going to introduce me, though. Aren't you?"

Carl walked away from his perch and back to his desk in the middle of the newsroom. "You don't know Megan. She'll introduce herself. She probably knows all about you anyway. That woman is telepathic where men are concerned."

Jake was getting bored with Carl's attitude. He said he disliked Megan more than he showed it, he thought.

While Carl went back to his work, Jake paced in front of his office and waited for Megan to walk through the newsroom door. From everything Carl had said about her, he knew she'd be pleased to find him waiting. And he *did* want to make a good first impression.

Eleanor walked through the door first and she was more animated than Jake had ever seen her. Her eyes sparkled and her laughter was light, but full. There was even more pep in her step. When he saw the tall woman with short, tight brownish-red curls next to her, Jake's heart dropped. This was Megan?

As Eleanor and the redhead approached, Jake became more certain the woman was indeed Megan. There was something blatantly sexual about her. He felt it even from a distance. She was the kind of woman who called out to men without opening her mouth. And she was the kind of woman to whom men always responded. But she wasn't the woman from the pool. Her hair was too short and the wrong color and she was too tall. No, she wasn't the woman from the pool.

When she saw him, she flashed him a smile he was sure made weaker men pant. He merely returned it with one of his own. He saw the change in her expression and knew his response was not what she'd expected.

Jake watched the two women approach him.

Eleanor and Megan were the Odd Couple, all right. Megan in her bright red miniskirt and jacket was fire, and Eleanor in her cold navy blue female version of the power suit was ice, or at least that's what they seemed.

"You must be Jake," Megan said, extending her hand to him.

He pulled her hand to his lips in mock Southern gallantry. Carl groaned at the action, then turned his chair away from them. Eleanor rolled her eyes. Megan merely took it as her due.

"Why, Jake, they told me you were a Northerner. Where did you learn Southern charm?"

Jake rubbed her hand with his thumb before releasing it. "I've always felt the woman brings out the charm in a man. Now, if they had women like you in the North, maybe Northern charm would be as well known."

"You're pouring it on a bit too thick," Carl muttered from his seat not five feet from them.

Megan leaned close to Jake, but spoke to him in a voice loud enough for Eleanor and Carl to hear. "Don't mind Carl. He was raised in the South, but he's no gentleman."

"I heard that, Megan," Carl said, still facing away from them. Jake noticed he was doing a pretty good job of showing disinterest.

Megan turned to Carl. "Jealous, Carl?"

"Of what?" He still didn't turn around.

Megan frowned then turned back to Jake without answering Carl's question. "Are you free for lunch? It looks like Carl will be too busy to go. What a shame." Her smile said that was the best news she'd had in days.

Jake laughed, then noticed Eleanor wasn't smiling. She was watching him and Megan as though she expected something. What? "Where are you going for lunch?"

"Virginia's," Eleanor answered. "It's Megan's favorite place."

Megan folded her arm under Jake's as if she did it every day. "And you must go with us. We have to get to know each other better."

Jake laughed. "I thought that was supposed to be my line."

"We don't stand on formality around here, Jake," Carl said, finally turning around. He stared directly at Megan though he spoke to Jake. "You'd better watch out, she'll probably make a pass at lunch."

"Carl," Eleanor chastised.

Megan said nothing. She merely stared at Carl, then flecked nonexistent lint from her jacket in Carl's direction and turned back to Jake. "If you two are ready, we can go. I don't see any need for Carl to tag along. Do you, Eleanor?"

Eleanor sure did see a reason for Carl to tag along. He could be her companion. From the way things were going so far, Megan and Jake would spend the entire lunch flirting. And she'd be sitting there like a fifth wheel.

She knew she could bow out, claiming she had work to do, but she didn't want to. She wanted to be there when Jake realized she was the woman by the pool. She could tell by the change in his expression when he saw Megan that he'd correctly concluded Megan wasn't the woman.

Eleanor knew too that Jake had done what most people did when she and Megan were together. He'd compared them. Strangely enough, she felt his comparison didn't find her lacking. That was a first.

"I can think of a good reason for Carl to come along," Eleanor said, getting back to Megan's question.

"What?" Megan's tone said she seriously doubted it.

Eleanor looked from Jake to Megan. "I'm just a chaperone. You two may need somebody to hose you down."

Sometimes Eleanor wondered how she and Megan remained friends. Today was one of those days. Megan was in rare form.

"You're so funny, Jake," Megan said for the umpteenth time, each time needing to touch Jake's wrist lightly as if to prove she was telling the truth.

Eleanor could have gagged. She shot a glance at Carl. His response was pretty much the same. He was on his fourth drink; thankfully he wasn't drinking alcohol.

"You're going to rub the skin off his wrist if you keep rubbing on it," Carl commented, then dropped his napkin on the table and stood up. "Excuse me," he said, "I need to get some air. It's getting pretty thick in here."

A part of Eleanor wanted to get up and follow Carl, but another part of her wanted to stay right there with Megan and Jake. Somebody had to keep the two of them in line.

"What's his problem?" Jake asked, referring to Carl.

Megan dismissed his question with a wave of her hand. "Carl has so many problems. Who knows which one is bothering him today."

Jake sat back in his chair and lifted his glass to his lips. "What's up with you and Carl? You two act like quarreling lovers."

Megan's eyes flashed anger. "Don't even go there. Carl is definitely *not* my type, wouldn't be my type if he were the *only* man on the earth."

Jake shot a glance at Eleanor and she read the question in his eyes. His perception surprised her. He'd figured out what it had taken her years to conclude. She nodded her head slightly and Jake directed his attention back to Megan.

Jake and Megan flirted for the rest of lunch, pausing occasionally to include Eleanor.

"I know you swim, Jake," Megan said, batting her eyelashes. "Eleanor has invited me over for a swim after work. Why don't you join us?"

Eleanor almost choked on her coffee. This was what she wanted, yet it wasn't. If Jake went swimming with them, he'd definitely figure out she was the woman in the pool. She'd hoped he would have figured it out during lunch but he hadn't.

Jake looked at her. "I don't have any games to cover tonight. You won't mind, will you, Eleanor?"

"Why would I mind?" she asked, with a shrug of her shoulders. "You're living in the house. You can use the pool when you wish."

Jake smiled at Megan. "I'll see you after work, then." He turned to Carl, who had returned to the table. "Are you game?"

Carl snorted. "I can only stomach so much of Ms. M. in a single day. I think I'll pass."

Jake smiled first at Megan then at Eleanor, before lifting his glass to them. "It seems I've lucked out, ladies. I'll have the two of you to myself. I'm enjoying living in Lamar more by the minute."

For the first time since she'd taken on the managing editor's job, Eleanor watched the clock for quitting time. She couldn't wait for the swim party this afternoon. She glanced over at Jake. She couldn't wait to see his reaction when he found out she was the woman by the pool. She hoped he swallowed his tongue.

Then she wondered what he'd do. Would he start to flirt with her like he'd been flirting with Megan? A part of her hoped he would, so she could shoot him down. Yes, it would give her great pleasure to be the one that got away from Jake Mason, Mr. Irresistible.

"We're going to have to start discussing plans for the paper," Jake said.

Eleanor looked up at him. "So soon? On Monday, you will have been here two weeks and you're ready to start making plans. That's kind of quick, isn't it?"

"I don't think so. Anyway, I said we needed to start, not that we needed to finalize anything."

"Okay, then. When do you want to start? This weekend?"

Jake shook his head. "Monday is soon enough. I plan to have some fun this weekend."

Eleanor wondered if he'd asked Megan out. No, Megan probably asked him to go dancing at the Farmhouse, a local hangout for the adult crowd. She'd have to wait and ask Megan about it because she definitely wasn't going to ask Jake.

"Monday's fine with me," she said after checking her calendar. "How about first thing in the afternoon? One o'clock, okay?"

"It works for me." Jake didn't bother to check his calendar. "Well, I'm outta here. I guess I'll see you at the pool."

"You sure will," she said after he left the office. She waited a good fifteen minutes before packing up her briefcase and following after him.

Eleanor heard the voices and splashing water before she reached the pool. She stopped a few steps behind the hedges that separated her yard from the pool grounds, adjusted the white thong swimsuit she'd worn the first day Jake had seen her, and took a deep breath.

She stepped from behind the hedges. "Hi, you two," she said in as calm a voice as she could muster. Megan, dressed in a red one-piece mallot, and Jake, in black trunks, sat on the far end of the pool. "How's the water?" She dropped her fluffy white towel on the plaid lounger and dived into the pool to join them.

The water was the right temperature to make her forget her worry. She used broad strokes to swim to the side of the pool and join Megan and Jake. When she reached them, she hoisted herself up next to Megan.

Pushing back her mane of dark hair, she smiled. "The water's great. Why aren't you guys swimming?"

Megan put a proprietary hand on Jake's knee. "I wore him out. He needed his rest."

Eleanor looked at Jake for the first time, and when she saw his expression, she wanted to shout her joy. From the cold look in his eyes, she knew he'd figured out who she was.

"Enjoying yourself, Jake?" she asked.

"It was you," he said, his voice full of accusation.

Megan looked at him. "What are you talking about?"

Jake wouldn't take his cold eyes off Eleanor. "You made a fool out of me."

Eleanor grabbed the towel behind Megan. "I did no such thing. You made a fool out of yourself."

"What are you two talking about?" Megan asked, clearly not liking being kept in the dark.

"Jake thought I was you."

"What?"

Eleanor explained about the day Jake had seen her at the pool.

Megan turned to Jake. "Why did you think she was me?"

Jake glared at Eleanor. "Who else could the woman I saw have been? I surely didn't think it was Eleanor."

"What's that supposed to mean?" Eleanor said, recognizing an insult when she heard one.

"Yeah, what does that mean?" Megan repeated.

"How come you didn't think it was Eleanor? She lives here, after all. I don't."

"I'd seen her pictures," Jake muttered.

"What did you say?" Megan asked.

Eleanor didn't have to ask. She'd heard him. He'd seen her pictures and had concluded there was no way it could be her. She was definitely insulted.

"I'd seen her pictures," Jake said more clearly.

Megan chuckled. "What pictures? When?"

Jake explained about the friendship between their two fathers and the pictures they exchanged each year at the publishing convention.

"What did her pictures look like?" Megan asked, clearly enjoying Eleanor's discomfort.

Jake's eyes roamed Eleanor from head to toe. What Carl had said was an understatement. Eleanor was more than beautiful. She was a toasted goddess. "I'm sure you've seen the ones on the piano in the living room. In them, she's certainly doesn't look like she's looking now."

Megan turned to Eleanor. "See. I told you to stop dressing like some old woman."

"I don't dress like an *old* woman, as you put it, Megan. I dress like a *professional* woman. If I listened to you, I'd be dressed like a hooker."

"You know that's not so. There are a lot of professional outfits you could wear that wouldn't make you look so stern and old."

"I think I'm old enough to pick my own clothes, Megan."

"From what you've been picking lately, I'm not so sure. Anyway, it's not so much what you wear. It's how what you wear hides who you are."

"And who am I, Megan?" Eleanor asked calmly.

Jake cleared his throat and both women turned to him. They had forgotten he was there. Clearly, this was an argument they'd had before.

"Sorry," Megan said sheepishly. "We always get carried away when we discuss this particular topic. But don't you think I'm right, Jake? She's gorgeous, but you'd never know it by what she wears every day. Tell her."

Jake read Eleanor's discomfort—no, it was more than discomfort—with the topic. "I don't think I want to get in this."

"You're already in it," Megan corrected. "You said that after seeing her pictures, you never would have thought she could look this good."

Jake shot a pleading glance at Eleanor. "That's not exactly what I said."

"Not in so many words," Megan relented. "But it's what you meant."

"Look," Eleanor said, tired of the entire discussion. "We came here to swim. Let's swim."

"You owe me an apology."

Eleanor's eyes flashed her surprise at Jake's statement. "I recognized you. It's your problem if you didn't recognize me."

"I didn't see your face," Jake murmured.

She shook her head in disgust. "And I can guess why. From what I saw, your eyes were focused on another part of my anatomy."

Jake's gaze dropped to her thighs and she knew he was remembering her upturned bottom. "Oh," he said.

"Yes, oh," she said, wishing he'd stop staring at her.

"Well," he said, recovering quickly. "That doesn't matter. You still owe me an apology."

"Surely you're joking."

"No, I'm not. You should have told me it was you. You've had me going on and on about meeting Megan since I've been here."

"Hold on a minute," Megan said. "This is beginning to sound like you're disappointed about meeting me. I don't think I like the sound of that."

Jake threw up both hands. There was no reasoning with them this afternoon. "Southern women. Who needs them?" He grabbed his towel and stomped off to the house.

Seven

Megan stared after Jake. "What's wrong with him?"

"Right now, I don't know and I don't care." Eleanor stood up. "I thought you came here to swim. Let's get in the water."

Megan jerked her friend's hand, causing her to sit back down. "You like him, don't you?"

"He's all right."

"This is me you're talking to, Eleanor. There's nothing wrong with it. He's a fine brother. And he seems interested in you, too."

Eleanor squashed the hope that sprang up in her chest. "He's interested in anything in a skirt."

Megan shook her head. "I know men. And that man is interested in you. He was probably curious even before he saw the *real* you."

Eleanor paddled her feet in the water and it splashed up her leg. "Now I know you're crazy." But memories of Jake's gazing at her in the last day or two flooded her mind. Was he interested in her?

"I don't see what the big deal is. He's a grown man and a fine one to boot. Go for it!"

Eleanor paddled faster. "There's nothing to go for. Anyway, I thought you were interested in him."

"I was, but only if you didn't want him."

"I don't want him."

"You may not want to want him, Eleanor, but you *do* want him."

Megan was too right. Eleanor's feelings for Jake had sneaked up on her. Sure, she'd been attracted to him from the beginning, but that was physical. In the past couple of weeks, she'd grown to like him as well. And she'd developed a begrudging respect for him after seeing the way he handled his sports assignments. But her emotions were too new to share with Megan right now. She'd share them, but not now. "What about your feelings for Carl?"

Megan's eyes jerked away. "Now I don't know what you're talking about."

"Sure you don't."

"What's that supposed to mean?"

"It means this game you and Carl are playing. When are you both going to admit that you care about each other?"

Megan snorted. "I also care about stray cats."

Eleanor decided to stop prying. Maybe Megan wasn't any more ready to talk about her feelings for Carl than she was ready to talk about her feelings for Jake. She stood and dived into the pool. What a pair they were!

"I thought you said they were beginning to like each other," Randolph said, thumping his Cross pen on the desk pad.

"They were until this little mishap this afternoon," Mathias responded with impatience.

"So what happened?"

"How do you expect me to know?"

Randolph jumped up out of his chair. "Hell, Mat, you're right there with them. Jake's living in your house. Eleanor's living in your backyard. And they both work for you. Why don't you know what happened?"

A moment of intense silence preceded Mathias's muttered response. "It was something to do with a swimming pool."

Randolph eased back down in his chair and waited for Mathias to tell his story. Mathias always did this when he was tense. No amount of pushing would make him speed up the telling of his tale. "What happened with the pool?"

Mathias explained the mix-up Jake had made with Eleanor and Megan.

Randolph chuckled. "So Eleanor's female vanity took a beating when Jake didn't recognize her."

"And Jake's male ego took a beating when he found out it was Eleanor in the pool and not Megan," Mat finished for him.

"That's a good sign. It seems to me things are moving along according to plan."

"Well, you must be seeing things I'm not seeing."

Randolph's secretary came in and beckoned him. "Stop worrying, Mat. Things are coming along fine. I've got to go."

Carl stood on his toes and let the basketball fly out of his hands. Swoosh! "That's the game, man," he said, grinning. "I told you I was good."

Jake dropped down on the pavement, grabbed the

blue towel next to him, and wiped the sweat from his face. "You're not that good. I'm out of it today."

Carl sat next to him, leaned back on his elbows, and stretched out his long legs. "Excuses, excuses."

"You'd better watch it. It's only a game."

"I bet you'd be singing a different tune if you'd won instead of me."

Jake shook his head. "Man, if I had on those red polka dot shorts, I don't think I'd be saying much of anything. Win or lose. Where'd you get those things anyway?"

"I don't really remember," Carl said, looking down at the his dotted shorts before looking over at the regulation New York Knicks shorts Jake wore. "Not everybody has designer sportswear."

"Don't even start. I've had enough arguing for one day."

Carl chuckled, then reached behind Jake for the water bottle. "Eleanor and Megan got you down."

Jake snorted, shaking his head. "Those two women are crazy. I didn't come to Lamar to get mixed up with crazy women."

Carl took another sip from the straw in the water bottle. "Why did you come to Lamar, Jake?"

Jake shot him a quick glance. "You know why."

"I know what you've said, but I have a feeling it's more than that."

Jake thought about playing off Carl's question, then decided against it. "Have you ever felt the need to prove yourself?"

Carl nodded. "I was the class nerd. I felt the need every day and I still do."

"Well, I was never the nerd. I was Mr. Cool. No

worries. No responsibilities." He stopped for a minute to gather his thoughts and was glad that Carl didn't interrupt those thoughts. "But that's not who I really was."

"So why did you act that way then? To get girls?"

Jake shook his head. "I wish it had been something as simple as that. No, my reasons were a bit deeper."

Again, Carl waited without questioning.

"It's almost like my father wanted me to be that. He seemed more comfortable with me in that role than me working with him."

"You were a kid, Jake. Your father probably wanted you to act like a kid."

Jake wished that were true. But it wasn't. He'd stopped being a kid a long time ago, but his father's attitude toward him hadn't changed. At least, it hadn't until this assignment in Lamar. Finally, his father had given him a job in Mason Publishing. And he was determined to present his father with a proposal for this merger that would make the older man question why he hadn't asked for Jake's help before.

Unfortunately, Jake had been in Lamar almost two weeks and he hadn't come up with a fresh angle on the deal. Not yet. But he knew if he kept digging, he'd find the angle he needed.

Carl punched him in the arm then stood up. "Come on, man. I think we both could use a cold beer."

"Strike!" the umpire called.

Jake grimaced. It didn't appear that his team was

going to win today. His team. He'd been Carl's assistant coach for less than an hour and he already felt it was his team. He already had plans for the next practice. The Johnson kid needed to loosen his grip on the bat. The Woods boy should have been playing third base instead of center field. Yes, he had some ideas he was sure could improve this team.

"Enjoying yourself, man?" Carl asked, coming back into the dugout.

"Great, man. Look at that kid's swing. He needs some work. He's gripping the bat too tight."

Carl clapped him on the back. "Does that mean you're going to work with us while you're here?"

Jake nodded. He was glad he'd called Carl yesterday after the women had sent him running from the pool. Their quick game of one-on-one followed by a night of beer drinking had helped to ease his anger at Eleanor's trickery. He admitted *trickery* might be too strong a word, but he still insisted Eleanor should have told him she was the woman at the pool.

He allowed his glance to slide over to the first row of bleachers, where Eleanor stood talking to a member of the cheerleading squad. She looked great in her white denim shorts and pink T-shirt. Jake smiled when he thought about a baseball team with cheerleaders. He'd never heard of that before, but Carl had explained that the parents of the boys on the team had daughters who wanted to participate but who didn't want to play. Thus, the baseball cheerleading squad.

"She looks good, doesn't she?"

Jake didn't bother pretending he didn't know who

Carl was talking about. "Very good." Good enough to eat, he thought to himself. He remembered then that this was the second time Carl had commented on Eleanor's looks. He'd assumed the two didn't really get along, but now he wondered. "You don't have a thing for Eleanor, do you?"

"Who, me? You must be kidding."

For some reason, Jake took exception to Carl's comment. "What's wrong with Eleanor?"

"There's nothing wrong with her if you want a woman who thinks she knows everything."

Jake laughed. Carl was right. Eleanor did think she knew everything. He wondered how much of that was real and how much of it was a part of her professional persona. "What about Megan? Does she think she knows everything?"

Carl snorted. "No, Megan thinks she *is* everything."

Jake shook his head. It was as he had figured. Carl had it bad for Megan. He had it so bad he didn't even realize he had it. The poor sod. Megan was making his life miserable and he didn't even understand why. Well, Carl didn't have to worry about Jake making a move on Megan. No, his interests lay a little closer to home. He glanced over at Eleanor again. She might think she knew everything, but he knew a thing or two himself. It'd be fun figuring out who knew the most.

"Strike three. You're out," the umpire yelled. Pulling off his cap and mask, he said, "Game's over."

As the boys marched out of the dugout, Jake clapped them on the shoulders. "Good game, guys. We'll get 'em next time." He heard Carl saying similar words and reminding the boys about their next practice.

"I don't know who feels worse, me or them," Carl said after the last boy had filed out.

"Take my word for it," Jake said, gathering the last of the equipment from the dugout. "They feel worse."

Carl picked up the ball basket. "Maybe you're right. Hey, you played sports in college, didn't you?"

Jake nodded. "I ran track. Almost made the Olympic team."

"That's right and you majored in drama."

Jake stopped and looked at Carl. He didn't talk much about his rebellious Yale days. He'd majored in drama to irk his father. Jake had thought his father would force him to choose a major that would be useful in Mason Publishing. But it hadn't happened. Randolph had only encouraged his interests. And Jake had been too stubborn to change his major after that. "How'd you know?"

Carl was silent.

"How did you know?"

Carl shrugged as if it wasn't important. "I must have read it somewhere."

"Come on, man. There's more to it than that. I'm sure you didn't read it *somewhere*. How'd you know?"

More silence.

"You did a background check on me, didn't you?" Jake didn't wait for a response. "Whose idea, Mathias's or Eleanor's?" Jake knew the answer but he asked anyway.

"Eleanor's," Carl answered reluctantly.

"Damn!" Jake slapped his cap against his thigh.

"I knew it. What's on that woman's mind? What right does she have to go digging around in my background?"

"Hey, man," Carl said, placing a calming hand on Jake's shoulder. "It wasn't like that. Eleanor was worried about your plans for the paper. You don't know what this paper means to her."

Jake sat down on the bench. "Why don't you tell me?"

Carl dropped the ball basket and sat next to Jake. "Eleanor's mother and father bought the paper when Eleanor was a baby. The paper was a weekly then. Anyway, a black couple owning a newspaper in a small, predominately white Southern town was a big thing at the time. They experienced some problems early on, though you wouldn't know it now. The people of Lamar have grown used to it and to them. The paper is her family legacy. Naturally, she has strong ties to it and she'll do anything to protect it."

"So why did Mathias agree to go into business with Mason Publishing?"

"That's the question Eleanor has been asking since she found out about the deal. That's why she asked for the background check on you. She was looking for anything that would help her understand her father's actions."

"And did she find anything?" When Carl hesitated, Jake added, "I'm not asking you to be disloyal. I'm trying to understand the real situation here."

"No, she didn't find anything. She still doesn't know why her father wants this deal."

"So she's not buying that he wants the money Mason Publishing has to offer?"

Carl stood up. "You'll have to ask her that. I've probably said too much as it is. Now let's get out of here."

Jake eased up from his seat and followed Carl out of the dugout. Eleanor and a pretty, dark-skinned little girl with a head full of braids were the only people left in the park.

"We're waiting for Kia's mother," Eleanor said when they asked why she was still there.

"How long will she be?" Jake asked solicitously.

"Oh, it shouldn't be long now. Don't worry about us. You two go on."

Jake looked at Carl. "You go on, man. I'll wait here with Eleanor and Kia."

"You don't have to do that," Eleanor protested. "I told you her mother'll be along any minute now."

Jake dropped down on the bench next to her. "Then I guess I won't have long to wait, now will I?" He smiled at the little girl. "Hi, Kia. Did you enjoy the game?"

The little girl, who couldn't have been more than seven, smiled a gap-tooth smile up at him and bowed her head up and down.

"Do you want to play baseball when you're older?"

She smiled but this time she shook her head.

"How about being a cheerleader?"

This time she bowed her head up and down vigorously.

"Can you do any cheers now?"

She looked up at Eleanor.

"You can talk to him. His name is Mr. Mason."

She looked back at Jake. "Miss Eleanor has been teaching me one, but I haven't learned it yet."

Eleanor tousled the little girl's braids. "You're getting better each time we practice. Before you know it, you'll be able to do all the cheers you want."

The little girl gave Eleanor a look of pure adoration and Jake's heart turned over. He was about to say something more when the little girl jumped up.

"Mommy, Mommy," she called in the direction of a late model, well-worn blue Ford Escort.

Eleanor stood and held the little girl's hand as the child's mother got out of her car and headed toward them. "Yes, it's your mommy."

"Thanks, Eleanor," the mother said, giving the little girl a hug. She was dressed in a brown plaid uniform so Jake assumed she was a waitress. "I'm sorry I'm late. I had a problem with the car."

Concern clouded Eleanor's eyes. "Nothing serious, I hope."

The woman shook her head, then glanced at Jake. Eleanor introduced him. "Winifred Carlisle meet Jake Mason. Jake's working at the paper for the summer."

"A summer job?" Winifred asked.

Jake smiled at her. "Something like that." He tugged at one of Kia's braids. "You have a great little girl here."

Some of the fatigue left Winifred's eyes as she smiled at her little girl. "The best. And I'd better get her home. You're probably tired, aren't you, punkin'."

"Can we get ice cream, Mommy?"

Winifred looked up at the adults. "I guess she's

not that tired. But I'd better get her home. Thanks again, Eleanor. Nice meeting you, Mr. Mason."

"See you next week, Kia," Eleanor said, waving goodbye to the little girl.

"I didn't know you were a cheerleading instructor," Jake said as much to himself as to her. There were a lot of layers to Eleanor and he wanted to peel each one of them away.

Eleanor turned back to him. "I'm not. Kia's a little girl who needed a friend."

"And you're a big sister."

She didn't smile. "You make it sound as if I'm doing something extraordinary. I'm not."

"Just doing your part, huh?"

She did smile then. "Something like that. How about you? When did you become a coach?"

He shrugged. "I've always been involved in sports. But I guess you already know that."

She had the decency to blush, and to him, it made her look even cuter. "How would I know that?"

He tugged on her arm and she plopped down next to him. "Give it up, Eleanor. Carl told me about his investigation."

"He had no right to do that. He's my employee. I'll speak to him tomorrow."

"You'll do no such thing. We're partners now and Carl will not be called on the carpet for telling me something I need to know."

"We're not partners," she muttered.

Jake leaned closer. "What was that? I couldn't hear you?"

"I said, 'We're not partners.' Yet."

"And you don't want us to become partners, do you?"

"How'd you guess?"

"I'm not stupid. You've expressed your dislike from the first day we met, but I thought you were warming up to the idea of our business relationship. Was I wrong?"

Eleanor stood up. "I thought you said we would talk about this on Monday. Let's keep to that schedule. I have plans tonight, and if we get into this discussion, my evening will be ruined. Deal?"

Jake stood up, resolved to wait until Monday to have their talk. "Deal."

Eleanor nodded and proceeded to walk to her car. He followed her. "So what are you doing tonight?" he asked casually. He really wanted to ask *whom* she was going out with. He didn't think she was seeing anybody.

She stopped walking and glared at him. "Going out." She resumed walking.

Okay, he could take a hint. Especially when it was as subtle as a sledgehammer. "Megan going with you?"

"If you're interested in Megan's schedule, you should call her. I'm sure she gave you her number."

"What if it's not Megan's schedule I'm interested in?"

She stopped again when she reached her two-seater sports car. After taking a deep breath, she said, "Don't even think about it. I'm not interested. Definitely not interested." She pulled the keys out of the pocket of her shorts, opened the door, and slid into the driver's seat.

When she reached to close the door, Jake held it open. "You can't run from me, Eleanor."

She jerked on the door and he released it. "Watch me." She turned on the ignition, quickly put the car in gear, and backed out of the graveled parking lot, kicking up dust as she left.

Damn, Jake thought. There was nothing he liked better than a challenge. He knew pursuing Eleanor was a tricky move since he was there on business. Business with her. He also knew he was about to do something he'd regret. But he couldn't stop himself. Eleanor drew him the way bees drew honey.

Eight

Jake looked up from his desk when Eleanor walked in the office Monday morning. "Good morning," he said with cheer.

Eleanor nodded. "Good morning."

He studied her dark suit, sensible shoes, and high-cut blouse but still wondered why he hadn't known she was the woman in the pool. Now that he knew who she was, it was obvious. When she removed her jacket and rose up on her toes to hang it on the coat stand, he noticed the way her blouse curved around her full breasts and the way her skirt clung to her generously rounded buttocks. It didn't take much effort to remember how the rest of her looked. The swimsuit she'd worn that day had left little to the imagination.

She turned around and glared at him. "Let's not forget this is a place of business."

He deliberately let his gaze wander teasingly from her trim ankles to the head that sported the usual bun. "And I've got nothing but business on my mind."

She opened her mouth to respond, but apparently changed her mind. She closed her mouth instead and went to her chair, dropping her morning papers on her desk.

Jake got up. "Want some coffee?"

She eyed him suspiciously, but handed him her cup. "Thanks."

"No problem," Jake said and left the office.

Eleanor slumped down in her chair. This was going to be harder than she'd imagined. Jake Mason did things to her. She had to be strong.

Jake returned to the office with her coffee. "Here you go."

When Eleanor took the cup, her fingers brushed against his and his gaze met hers. "Sorry," she mumbled, not knowing which was hotter, the coffee or his hand.

"No problem," he said, looming over her.

She turned around to her computer and pulled up the latest AP stories, hoping he'd take the hint and she wouldn't have to tell him to get away from her.

"What's new this morning?" he asked, leaning over her shoulder, so close she could smell his cologne.

She mumbled off the titles of the first few articles.

He pointed his finger to an article on redistricting. "Open that one."

She wanted to tell him to go to his own terminal and look at it; instead, she hit the space bar twice and the file opened.

"Those are some good quotes from your esteemed senators. Are you going to use them?"

She shook her head. "I'll let Carl decide. He's doing a story on local response to redistricting. If he wants to incorporate the quotes, we'll do that. If not, we'll run them as a separate story."

She breathed her relief when Jake picked up his cup and moved away from her.

"Are we still meeting after lunch?" he asked.

She'd forgotten about the meeting. "Sure."

He nodded and went back to his desk and to work. She watched him covertly while she pretended to go through her morning ritual of reading the papers. If only he—

"Eleanor," Maxine's voice on the intercom interrupted her thoughts, "they need you in composition. They're having a problem with the layout."

Eleanor went to composition. After solving the problem there, she spoke with Carl about his story, then one thing led to another, until the paper was ready and sent to the press. When she was done, she wanted more than anything to go home and take a cool dip in the pool. But she had that meeting with Jake.

"Lunch?"

She jerked her head away from her terminal and her thoughts back to the present. "What are you doing here?"

He grinned a wide mouth grin. "My office."

She rolled her eyes. "What are you doing back so soon? I thought you had an interview."

He flopped down in his chair. "I did. It didn't take long. The coach is an easy guy to talk to. How do you guys keep him in Lamar?"

She shook her head. "Really, Jake, you make it sound like he's in a cage. He's here because he wants to be."

"If you say so."

"It's hard for you to believe people actually enjoy living here, isn't it?"

"Not people. The coach. I'm sure he could get a position in a bigger town, a bigger school, more prestige."

"Bigger doesn't necessarily mean better. The man is living here because he likes living here."

"Are you here because you like living here, Eleanor?"

Memories of the night Jake had arrived in Lamar filled her mind. He'd shown his distaste for her decision to continue living at home then. "Yes, I'm here because I like it here."

"Maybe you're here because you're afraid to go anywhere else?" he murmured under his breath.

"What did you say?"

"Nothing."

"I heard you," she accused. "What do you have against small-town living, Jake? Have you ever considered that you're the one who's afraid? It's much easier to hide in a big city than it is in a small town."

Jake was still thinking about Eleanor's words when they met for their afternoon meeting. For some reason her accusation that he was hiding stuck with him. He wondered what signals she'd picked up to make her say that. When she entered the closet-size room they called a conference room, he had to force himself to discuss the scheduled topic when he really wanted to discuss her comments.

"Have you thought much about this merger?" he

asked, once they were settled across the conference table from each other.

"I've done nothing but think about it since Dad mentioned the plans to me."

He lifted a brow in her direction. "I've got a feeling I'm going to have to listen to your little jabs all afternoon. So why don't you get it all off your chest before we get started?"

She leaned toward him. "Okay, let's do that."

He tossed his pen on the table. "Shoot."

Eleanor picked up his pen and pointed it at him. "Number one. My father and I have prided ourselves on running this paper with no interference. We do what we want, when we want—"

Jake lifted a finger. "Correction. You do what you want when you can get the money. I think that's why I'm here."

She shot him a warning glance. "We don't want to, will not, lose that autonomy."

She waited for him to interrupt again, but he only nodded.

She took a deep breath. "Number two. We're concerned that though Mason Publishing initially agrees with number one, somewhere down the road things will change."

"That's why we have contracts," Jake said, interrupting again.

She ignored that comment. "Number three. You and I have to be the voices of reason here. Our fathers' friendship is the basis for the business relationship and that makes it a risky proposition. I don't think either of them has really thought this through."

Jake nodded. "You might have a point there."

Her eyes registered her surprise. "You're actually agreeing with me?"

He leaned toward her. "You've gotten our roles confused. You've been the one with the hostility, not me."

"Touché."

"Have you talked to your attorney about your, ah, three points?"

"Of course. Now what's on your mind?"

He reached for his pen. "Number one," he said and she knew he wanted to grin. "Mason Publishing cannot afford for this newspaper to become a money pit."

"A money pit? What are you talking about?"

"You've mentioned before that the one positive for this whole deal is the dollars Mason Publishing brings to the table. Well, each expenditure must be justified. We can only spend money where we think we can earn it back."

"So, you're a bottom line kind of guy?"

"Aren't we all? You have an MBA. You know how businesses work."

"How did you know I had an MBA?"

"You aren't the only one with access to an investigating staff."

She was impressed. "Two for you."

He grinned. "Number two, which is really related to number one. This is a business deal, not a personal one. All decisions will be made on the basis of what's best for the business, all the businesses, of Mason Publishing."

She pointed her finger at him. "And that point

conflicts with my points one and three. I cannot and will not abdicate control of the *Lamar Daily* to Mason Publishing. We must keep control. On that point, I'm inflexible."

"It's also a point on which I'm inflexible. Our fathers agreed on some basic tenets which I'm forced to uphold. Beyond that, you're going to have to trust us, Eleanor."

"Trust *you?*"

"Yes, trust us to make good decisions."

Eleanor wanted to dismiss Jake and end this meeting, but she couldn't. Her father wanted this deal and it was up to her to fight for the best terms possible. She had to compromise with Jake. She hoped she didn't live to regret it.

"What do you say? Will you trust me?"

Eleanor looked into his eyes and she understood he was asking about more than their business negotiation. "Let's take it day by day. If you show yourself to be trustworthy and if you work in good faith toward the paper, maybe then we can talk about trust."

Jake nodded, seeming to understand that was all he was going to get. "All right. Let's go through your points again in a little more detail. I'll have our accountants in New York run the numbers and we'll see where we are."

Jake stared at the calendar on his desk. Five weeks. He'd been in Lamar five weeks and he hadn't made much headway on his plan to impress the hell out of his father. All he'd done was get frustrated by a stern miss who was a knockout in a white swimsuit.

Maybe it was because she was the first woman he'd seen in Lamar, Jake reasoned. Maybe that was why she stayed on his mind all the time.

Jake shook his head. There was no use lying to himself. The woman at the pool had stayed on his mind true enough, but Eleanor had become an obsession. And when he'd asked her out, she'd had the nerve to turn him down as if he were some horny schoolboy.

But it was her supposed disinterest over the last week that irked him most. He'd never been treated with disinterest by a woman before.

So he had a plan to turn Eleanor's disinterest into interest. Although it wasn't an entirely ethical plan, it was close enough to one that he could execute it without too much guilt.

When he saw Eleanor glide down the hallway toward their office, he garnered enough courage to execute the first step of his plan.

"How's it going?" she asked, entering the office.

"I need to talk to you about something, Eleanor." He shut their office door and closed the blinds on the glass window facing the newsroom.

"Is something wrong?" she asked, anxiety filling her words.

"In a way," he said in a whisper.

"Speak up, Jake."

He moved closer to the desk, but didn't raise his voice. "It's about Carl and Megan. I think they need our help."

"Carl and Megan? What are you talking about?"

His look said he thought she was dense. "You do know he's in love with her, don't you?"

"In love? Carl's in love with Megan?"

Jake nodded his head. "I know when a man's in love."

She smirked. "I bet you do."

"Look, this isn't about me. It's about Megan and Carl. I like them both and I hate seeing them so miserable."

Megan didn't seem to be miserable. She had gone out with two different men over the weekend. "What do you think we can do about this anyway?"

"Matchmake," he said, as if he'd originated the idea. "You and I could be matchmakers."

"No way." She shook her head. There was no way she was going to get mixed up in Megan's love life. Sure she thought there was more to Megan and Carl than Megan would admit. But Eleanor knew her friend well enough to know she wouldn't appreciate any interference.

"I thought you were Megan's friend."

"I am her friend. Her best friend. That's why I'm not getting involved in any matchmaking scheme you may have in your mind." She lifted a brow. "If you're smart, you'll stay out of it."

He collapsed in his chair. "I can't just do nothing. Carl is driving me crazy complaining about Megan. If you won't do it for him, do it for me."

She had to smile. "It can't be that bad."

"It's worse than that. That man has it so bad he doesn't know if he's coming or going." Jake knew he was pouring it on a little thick but he couldn't stop himself. "Can't you see it?"

She nodded slowly. "They argue too much for there not to be something there."

"Yes, it's either love or hate. And I don't think it's hate."

"Well," Eleanor hesitated. "Neither do I."

"So you'll work with me?" Jake pressed.

"I'll think about it."

Jake grinned as if he'd won the lottery. "We can't discuss this too much at work." He motioned toward the door and the glass window. "The staff is probably wondering what we're doing in here now. Why don't we get together over dinner and discuss it? How about tonight?"

Nine

Mel's Diner. The name on the revolving sign in front of the faded white diner was vaguely familiar to Jake. He rushed around to the passenger door of his leased sports sedan in time to close the door behind Eleanor.

"I can do some things for myself," she said to his unasked question.

"So I see." He put his hand to her back and ushered her through the screened door. He thought he'd stepped back in time when he saw the three white men in beige painter's outfits seated on the faded blue plastic seats of the metal bar stools. His gaze roamed to the score of people seated in the matching booths. It occurred to him that he and Eleanor were the only black faces in the place.

"You come here often?" he asked with obvious sarcasm.

Ellen gave a light chuckle. "All the time."

"Do we take a seat or wait to be seated?"

"We wait. Somebody will take care of us soon."

Jake noticed the two women in short, pink, apron-covered waitress uniforms busily serving the already seated customers. One was a kooky-looking brunette

with beady eyes. The other was a nondescript redhead with a welcoming smile.

"Hi there, handsome. Nice buns."

Jake looked to his left and saw a bleached blonde
with a beehive hairdo and a mouth full of chewing
gum giving him the once-over.

"Where'd you find this one?" the gum-chewing
beehive asked Eleanor.

"This is Jake. He's working with us down at the
paper. I thought you would have heard by now."

She looked Jake over again and he actually felt as
if she was undressing him with her eyes. "Well, now,
maybe I did hear something."

Eleanor looked up at Jake and chuckled at the
expression on his face. "You'd better leave him
alone, Flo. I don't think he can take it."

Flo continued to smack on that gum. "I kinda
think Jake, here, could handle anything. And I get
the feeling he's handled a lot."

Eleanor laughed again. "Show us to a booth before Jake passes out."

As Jake followed Eleanor and Flo to a booth in
the middle of the restaurant, he couldn't help but
notice the exaggerated movement of Flo's hips.

"Here you are, folks," she said, handing them
each a laminated menu. "Just holler when you're
ready to order."

Jake watched Flo's switch as she walked away from
them and to another table.

"See something you like?" Eleanor asked.

Jake turned to her and saw the humor in her eyes.
"She's a piece of work."

Eleanor laughed, then slipped out of her navy

jacket and placed it on the seat next to her. "That's an understatement. Flo's a landmark around here."

"Mel's Diner. Flo. Somebody in this town got a TV complex or something?"

Eleanor nodded. "I wondered if you'd even notice. Didn't know if the TV show *Alice* went over well with you Northerners."

"It didn't. At least, not at my house."

She ignored the comment. "Mel McKissic was a big fan of the show. When it was canceled he begged, borrowed, and some say stole to get the money to open this place. When it opened, Flo was here. Nobody knows where he found her."

"You're kidding."

She shook her head. "It was a big thing last year when Mel and Flo got married. It took up the entire page of the Thursday Living section."

"That much space, huh?" He chuckled.

Eleanor nodded. "That kind of story would have run in the Sunday edition, if we did a Sunday edition."

Jake raised his hand. "This meal is to discuss Carl and Megan, not the newspaper. Let's save that for the office."

"Okay, what do you want to eat?"

Jake picked up his menu. "What do you suggest?"

"The meatloaf is the best."

Jake scanned the items on the menu. Liver and onions, chicken steak, chicken gizzards. "I think I'll take the meatloaf."

Eleanor picked up his menu and hers and waved them in the air. Flo was at the table in a matter of seconds. She took their orders and left.

"Waving the menus above your head is a unique way of getting the waitress's attention," he commented.

"You should tell Flo that. It was her idea. She said people waving their hands confused her since people in Lamar were waving all the time. She didn't know if they were waving for her to come over or if they were waving at one of their friends across the room."

"I'm getting scared," he said.

Her eyes widened. "Why?"

"That explanation actually made sense."

Eleanor laughed and her face brightened and softened. He'd love to see her like that when she sported that white swimsuit. Then he'd want to see that sparkle in her eyes dim with passion.

"Do you really come here often?" he asked to keep his thoughts away from dangerous subjects.

"Not often. Just when I need to get away and think."

"So why'd you bring me here?"

She lifted her shoulders slightly. "It's private, in a way, and we can discuss Megan and Carl without worrying about the wrong people overhearing," she said, wondering if there was more to it than that but not yet ready to think about it.

He seemed to accept that answer, but his eyes searched hers as if trying to find out more. He clasped his hands and leaned forward. "Now what are we going to do about Carl and Megan?"

Eleanor shifted back on her bench seat. Was it her or was Jake invading her space again? "This dinner was your idea. I thought you were the one with the plan."

Jake relaxed and sat back. "I can't believe you don't have one. How have you lived with those two this long?"

Eleanor lifted a hand to her hair, brushing it lightly. It was time to take the bun down; it was starting to itch.

"Why don't you take it down?" Jake said as if he'd heard her thoughts. *And unbutton a few buttons on that blouse while you're at it,* he added to himself.

Eleanor looked at him, not sure if she should take his suggestion, then she smiled and got her purse. "I'll be back in a minute."

Eleanor felt Jake's eyes on her as she made her way to the women's room, and she liked the feeling. She pushed open the door then walked to the mirror above the first sink.

She placed her purse on the metal ledge above the sink and took the pins out of her hair. After placing the pins in her purse and taking out her brush, she shook her head, causing her mass of dark brown hair to fall about her shoulders.

Eyeing herself in the mirror, she toyed with the top button on her blouse. "What the hell," she said and undid first the top button, then the second. "That should keep Mr. Mason on his toes."

She brushed a few unruly strands in place, then put her brush back in her purse and left the rest room. Flo was seated at their booth when she got back and Jake was laughing.

Flo looked up at Eleanor. "Back already? Jake and me were getting acquainted some." Flo stood up and Eleanor slid back in the booth. "Loosening up, are you, honey?" Before Eleanor could answer, Flo went on. "Well, I can see how this man could make you unbutton your blouse. Hell, he'd make me do a little more than loosen a few buttons. And he just might be the one man, other than Mel, that is, to see me without this beehive."

"Mel's a lucky man," Jake said, taking Flo's hand in his larger one. "If I thought I had a chance, I'd give him a run for his woman."

"Go on with you," Flo said, pleased with Jake's comment. Eleanor didn't miss the slight squeeze she gave his hand before she released it.

Unless Eleanor's eyes were deceiving her, Flo's strut had gotten worse. She rolled her eyes. "What did you do to her?"

Jake poured each of them a glass of iced tea from the pitcher Flo had brought. "I didn't do anything to her. She's a nice woman. We were having a little fun. You do know about that, don't you?"

"About what? You making a pass at everything in a skirt?"

"No, having fun. That is a concept that you understand, isn't it?"

"What do you think?" Eleanor watched his gaze travel from her hair to the top of her breasts. It took all her strength to keep from fastening one of the buttons on the bone collarless blouse she'd worn with her navy suit.

"I think you're gorgeous."

She cleared her throat. It got so stuffy in the diner she wanted to fan herself, but she wouldn't give Jake the satisfaction of knowing how much he affected her.

Flo returned with their meals and saved her from having to respond to his comment.

"About Megan and Carl," she said once she'd recovered her composure. "What do you think we should do?"

"We need to keep putting them together. They don't see each other enough."

"But when they do, they argue and take shots at each other the entire time. Remember the day Megan came to the paper?"

Jake laughed. "Of course I remember. They're a real fire and ice couple."

"More like oil and vinegar."

"You aren't fooled by their show, are you? Those two love each other."

Eleanor took a pat of butter and smeared it across her dinner roll. "And you think if we put them together enough, they'll finally admit their feelings."

Jake nodded. "It's takes a lot of energy to fight against their emotions the way they do. If nothing else, they're going to tire themselves out. Then they'll have to face their feelings."

There was some merit to Jake's idea, but there was also a major hole. "But who's going to referee in the meantime?"

"Us."

"I kinda thought that's where you were going."

"Cheer up. This could be fun. They may even make us godparents."

"You like kids a lot, don't you?" she asked, thinking about him helping Carl with the Little League team.

He nodded. "Part of being an only child, I guess."

It was the same with her. As a child she'd often wished for a brother or sister and she'd always loved babies. Children were still dear to her, which was one of the reasons she spent time with little girls like Kia.

"You know about that, don't you?" he asked when she didn't say anything. "We do have something in common."

Eleanor knew he was talking about their mothers and having lost them when they were young. "I think our mothers, even more than their shared childhoods, is the bond between our fathers."

Jake nodded. "My father thinks a lot of Mathias. I know they talk on the phone a lot and they see each other every year at the damn conference."

"Yeah, I remember the first year Dad brought home a photo of you."

Jake grinned. "You do?"

She arched a brow. "I bet you don't remember the first one your dad brought home of me."

"Oh, yes I do. I think that's who I still expected you to be. A little girl."

"I'm not that, am I?"

He grinned. "Not in the ways that count."

Heaven help her, she blushed. "You haven't changed much over the years."

"Now that has to be an insult."

"No. I was about eleven at the time. You must have been about fifteen. And I thought you were the handsomest boy I'd ever seen, my own personal knight in shining armor."

"Girlish infatuation," he said in earnest. "What do you think of me now that you're a woman of the world?"

Eleanor smirked. "Now, I think you're fishing for compliments."

He laughed and she felt tremors along her spine. "You can't blame a guy for trying."

She sobered. "No, I guess I can't."

They ate in companionable silence. After they had placed their dessert order, Jake asked, "Do you miss her much?"

She knew he was talking about her mother. "All the time. You?"

"Not all the time. But a lot."

They were silent again and in that silence a bond formed between them. They both hoped it would last.

Eleanor stepped out of the shower, grabbed a towel, and ran to answer the ringing phone.

"Where have you been? I've been calling you all night."

She put Megan on the speakerphone and dried herself with the towel. "Sorry about that."

"Take me off that speakerphone. You know I hate it."

Eleanor tied the towel around her chest, clicked the speaker button, and picked up the receiver. "Satisfied?"

"Now that's more like it," Megan continued. "Where were you?"

Eleanor had hoped to keep her meeting with Jake a secret, but now she realized that was merely wishful thinking. "I had a dinner meeting."

"No, you didn't. You went out with Jake, didn't you?"

Damn. "We had a dinner meeting."

"You can't fool me. If it had been a simple dinner meeting, you would've told me. There was more to it than that."

The accusation in Megan's voice made Eleanor wonder why she'd agreed to help with Jake's plan. "How are plans coming for Jake's welcome party?" Though she'd back-peddled on this party from day one, she knew it was the only topic Megan would warm to quickly.

"I know you're changing the subject, Eleanor, but fortunately, it's a subject I want to talk about. Everything is on for this Saturday."

"Has everyone been invited?" Eleanor asked, realizing that by the time of the party Jake's visit to Lamar would be half over.

"Yes, yes."

"Did you invite Carl?"

"Sure," Megan answered, a little too quickly.

"Megan—"

"Do we have to invite him?"

"You know we have to invite him. He's practically Jake's best friend in this town."

"Okay, okay. I'll call him myself."

"And be nice."

"I'm always nice."

"To most people, but not to Carl. Why is that, Megan?"

"All right, if you talk to me about Carl, I get to talk to you about Jake."

Eleanor was silent. She had the sneaking suspicion Jake had set her up. "I told you nothing's going on."

"Yeah, right."

Carl picked up the baseball bats and placed them in the rack stand. "So you went out with Eleanor last night. How was it?"

Jake leaned back on the bench. The little guys had all gone home from practice and he and Carl were cleaning up. Well, Carl was cleaning up while he watched. "It was a date."

Carl sat next to him. "I thought you were interested in Megan."

Jake shot him a sideways glance. "Would it bother you if I was?"

"Why should it bother me?"

"I don't know. Maybe you're interested in Megan."

Carl shook his head. "Never. Megan is nothing but a tease. Always has been. Always will be."

"I don't think so, Carl. She's a nice woman who likes to have fun. What's wrong with that?"

"She's not *my* kind of woman," Carl said with finality.

Jake decided to take another tack. "What do you think about Eleanor?"

Carl snorted. "In her way, she's as bad as Megan.

You're the first man that's come along to shake her up a little." Carl punched Jake in the shoulder. "Thanks, man. It's good to see old Eleanor rattled."

Carl's words encouraged Jake, though he wasn't sure how accurate they were. "I don't know about all that."

"Take my word for it. I've never seen Eleanor so taken off balance by a guy. Where Megan's MO is to come on to everything in pants, Eleanor's is to push 'em away before they get too close." Carl laughed.

"What's so funny?"

"I used to think Eleanor was bossy by nature. Heaven knows, she bossed me around in those Before Megan days. But I figured out her bossiness is a tool she uses to keep people at a distance. The only people to get close are Megan and her father. Even knowing that, she still gets on my nerves."

Jake smiled. "Don't let 'em get to you so much, Carl. I think they like it. I bet Megan likes to set you off. Maybe if you pretended she didn't bother you or if you came on to her the way she comes on to men, she wouldn't bother you so much."

Carl looked at Jake and shook his head. "I guess I didn't tell you everything. Megan flirts with everybody. But me. Obviously, I'm not worth her energy."

"That's my point. Either you show her it doesn't matter or you give her the treatment she gives all the other men."

Carl seemed to think about Jake's suggestion. "And what would that get me?"

"You say you get satisfaction from seeing the way

I keep Eleanor off kilter. Think how much satisfaction you'd get from seeing Megan off kilter."

Carl got up and grabbed the ball basket. "I'll think about it. Let's go."

Ten

Jake admired Eleanor's firm hips and legs as she turned over on her back. It was time to execute step two of his plan.

"You've got to be kidding."

Jake handed her a towel. "No, we have to do this."

Eleanor took the towel and wrapped it around her chest. "We have to pretend to be a couple to help Carl and Megan? I don't think so, Jake. This sounds like some cheap trick on your part."

Jake threw up his hands. "If that's the way you feel about it, we won't do it. But I'm telling you, when Carl sees my success with you, it'll encourage him with Megan."

Eleanor eyed Jake suspiciously. "Explain to me again how this is going to help Megan and Carl."

"Well, we can go out and invite them to go with us."

"We could do that without being an item."

Jake shook his head. "I don't think so. Why would we be together so much?" He cleared his throat. "My reputation leads Carl to believe I'd have a romantic relationship with a woman, not a platonic one."

"Your reputation?" Eleanor sighed. "Carl's probably right."

"And the way I figure it, if I'm not interested in somebody, your friend Megan is going to be putting the moves on me so hard she and Carl won't have time to focus on each other."

Eleanor knew he was right about that. Megan had already promised to take her sights off Jake if Eleanor was interested. "So, what's our first step?"

Jake grinned. "You're going to go along with it?"

She shrugged, knowing he had the upper hand. "What choice do I have?"

"That's my girl. I figure our first event will be this 'Welcome to Lamar' party that you and Megan are planning. You can be my date."

She held up her hand. "Wait a minute. Everybody doesn't have to know about this ruse. Why can't we keep it to Megan and Carl?"

Jake sat down on the chaise next to her. "You yourself said there are no secrets in Lamar. Plus, if everybody knows, we have more legitimacy."

"Yes, and more people nosing in our business. You don't know about small-town romances, Jake. They become the fodder for local gossip."

"Look at it this way. We may not be able to control what people say, but we can definitely control what's printed in the paper."

Eleanor totally missed his attempt at humor. "What about my father? What's he going to think? Maybe we should tell him."

Jake hadn't thought about the fathers. He certainly didn't want them getting any ideas. "Yes, that's a good idea. Why don't we tell Mathias tonight? How do you think he'll respond?"

"He'll think it's a stupid idea, but he'll go along with it because he likes Megan and Carl."

Jake rubbed his hands together. "Well, then, it seems we have it all planned. Let's go for another dip." Jake dropped his towel and dived into the pool.

Eleanor watched as he swam the length of the pool in record time. Slowly, she dropped her towel, walked to the edge of the pool, and dived in. Why did she feel as though she'd dived into the biggest mess of her life?

"Hell, Mat, they aren't supposed to be matchmaking. They're supposed to be falling in love."

Mathias leaned back in his chair. Their scheme seemed to be falling down around their heads every day. "Don't tell me, I know. Now what are we going to do?"

"I don't know, but leaving them to their own devices is not working. We have to do something."

"We've already done something, Randy. We're the ones who set this whole thing up. Maybe we've done enough."

"And maybe we haven't. I have an idea."

Mathias rubbed his head. "Oh, no, not another one."

"Come on, Mat. Work with me on this. I'm hosting a gala next Friday and I think Jake and Eleanor need to attend."

"And how, pray tell, are we going to convince them to do that?"

"Tell them I'm interested in a progress report on their work on the merger. That should do it."

"Won't it seem strange that you're inviting Eleanor?"

"No, I don't think so. Tell her it's a chance for her to meet me and some of the players in the New York office. If she's as skeptical about this venture as she was in the beginning, she'll jump at the chance."

Mathias knew that part was right. Eleanor would consider it her duty to attend and to check out Randolph and his business. "Maybe I'll come along, too."

"Not this time, Mat. Make some excuse for not coming. Your Eleanor needs to do this one alone. Maybe being away from you and her familiar surroundings will push her and Jake closer."

"I'm not too sure about that," Mat said slowly. "Eleanor has this friend in New York. Some man who's been in touch with her over the years. He even came to Lamar one time."

"Damn. It could be a problem if she's with another man instead of Jake."

"Hey, what if you invited Carl and Megan along on this trip? Since Jake and Eleanor are pretending to be a couple for their sakes, they can't very well spend all their time with other people."

"You're a genius, Mat. That should do it."

"So what excuse will you use to get Megan and Carl to make the trip? Megan's not exactly involved in the newspaper business."

"Not me, Mat, you. You know both of them. Think of something. I'll talk to you later."

"Just pretend you're in Victoria's Secret," Megan said, tugging on Eleanor's arm to get her into Modern Woman, the trendy clothes shop for professional women.

Eleanor's pulse raced as she entered the upscale shop. The mannequins in the conservative yet modern miniskirted suits practically called out to her. It wasn't that she didn't like this kind of clothing. She did, but didn't think it was right for the office. She needed to project a strong, business image at work, and she didn't think a miniskirt provided that image.

Megan approached a mannequin dressed in a deep burgundy linen-silk blend suit near the front of the shop. "Now this is you."

Eleanor reluctantly touched the fabric and closed her eyes. It felt so good to touch, sensual almost.

"See, I knew you would like it," Megan said. "This *is* you."

Eleanor opened her eyes, her hand still touching the fabric. "The fabric feels good, but I'm not sure about the skirt."

Megan walked over to a rack and flipped through the suits. "Here's one in your size. Try it on."

"I don't know, Megan," Eleanor said, taking the suit in her hand. "I can't wear this to work."

"Sure you can," Megan said, leading the way to the dressing room. "Women are doing it every day. Come on, Eleanor, this is the nineties. Women don't have to dress like men or like schoolmarms to show their authority."

Eleanor slipped into the dressing room and quickly removed her tan slacks but kept on her matching silk shirt.

"While you're trying that on, I'll look around for some others things you might like. Keep that on until I get back though," Megan warned from outside the dressing room door. "I want to see you in it."

Eleanor stepped into the skirt first, pulling it up over her silk panties, then positioning it at her waist. After she'd zipped and fastened the button, she evaluated herself in the mirror. She admitted her legs looked good in the short skirt, but when she thought about Maxine and the others in the office, she began to tug on it to see if it would go farther down her thighs. No such luck.

Megan knocked on the door as she slipped on the jacket. "Let me see," she said.

Eleanor quickly fastened the double-breasted jacket and twisted the lock on the door. "Come on in."

"Wow," Megan said, her hands full of clothes. "You look great. We should have done this a long time ago."

Eleanor tugged on the skirt again. "It looks good, but the skirt is way too short to wear to work."

Megan hung the clothes on the hook next to the mirror, then swatted Eleanor's hands. "Leave the skirt alone. That's the way it's supposed to fit. And nobody's going to say anything except to ask why it took you so long to stop dressing like an old woman."

Eleanor rolled her eyes. With friends like Megan,

a girl didn't need any enemies. She pointed to the clothes Megan had brought in. "I suppose you want me to try on all of those?"

Megan grinned. "This is only the beginning. We have all day."

"Aggg . . ." Eleanor groaned, then reached for the white sheath that dipped low in front and back. "And where will I wear this?" she asked. "Surely you don't think I can wear it to work?"

"No, silly," Megan said, easing out of the dressing room. "You can wear it to Jake's welcome party. I can't wait to see his face when he sees you in it. You'll knock him dead."

Eleanor put the sheath back on the hook while she removed the suit, ignoring the frisson of pleasure that teased her belly at the thought of Jake's response to her in the sexy white dress.

She studied the suit after she'd put it back on its hangers. Yes, she'd take it. Maybe she'd wear it on their trip to New York.

That settled, she turned her attention to the white sheath and she couldn't stop the grin that spread across her face. She couldn't wait for Jake to see her in it.

Jake's arm resting on her waist distracted her. She'd been so anxious to see his reaction to her new outfit that she hadn't considered the effect Jake in a casual black suit and black shirt would have on her. "Nobody's looking," she whispered, glad for an excuse to put some distance between them. "You can drop your hand now."

"But it feels so good." He grinned down at her, squeezed the small of her back, then dropped his hand.

She stepped away from him, resisting the urge to tug on the short, form-fitting white sheath Megan had convinced her to buy. The man had a way of making her feel naked, which was odd since she was a woman who normally reveled in her nudity. "How are you enjoying your party?"

His eyes caressed her body. "I couldn't have asked for anything more."

She felt her skin warm to his words. Though she was sure this was a practiced assault, it didn't lessen its effect. "I'm sure my father will be glad to know you're having such a great time." Eleanor's eyes roamed the room and found her father trapped in discussion with Mel and Flo. A short space from him, Ms. Delaney and Maxine huddled together.

"How about you? Are you glad I'm having a good time?"

"So, so," she said, distracted by the whispered argument that seemed to have developed between Maxine and Ms. Delaney. She wondered what that was about.

"You sure know how to crush a guy's ego."

She placed her hand on his arm. "That's not it. It's just that I don't think Carl and Megan are paying us any attention." She inclined her head in the direction of the dance floor where Megan, in a fire-engine-red cocktail dress, danced with Winifred's brother, Wesley. "Megan's having a great time. Without Carl."

Jake moved a step closer to her. "It sure seems that way. Where's Carl?"

Eleanor pointed to a corner near the punch bowl where Carl, in what could best be described as a basic black Sunday-go-to-meeting suit, stood conversing with Mrs. Thompson and Tempest Tanner. "I don't think he cares about us or Megan."

Jake massaged her bare shoulder, his hand burning the skin he touched. "Don't worry so. I'm sure they're very aware of each other. Why don't we hit the dance floor? Maybe that'll get their attention."

She gave him a skeptical look, but allowed him to lead her to the dance floor Megan had made out of the Sanders living room. Megan had outdone herself with this party. The small tables surrounding the dance floor and the serving tables aligning the walls made the room seem almost like a nightclub. The banner proclaiming WELCOME TO LAMAR, JAKE across the mantel made it clear who the star of this event was.

As her luck would have it, a slow tune played as soon as they hit the dance floor. She looked up at Jake. "Did you plan this?"

He pulled her into his arms. "I'm lucky."

Eleanor didn't bother to comment. She rested her head on his chest and enjoyed the feel of his body against hers.

"You're the softest woman," he murmured against her hair as his arms caressed down her back.

She smiled against his shirt and tightened her hold on his waist. "You don't feel so bad yourself."

"Hey, are you flirting with me?"

She heard the grin in his voice. "If you have to ask, I must not be doing a good job of it."

"Well, well, well."

"Don't get carried away," she warned, responding to the smugness in his voice. "This is an act for Carl and Megan, remember?"

"Now that wasn't nice. You get my hopes up. Then you dash them. You could break my heart."

Eleanor didn't think it would be his heart that would break. More than likely it would be hers. "I bet you've broken a lot of hearts."

"Not me," he said in earnest. "I don't make promises I can't keep."

"Somehow I don't quite believe there aren't some hearts out there with your knife in them."

He squeezed her to him. "You'd be wrong. And I must be losing my touch. You're standing here in my arms in this romantic atmosphere and you're talking about other women in my life. I know I'm losing my touch."

She chuckled. "I don't think you have anything to worry about in that department."

"Does that mean I'm getting to you?"

She considered avoiding his question, but decided against it. "It means you could get to me if I let you."

"And why won't you let me?"

"Because I don't want my heart broken."

He tilted her chin up and brushed her hair back so he could see her face clearly. "I wouldn't break your heart, Eleanor."

The sincere words made her knees weak. His gaze rested on her lips and she knew he was thinking about kissing her. Heaven help her, she was thinking about kissing him. Instead, she cleared her throat and lowered her head back to his chest.

When the dance was over, he took her hand in his and led her over to where Carl still stood talking to Mrs. Thompson.

"You look so lovely tonight, dear," Mrs. Thompson said, reaching for Eleanor's hand. "You should wear your hair down more often."

Eleanor accepted the compliment easily. Almost all of the guests had complimented her new look.

"I'm glad to see at least one of my most favorite young people is finding romance," the older woman continued. "Carl, here, has spent the entire evening talking to me when he should be finding himself a young lady."

Carl groaned.

"Maybe he's looking for a woman with a bit more experience, Mrs. Thompson," Jake suggested with a masculine twinkle in his brown eyes.

"Oh, go on, Jake," Mrs. Thompson said, then slapped his hand coyly. "I was telling Carl there are quite a few available young women here in Lamar."

"I can find my own women, Mrs. Thompson," Carl said with a tinge of annoyance.

"Well, you don't seem to doing a good job of it, young man. How many of these young women have you talked with tonight?"

"That doesn't—"

"Yes, it does, young man. It tells me you need my help. Now, I'm going to mingle around here and find a young woman for you. You wait and see."

"But Mrs. Thompson—"

She patted his cheek. "You can thank me later, son. Now let me get out here and find you a young woman."

Eleanor and Jake laughed at Carl's chagrined expression.

"You'd better follow my lead and find your own woman, man," Jake said, pulling Eleanor closer to him.

Carl placed his glass on the lace-covered refreshment table. "I've had it. I'm out of here."

"Carl," Eleanor called after him, but he didn't stop. He headed straight for the door, then practically ran out of it.

"I thought he'd never leave," Megan said from behind them.

Eleanor turned around. "Where'd you come from? I thought you were dancing."

"I was, but the guy I was dancing with had two left feet and fifty arms." She lifted her hands and examined her nails. "Not exactly my type."

Eleanor leaned into Jake. "Sometimes what we're looking for is right under our noses."

"Well," Megan said, "the only thing under my nose right now is my top lip. Believe me, if there was another one like Jake around, I'd know it."

Eleanor looked up at Jake. "I think that's a compliment."

"Thanks, madam." Jake gave an exaggerated bow.

Megan reached for Jake's hand. "Mind if I borrow your man here for a whirl around the dance floor?" she asked Eleanor.

Eleanor slipped from under Jake's other arm. "Of course not."

Jake planted a quick peck on her lips and whispered, "Don't be jealous now. You're the only one for me."

Eleanor touched her hand to the place he had kissed and wished she was the only one for him.

Jake slapped his hand on the steering wheel. "Shut up! Both of you, shut the hell up!"

"Jake . . ." Eleanor said, placing her hand on his arm to calm him.

Jake shook her hand off. "I've had enough of them, Eleanor. They're worse than kids." He wondered why he'd been crazy enough to think Megan and Carl loved each other. In the week since the welcome party, they'd almost driven him insane with their constant bickering. Now, this drive to Atlanta was turning into a nightmare.

"I don't know why you invited her on this trip in the first place," Carl sneered. "What does she know about newspapers anyway? What does she know about anything?"

"Do what Jake said and shut up, Carl," Megan shouted. "Mr. Mason invited me because I'm Eleanor's best friend. And if you don't like it, you can go back to Lamar. We'll have a much better time if you don't come."

Eleanor turned around in her seat and pointed at them. "Jake is about ready to pull this car over and throw you both out. Now get yourselves together."

Megan crossed her arms and moved closer to the door—any closer and she would have to get out. "It's his fault."

Carl shot Megan an accusing stare. "You need to grow up, Megan. Look at yourself, pouting like a child."

"You don't—" Megan was about to get wound up again.

"If you two say one more cross word to each other," Jake said through tight lips, "I'm going to stop at the next exit and put you out. You got that?"

"Yeah."

"Yes."

Eleanor turned back around in her seat. "Do you think that was necessary?"

Jake glanced at her. "It made them shut up, didn't it?"

"But you don't mean it, do you?" Eleanor whispered.

"Like hell I don't," Jake answered, loud enough for Megan and Carl to hear. "One more set of cross words from them and they won't be going to New York. At least, not with us."

This time Eleanor believed him. She turned once more to look at Megan and Carl. They hugged their respective doors, staring out the windows with smirks on their faces. They were about an hour from the Atlanta airport and Eleanor wasn't sure they were going to make it.

"What are they doing?" Jake whispered.

Eleanor turned back around in her seat. "I think it's called a Mexican standoff."

Jake chortled. "Enough about the dueling brats. Are you excited about this trip?"

If Eleanor could talk freely, she'd tell Jake she was disappointed Carl and Megan had come along.

Their presence meant she and Jake had to continue their roles as budding lovers and that meant Eleanor couldn't spend time with her old college friend, Franklin. "I'd be more excited if we didn't have to baby-sit."

Jake grimaced. "I know the feeling." He'd been excited about having Eleanor to himself in New York. But when he'd found out she intended to spend all her time with Franklin, he'd been disappointed. Learning Carl and Megan were coming had restored his excitement. But in spite of what their presence would mean in New York, he was dead serious about leaving them if they acted up again.

Eleanor touched his arm. She'd started to do that a lot lately. She was really getting into her role. "You must be happy to get back to your old stomping ground."

"I am. I'm also looking forward to showing you the sights. I'll love seeing the city through your eyes."

That warm feeling that was becoming her constant companion filled Eleanor's stomach. "I've been to New York before."

"Not with me. I want you to see *my* New York."

They were both silent for a while, enjoying each other's company. Eleanor reveled in the masculine approval Jake had given her new burgundy miniskirt suit. Though she had to fight the urge to tug on the skirt, she was glad she'd given in to Megan's urgings and updated her wardrobe.

"You've traveled a lot, haven't you?" Eleanor asked a while later.

Jake smiled at the memories. "For as long as I can

remember. After my mom died, I started going with my father on business trips. We didn't go far because we didn't have much money, but where he went, I went."

"That must have been great. I know I loved spending time with my dad when I was younger. As a matter of fact, I still do."

"Yeah, those were good times. As I got older, Dad decided I needed more structure in my life so we stopped traveling as much and I settled down to the life of an ordinary child. Not as exciting."

"Did your dad still travel?"

Jake gripped the steering wheel with both hands. "That was the downside. By then, we had more money and his trips were for longer periods of time. But he made up for it during the summers. That's when we traveled together."

"Sounds like you and your dad are close."

"We were."

"What happened?"

Jake had asked himself that question. He wasn't sure if there was an answer. "Things changed. I got older. Dad got busier."

"That's too bad," she said, and he felt she meant it.

"It's all right. Overall, Dad's a good guy," Jake said absently. "He wanted me to be happy, but he didn't understand that being with him made me happy."

Sounded like her dad, Eleanor thought. "My dad always said he wanted me to travel, get away from home, but I never got the feeling he meant it. He wanted me with him."

"You liked that?"

"A lot."

"I hear a 'but' in there somewhere."

She looked out the window. "Sometimes I wonder what my life would be like if I hadn't come back to Lamar when I graduated from school."

"Where would you have gone?"

"New York."

"Your friend Franklin?"

She nodded. Franklin seemed so long ago. He'd been the first man she'd ever loved.

"Was he more than a friend?"

"He asked me to marry him."

The words hit Jake like a sucker punch. He was taking Eleanor back to the arms of a guy who'd asked her to marry him. "Why'd you turn him down?"

She smiled. "I didn't want to leave Lamar. My dad needed me."

"Do you ever regret it?"

"Not marrying Franklin?"

She'd asked herself that question many times over the last few years. "I don't regret not marrying Franklin, but I do wonder how different my life would have been had I been a bit more adventurous."

Jake wondered if she still had feelings for the guy. "How did you and Franklin meet?"

Eleanor smiled. "Jealous?"

"I think it's natural. The new beau is always a little jealous of the old beaus. Especially the ones who made marriage proposals."

"The new beau?"

Jake inclined his head in the direction of the backseat to remind her of the roles they were playing for the benefit of Carl and Megan. "Don't you think I'm entitled to be a little jealous, Carl?"

"I say always keep a man a little jealous," Megan chimed in.

"He wasn't talking to you, Megan," Carl explained calmly. "He was talking to me. Do you think everything has to revolve around you?"

Jake looked at Eleanor and they both grinned. Thank God, they were almost at the airport.

Eleven

Jake saw his plans for the weekend begin to disintegrate right before his eyes. "You can't go back to Lamar. We're here. We've checked our luggage. We have our boarding passes. They're boarding the plane now."

Megan glared at Jake. "You don't tell me what to do. *You* threatened to dump me out of the car. I'm not going."

"Megan," Eleanor said, "be reasonable. How will you get back to Lamar?"

"Who said I was going back to Lamar? I have friends in Atlanta. Maybe I'll get a room and stay here until you guys get back on Sunday."

"Well, I'm ready to get on the plane," Carl said cheerfully. "She's right. She's a grown woman. If she doesn't want to go, she doesn't have to."

Jake didn't know who he wanted to strangle first: Carl or Megan. "This is childish, Megan. Get on the plane."

"I am not." Megan kissed Eleanor on the cheek. "You have a good time in New York." She shot a glance at Jake, then said loud enough for him to hear, "And I hope you see Franklin while you're there."

Eleanor grabbed one of Megan's hands. "Are you sure?"

"I'm sure. Now get on that plane before it leaves you."

"Okay," Carl said, taking Eleanor's other hand. "We're boarding now. Have fun in Atlanta, Megan. We'll see you when we get back."

Carl escorted Eleanor to the jetway and Jake followed. Megan stood behind waving.

"We can't leave her, Carl," Eleanor said.

"Of course we can," Carl whispered. "Anyway, you know as well as I do she's going to make a late entrance on the plane. Let's not beg her. She's coming. Megan wouldn't miss a free trip to New York and a Mason Publishing party for anything."

"I'm not sure about this, Carl. I don't think she's coming."

Carl shot Jake a glance. "It's your call, man. Do we play it her way or mine?"

Jake looked back at Megan. She was still smiling. "Let's board."

When the stewardesses began closing the overhead compartments, Eleanor said, "I don't think she's coming."

"She is," Carl said, but some of his confidence was gone.

"She'd better hurry," Jake added.

Carl stood up. "I'll go get her. But this is the last time."

"Carl . . ." Jake said, but Carl was out of his first-class seat and through the door. "Damn, now they're both going to miss the flight."

The flight attendant closed the front cabin door as soon as the words were out of Jake's mouth.

"I'd say you're right," Eleanor said as the pilot began his push back from the gate.

"Damn!"

Eleanor touched his arm again. "Don't worry so. It's not that bad. Maybe they'll come to an understanding while we're gone."

Jake stared at her. "Do you really think so?"

She shook her head. "I'm beginning to wonder if this plan of yours is worth it. Megan and Carl may be a lost cause."

"Let's not give up yet." Jake didn't want to agree with her since he had ulterior motives for the plan, but he thought she was right. In his opinion, Carl and Megan were too inflexible to ever get it together. He didn't think they'd find *anyone* who'd put up with them.

"At least it works out for us."

"Works out?"

Eleanor took a magazine out of the seat pocket in front of her. "Yes, now we don't have to pretend to be a couple. You can visit with your friends and I can spend some time with Franklin."

Franklin. Exactly what Jake hadn't wanted. "Yeah, lucky us."

She looked over at him. "I'm sure your little black book must be burning a hole in your pocket. Do you think you'll be able to see all of your women this weekend?"

Jake could do nothing but go along with her. He wasn't about to admit he wanted to spend time with her if all she could think about was Franklin. "I'll hold a lottery. The winner gets to see me this weekend."

Eleanor laughed. "You're too much, Jake."

Jake laughed, too, but it was an empty laugh. His trip to New York was doomed. He wanted to strangle Megan. And he probably would as soon as he got back to Lamar.

He leaned back in his seat and closed his eyes. It had been a hell of a day.

Jake and Eleanor took a limo from LaGuardia Airport to the Mason estate in White Plains. During the thirty-minute ride, Eleanor questioned Jake about his father.

Jake's accessing gaze traveled from her crossed legs to the choker around her neck before meeting her eyes. "Why all the questions? I'm sure you've had Carl put together a file."

"Of course," Eleanor answered, uncrossing her legs and shifting slightly to pull her skirt farther down her thigh. "But I want to hear it from you."

A smile touched Jake's lips then he sank back in the seat and closed his eyes. "Next question."

Eleanor liked the relaxed look of his features. It made him appear more approachable. Vulnerable, even. "Why haven't you been more involved in your father's business?"

The twitch in his jaw told her the question was painful for him.

"My father didn't want me involved," he answered simply, but she sensed there was nothing simple about it.

"Why was that?"

Jake opened his eyes. "You're full of questions, aren't you?"

"You didn't answer me."

He closed his eyes again. He didn't want to discuss this with Eleanor because he had some of the same questions himself. "Why don't you save it until you meet my father. You *do* want to have something to ask him, don't you?"

Eleanor touched his knee. "But I want you to answer this one."

Jake grinned. "You're beginning to sound like Megan."

"Now that was a low blow," she said, allowing him to deflect her question.

"Ah, but it's true." Jake chuckled. "You and Megan are quite a pair."

"You can't seriously think I sound like Megan."

"You make it sound like an insult. It's not. It's merely an observation."

"Yes, but I was in the car with you while Megan behaved like a petulant child."

Jake opened his eyes and sat up. "You're being kind. She was at her best today."

"Don't try to change the subject. Do you seriously think Megan and I are alike?"

Jake nodded.

"You're the first person to say that. Most people think we're exact opposites. I suppose you know they called us the Odd Couple in school."

He nodded again. "I can see why they did that. That's the impression you two give. But it's a false impression. You're very much the flirt and spoiled little girl that Megan is and she's very much the re-served, stern woman that you are."

"Me, a flirt and a spoiled little girl? I don't think so. You must have me confused with someone else."

Jake rubbed her arm. "Now don't get mad with me. You did ask. Do you want me to continue?"

Eleanor nodded. "You certainly can't stop now."

"Take that evening at Mel's Diner. You wanted to play the flirt then, but you weren't sure about doing it."

Eleanor remembered taking her hair down, un-buttoning a couple of buttons of her blouse, and hoping Jake would notice.

"And don't forget that white bathing suit you wear. Definitely designed to get a man's attention."

"But that doesn't make me a flirt."

He ignored her comment. "And look at you now," he said, allowing his gaze to meander from her feet to the hair on her head. "Your legs were made for short skirts. And the way your hair falls in curls on your shoulders is maddening."

"Jake . . ." she pleaded, a warm breeze of passion raising her body temperature.

Jake stared into her eyes and she wondered if he knew the effect his words were having on her.

"I bet you were a virgin until you met Franklin. Right?"

Eleanor averted her eyes. He was right, but it wasn't his business, she decided. She wondered how he knew anyway, but she wasn't going to ask. She was sure she wouldn't like his answer.

He didn't wait for her response. "And my guess is, Megan is *still* a virgin."

Again he was right, though most people guessed Megan was sexually active. She liked men. A lot. But she didn't sleep around. She'd die if she knew Jake knew. "You'll have to ask her that," she said, wondering again how Jake knew so much. The man must have ESP where women are concerned, she concluded.

When he didn't continue, she met his gaze with her own. "Go on," she said. "I know you're not finished."

"When men look at Megan, their first thought is she's a firecracker. When they look at you, their first thought is she's uptight. What they don't know is you're probably hotter than Megan."

Eleanor felt herself grow warmer. "And how do you figure that?"

"That bathing suit. I doubt Megan would wear anything that revealing, even in the privacy of your pool. I'm hoping the only place you wear it is in the privacy of your own pool. Please tell me I'm right."

She wouldn't have answered him, but he sounded so grave she took pity on him. "You're right. Not that it matters."

"Oh, it matters, all right."

Eleanor refused to ask what that meant. "So you've got Megan and me all figured out?"

Jake nodded. "As much as a man can figure out any woman."

"And I'm sure you've been through your share of women."

He caught her gaze. "Why don't you ask me?"

Eleanor knew what he was talking about. "I know

you've been through a lot of women. There's nothing to ask."

"If you ask, I'll answer."

"Why?"

"Because I'm basically an honest guy. I don't make promises and I don't lie. Keeps life simple."

She didn't know why she had to ask, but she did. His eyes told her he'd tell her the truth. "Have you loved any of them, Jake?"

He smiled as if he'd known that was the question she'd ask. "I've loved them all."

"Eleanor, dearest," Randolph Mason said, pulling her into his arms. "It's about time we met." He pushed her back and grinned at her. "I knew it. You're gorgeous."

Eleanor believed he meant it and his words made her feel gorgeous. She silently thanked Megan for coaxing her into the burgundy tailored suit with the miniskirt.

"You're not so bad yourself," she said and meant it. Randolph Mason was a very attractive man. His salt-and-pepper hair, his bright eyes and sparkling teeth. Not to mention the broad shoulders set off by his tapered suit. Jake got his good looks from his father.

"Hey, watch it now," Jake warned. "There are children in the room."

Eleanor saw the teasing glint in Jake's eyes. "I apologize, Jake. I see where you get it from."

Jake laughed.

"I know an insult when I hear one," Randolph

teased. "My son is a perfect gentleman and so am I."

Eleanor rolled her eyes and spoke in an exaggerated Southern drawl. "Oh, is that what ya'll call it up North?"

Randolph's eyes danced. "What do you call it in Lamar?"

"Calculated charm."

Randolph laughed, then spoke to Jake. "She's a tough one, son. Are you surviving down there?"

Jake passed her a teasing glance. "We've had our moments. But I think we're on the right road now. What do you say, Eleanor?"

She nodded, getting into the spirit of the moment. Jake and his father's relaxed relationship warmed her. Maybe she'd misread the comments Jake had made during the ride from the airport. "It was touch-and-go for a while, but I think I have him trained now."

Randolph shot Jake a glance. "Trained, huh?"

Jake raised his arms in surrender. "What can I say? She's a slave driver."

"Well, this slave driver needs to freshen up," Eleanor said. "If you'll excuse me?"

"I don't know what I was thinking about, dear," Randolph said. He pressed the intercom and a uniformed manservant appeared in the door. "Jeffrey will show you to your room."

Jake watched as Eleanor left the library behind Jeffrey. When the door closed, his father said, "She's nothing like her pictures, is she?"

Jake turned to his father. "Mathias told you about the woman at the pool?"

Randolph nodded and walked around to his desk. "So what's been happening?"

Jake dropped down on the couch in front of the wall of built-in bookcases. "Not much. I've been trying to understand the paper."

"What do you think?"

"It's a nice, small-town paper, but I still don't see why you want it. Will you explain that to me again?"

"There's nothing to explain. Mat and I have been friends forever. We want this merger because of our friendship. It's your job to make it work as a business deal for Mason Publishing. Are you going to be able to do it?"

"Definitely," Jake said with confidence. He was still determined to do more than his father expected.

"Good, I'm counting on you."

Jake's shoulders set up a little straighter at that comment. His father was counting on him. There was no way he would let him down. In fact, he planned to impress the hell out of the older man. Once he knew from which angle to approach the new magazine that he and Eleanor had discussed, he'd be better able to draw up his deal-of-the-century. He couldn't wait to present his father with the final proposal.

Jake scanned the hotel ballroom later that night looking for Eleanor and wondering where she was. He wanted to see her, but he also wanted to see this guy who had spoiled his plans to be Eleanor's date for the gala.

"Are you looking for somebody, Jake?" Sherise's honeyed voice asked.

Jake looked at her and wondered when he'd lost interest. She was still the attractive, leggy, demure yet fun-loving diva he'd first met, but now his tastes hungered for someone with more mouth and less height. "I told you about Eleanor. She's supposed to be here tonight. Dad wants to introduce her around."

"Are you sure there isn't more to it than that?"

That got Jake's attention. "Jealousy doesn't become you, Sherise."

"And you're turning into a bore. I get the feeling I'm being used."

Feeling guilty, Jake immediately slid his gaze from her. She was right. He'd only invited her after he'd learned Eleanor was bringing Franklin. His plan had been to make Eleanor jealous. Now he realized how stupid that was. And how unfair to Sherise. "Look, Sherise, I'm sorry. Do you want to dance?"

Her eyes twinkled and he knew all was forgiven. He took her hand and led her to the floor. Luckily for him a slow Barry White tune played. He pulled her into his arms, glad they didn't have to talk anymore.

He sensed Eleanor's entrance into the ballroom and his head went up.

"Watch it, Jake," Sherise chastised. "Those are my feet you're stepping on."

"Sorry," Jake mumbled, his eyes still on Eleanor. He'd thought she was gorgeous before but tonight she'd gone beyond that. White was definitely her color, though he thought the strapless white gown could have used a little more material up top.

And he thought the guy on her arm looked a little bit too happy. He wondered what Eleanor had done to make the guy grin like that.

"Is that her?"

Sherise had stopped dancing and was now looking at Eleanor and her date.

"That's her," Jake said, taking Sherise's hand and leading her in Eleanor's direction. "I'll introduce you."

Randolph and his date for the evening reached Eleanor before Jake did.

"Here you are," his father said to him. "Good to see you, Sherise. Have you met our Eleanor?"

Randolph made the introductions then Eleanor introduced the tall, well-groomed man with her as Franklin.

Jake took his hand, sizing him up. "Glad you could make it. Eleanor speaks of you often."

Franklin placed an arm around Eleanor and pulled her to himself and smiled. "All good, I hope."

Eleanor touched the string of pearls around her neck and gave Franklin an intimate smile that made Jake's insides clench. "I only told the truth."

Franklin rewarded that answer with a kiss on her forehead. "Thank you."

Randolph took Eleanor's arm. "Come on. There are some people I want you to meet."

"Franklin?" Eleanor asked.

"No, you go on," he said, waving her away. "I'll be okay."

"Are you sure?"

Franklin winked. "As long as you look for me for the first dance."

"Deal," she said and let herself be escorted away by Randolph.

"Do you live in New York, Franklin?" Sherise asked, flashing the man a brilliant smile that Jake thought was exaggerated.

"All my life. You?"

"Brooklyn."

Jake observed Franklin as he talked with Sherise. What was it about this man that attracted Eleanor? Jake admitted he was handsome. And tall. And well groomed. Probably very successful, since Jake guessed his tuxedo wasn't a rental. And the guy was personable. Jake had to give him that.

But Jake didn't like him. And he knew why. Franklin had been engaged to Eleanor. And in Jake's opinion, that erased all the other positive attributes the man had.

Eleanor's jaw hurt from so much smiling. Randolph had introduced her to what seemed like over a hundred people. Thankfully, he did most of the talking so all she had to do was nod and smile. At other times that would have rankled her, but not tonight. Tonight she was glad because it gave her time to think.

So Sherise was the kind of woman that attracted Jake. She was surprised. For some reason, she'd thought Jake went in for blatant sexuality, not the demure sophistication she sensed in Sherise.

She guessed one really couldn't judge a book by its cover. She smiled at the thought and at the bald-headed man and his wife Randolph was now introducing. Jake always surprised her. First, his attitude at the paper. Then, his genuine concern for Megan and Carl. Now, his choice in women. Jake Mason was not a man to be pigeon-holed.

"I think I've waited long enough," a firm masculine voice whispered close to her ear.

She turned and smiled at Franklin. "I'm sorry I left you for so long. Thanks for being such a good sport about it."

Franklin took her drink from her hand and placed it on the passing tray of the floating waiter. "Now it's my time."

She turned to Randolph. "Please excuse me for a while," she said.

"Oh, sure, dear," Randolph said, looking from her to Franklin. "But be sure to come back in a little while. There are still people for you to meet."

Franklin placed his hand on her elbow and escorted her away from Randolph and company and onto the ballroom floor. "If I didn't know better," he said, "I'd think the elder Mason was trying to keep you away from me."

Eleanor stepped into his arms. "You've got to be kidding."

Franklin slipped his arms around her waist and pulled her close. "He wouldn't be the first older man interested in a pretty young thing like yourself."

"Pretty young thing?" she repeated. "You'd better

be glad I'm in a festive mood or I'd have to call you on that phrase."

"Politically correct phrasing or not, the older Mason could be interested in you."

"No way. The man is my father's best friend."

"So?"

"So, they're practically brothers."

He turned her in a fancy turn. "There could be another reason for his interest."

He turned her again.

"And what's that?"

"Maybe he wants you for a daughter-in-law."

Eleanor stopped moving and looked up at him. "Now that's crazy."

He urged her into the dance step. "What's crazy about it? Maybe your fathers want to merge more than their businesses."

Eleanor shook her head. This conversation was ridiculous. "Are you jealous, Franklin? Is that what this is about?"

"Why would I be jealous? You're not my girl anymore."

He *was* jealous. She'd thought Franklin had gotten over their failed romance, but obviously he hadn't. "Maybe it was selfish of me to invite you tonight, but I wanted to see you."

He hugged her closer and she felt him relax. "I'm glad you invited me. You're very special to me, Roni." It was the first time he'd used his pet name for her in years.

"Oh, Franklin . . ."

He squeezed her. "There's no need for that. I'm

fine. I'm not pining away for you, if that's what you're wondering."

The levity in his voice made her smile. "I'm glad to know that."

"I'm seeing somebody," he said a few seconds later.

"Is it serious?"

"More serious than any relationship I've had since you. I think she could be the one."

"Oh."

"Yes, oh. You'd like her. She's a great woman." He looked down at her. "A lot like you."

"Are you happy?" Eleanor questioned.

"Very. I didn't think I'd get over you, Eleanor. You broke my heart when you decided not to come to New York. I loved you, you know."

"I know," she said softly. She was happy for Franklin, but a part of her hated that soon he would no longer be hers. There was a sense of security in knowing somebody out there loved her. "Does she mind your being out tonight?"

He shook his head. "I told her the three of us would get together sometime this weekend. She wants to meet you."

"She does?"

He nodded. "She said she wants to meet the woman who helped make me a man."

Eleanor looked up at him. "You told her that." It was something he'd often told her though she never really believed he meant it.

When the song ended, Franklin led Eleanor out to the terrace. She sat on the marble bench and he leaned on the marble railing in front of her. The night was clear and cool and the sky shone with stars.

"You've changed," he said.

"I'm older."

"And a little wiser," he added.

"I hope so."

"He'd be a good match for you."

"What are you talking about?"

"Jake."

"Jake?" she repeated.

"I think you already know that."

She didn't answer. She'd be lying if she said she wasn't attracted to Jake. He was an attractive man and that tuxedo showed off the contours of his body so well that her pulse raced. But finding him attractive and having a relationship with him were two different things.

But heaven help her, she had wondered about loving Jake Mason. He had a charm that practically disarmed her. And she sensed he was drawn to her as well. If they had met under other conditions, maybe—

"This is Franklin you're talking to, Eleanor," he said, interrupting her musing. "I think I know you better than anyone else in the world."

"But you're wrong this time."

Franklin sat next to her and took her hand in his. "I don't think so. Love doesn't always happen twice, Eleanor. I've been lucky. I loved you, but you didn't love me. Then I found Vicky. I love her and she loves me. I want you to find that. I want you to love somebody so much it hurts."

"Why do you want me to hurt?" she asked, deliberately misunderstanding what he meant.

"You know it's real when it hurts, when you've given all you think you have and you still have to give more. You know it's love when you're willing to dig deep to find the extra strength it takes to make the relationship work."

Twelve

Jake heard her laughter before he opened the door to his father's library. He was relieved she was back, glad she hadn't spent the night with Franklin.

"What's so funny?" he asked as he entered the library. Eleanor and his father sat on the leather couch studying what he recognized by its tattered cover as the family scrapbook. "Or do I have to ask?"

Randolph eased back on the couch and Eleanor closed the book. "Don't ask," Randolph said. "I was catching Eleanor up on the family history."

He had been telling Eleanor about his wife, Jake's mother. That meant he liked Eleanor. A lot. He discussed his late wife with very few people. "Don't believe anything he said about me."

"Oh, I didn't. He sounded too much the proud father. He had to be exaggerating."

Jake studied his father, wondering what he'd said and wishing he'd heard some of it. "What have you been saying?"

"I'm an old man," he said, standing up. "I'm entitled to say whatever I want."

Eleanor chuckled. "I see my father isn't the only one who's not above using age to get his way."

"Watch it, young lady," Randolph warned. "I'd hate to have to report you to your daddy."

Eleanor rolled her eyes. "Another similarity to Dad. You both seem to forget I'm an adult."

"Humor us. If you're lucky, you'll have children of your own someday and you'll understand." Randolph looked at Jake. "Entertain Eleanor for a while. I'm going to bed."

Jake saluted. "Yes, sir."

"Jake, you don't have to—" Eleanor interrupted.

Randolph waved his hand. "He wants to. If he didn't, he'd be at his apartment or still out with Sherise."

"Dad—"

"Okay, I'm going. See you two at breakfast."

As Randolph closed the door, Jake took a seat next to Eleanor and rested his arm on the couch behind her. "Did you have a good time tonight?"

"I sure did. Your father's a great host." She yawned. "I don't think I've ever met that many people in a single night before."

Jake chuckled. "How many names do you remember?"

She waved a finger in the air. "I remember a lot of names. Matching those names to faces, now that's another matter."

Jake casually propped his right leg over his left. "So, ah, did Franklin enjoy himself?"

Eleanor glanced at him. "I think so."

"That's good."

"I liked Sherise. She's a nice woman."

"Yes, she is." Jake checked Eleanor's eyes, hoping

to see at least a trace of jealousy. Unfortunately, he found none.

"Is it serious?"

Jake caught her gaze. Maybe there was a trace of the green devil, after all.

"You don't have to answer that," Eleanor amended and he knew she wished she could take her question back.

"Oh, I don't mind. No, it's not serious. We're friends. She dates other people and so do I. We enjoy each other's company. Nothing more."

Eleanor nodded as though his answer didn't mean much to her. "I see."

He wasn't fooled by her gesture. "Do you?"

She gazed up at him, her eyes bright and her lips wet. He wanted to kiss her. He uncrossed his legs and decided to try it.

When he leaned his head down to her, Eleanor's mouth dropped open. "It's okay," he teased. "I don't bite."

She scooted back on the seat, away from him. "I don't think we should do this."

Jake followed her. "Do what?"

She looked up at him again and he took advantage of her open mouth and kissed her. When his lips met the softness of hers, sparks shot through his body. She was so soft, so sweet.

She didn't respond immediately, so he increased the pressure slightly, encouraging her to participate with him.

She pulled her mouth away from his. "Jake—"

"Don't talk. Kiss me," he ordered, taking her mouth in his again.

This time she gave. A little. Enough to make him want more. He leaned closer until he had her pressed into the back of the sofa.

"That's it," he encouraged. "Kiss me."

Eleanor moaned into his mouth and he felt her hands go up to his shoulders, pulling him closer.

"Oh, yes," he murmured, increasing the pressure even more. "I want you, Eleanor."

Her arms dropped from his shoulders and she eased her mouth away from his. When she lifted her gaze to his, he saw that her eyes were damp.

He touched his finger to her cheek. "I *do* want you," he repeated softly.

She looked up at him with clear eyes. "I want you, too."

He grinned. Hell, he felt good. "I kinda guessed that."

She grimaced. "How nongallant of you to say so."

"You're beautiful," he whispered, his finger tracing a path down her jaw. "And you smell so good."

She released her smile. "Now that's a lot better."

"What are we going to do about it?"

"Nothing."

"Nothing? We're both adults. What's stopping us?"

She eased away from him and stood before his father's desk. He liked the look of her—wet lips, hair ruffled from his hands.

"There's a lot stopping us," she said.

"Name one thing."

"Your plans for my paper."

He sank back into the couch, realizing they were going to do nothing about it. "That's business. This is personal."

She smiled sadly. "That's where we differ. The paper for me is personal."

He knew there was nothing he could say to change her mind. He wasn't sure he wanted to. He couldn't make any promises about the paper beyond the ones he'd already made. What he did there had ramifications far above the merger her father and his father had planned. No, what Jake did in Lamar was, to him, proof of what he could accomplish when he set his mind to it. It was evidence he could present to his father to show he was more than capable of doing a job well. No, there were no more promises he could make to Eleanor. "I understand," he said softly.

She gave another crooked smile and quietly left the room.

Eleanor eased up the stairs to her room, her senses still taut from her encounter with Jake. She wanted him in the worst way. She admitted to herself that what she felt had been building since she'd first seen his picture when she was a little girl.

Eleanor and Jake. She'd dreamed of kissing him long ago, but she'd never imagined how powerful such a kiss would be.

Eleanor and Jake. Colleagues and competitors. There was no way they could sustain a love affair given their working relationship. Jake had a job to do and she had to protect her paper. She couldn't let anything cloud her judgment about that. She couldn't let Jake use her for his purposes.

That thought took her by surprise. What if Jake

was using her? Though she didn't think that was the case, she couldn't immediately dismiss it. Maybe if she held on to it, she'd be able to fight her attraction for Jake.

She undressed and climbed into bed. When she closed her eyes, visions of Jake loomed above her and her mind took her to the place that held the beauty of what it would be to share her body with him, to indulge herself with his body. Yes, she wanted him. And though she wasn't that experienced, she knew enough to know that making love with Jake would be exquisite.

She knew she had to stop thinking about him. If she didn't, she'd find herself going back downstairs to him. She wondered what he would do if she did. It didn't take much imagination to figure out that answer.

Her breathing increased when she heard him ascend the stairs. It stopped altogether when he paused outside her door. If he knocked, she didn't know if she'd have the strength to turn him away. She started breathing again when he left the door. She didn't know if she was glad or sad that he had gone.

She closed her eyes once again and tried to sleep. No such luck. Giving up, she climbed out of bed and went to take a shower. A cold shower.

"I'm telling you, I think we're getting someplace. Jake couldn't take his eyes off Eleanor all night."

"Are you sure, Randy?"

"Of course I'm sure. I think he kissed her tonight."

"At the party?"

"No, in my library here at the house."

"Did you see them?"

"Not exactly," Randolph hedged.

"What do you mean, 'not exactly'?"

"I left them alone in the library, then I listened outside the door."

Mathias chuckled. "No, you didn't."

"Well, for a few minutes I did," Randolph explained. "I wanted to know if we were getting anywhere. And we are."

"That's good. Be careful and don't get caught. Remember, they're not supposed to know we're matchmaking."

"I know, Mat. I'll talk to you tomorrow."

Eleanor bumped into Jake when he stopped suddenly at their arrival gate in the Atlanta airport.

"Why'd you stop?"

"I don't believe it."

She looked around him to see what had his attention. Her mouth dropped open when she saw Carl and Megan seated, practically in the same seat, swallowing each other's face.

"Do you think they were hit on the head and lost their minds since we left them on Friday?" she asked.

Jake recovered and started in the direction of Carl and Megan.

"I see you two didn't kill each other," he said.

Megan pulled away from Carl and stood up. Eleanor noticed she didn't let go of his hand. "Welcome back, you two. Did you have a good time?"

"We did," Eleanor answered. Jake and Carl, wearing a Cheshire-like grin that she'd never seem him sport, had some male eye discussion going so she knew he wasn't going to answer.

Megan smiled up at Carl. "I guess we're ready to go, sweetie." Carl rewarded her with a kiss.

Eleanor shot Jake a bewildered glance. "Sweetie?" she whispered.

Jake shrugged his shoulders, indicating he didn't know what was going on.

"So are you two going to tell us what happened?" he asked.

Carl draped an arm around Megan's shoulders and pulled her close. Leaning into him, she slid her arm around his waist. "It's a long story," Carl said. "We'd better walk while we talk."

Thankfully, the concourse wasn't crowded. If it had been, there would have been no way for them to walk four-abreast. And it seemed Carl and Megan were not about to release each other.

"Do you want to tell him or should I?" Megan asked Carl.

"You can start, cupcake." He kissed the tip of her nose. "I'll finish."

Eleanor saw the look that passed between them and knew there was a memory of sexual adventure associated with the words. Megan was no longer a virgin. She'd bet on it.

"Okay," Megan began. "I sat around for a few minutes after you guys had gotten on the plane, then I went to the phone to find a rental car and a hotel room. There were no cars available anywhere."

"She was muttering curses to herself when I found her," Carl said, his voice full of warmth.

Maybe aliens have invaded their bodies, Eleanor speculated silently. Surely this couldn't be the fighting couple she and Jake had left in the Atlanta airport two days ago.

Another affectionate smile passed between the couple. "Well, Carl came along and solved all my problems."

Carl chuckled. "Megan's memory is colored by the good time I showed her this weekend."

"Well," Megan agreed, "maybe I did scream at him a couple of times as he followed me down the concourse."

Carl laughed.

"And I may have slammed the cab door on him and ripped his jacket."

Carl laughed harder.

"And maybe, just maybe, I told the hotel desk clerk he was a pervert who'd followed me all the way from the airport."

Carl laughed yet harder.

"But the worst thing I did to my sweetie is that I locked him out in the hall when all he wore were his briefs."

Carl sobered. "Now that wasn't funny, cupcake."

Megan put a finger to his lips. "But I made up for it, didn't I, sweetie?"

"Yes, you did," Carl said, kissing her finger.

When they reached baggage claim, Megan and Carl volunteered to get the car while Jake and Eleanor waited for their luggage.

"Looks like I was right," Jake said as soon as the other couple was out of ear shot.

"About what?"

"All that tension between Megan and Carl. I think they're in love."

"Or lust."

"What's the difference?"

Eleanor's eyes widened. "If you don't know, there's no way I can explain it to you."

"Are you upset about something?" Jake asked, giving her a quick glance before focusing on the conveyor that delivered the bags. "You've been acting weird all day."

Yes, something was wrong with her. Her cold shower the night before last had done nothing to quell her desire for Jake, while he seemed to have recovered with little effort. Obviously, he hadn't wanted her that much. "I'm fine. I just want to get home."

"So do I."

"You think of Lamar as home?" she asked, surprised at his words but also warmed by them.

He shrugged it off. "I like it there and I miss my team. Maybe there's something to be said for the slower pace. Hey, isn't that your bag?"

She watched as he retrieved first her bag, then his from the carousel. "Let's wait for them outside," he said, motioning to the door.

She followed him out, all the while thinking about his comments on Lamar. Was Jake becoming a country boy, after all?

Thirteen

"You're blushing," Jake teased. They were about halfway to Lamar and already Carl and Megan had put on quite a show.

Eleanor lowered her head. "It's the moaning. Can't they kiss in silence?"

"When it's good, it's good. Why don't you talk to me? Maybe we can ground them out."

"What do you want to talk about?"

"Us."

There is no us, she said silently. "Okay, let's talk about the paper."

Jake chuckled. "If you insist."

"Did you tell your father about my plans? Every time I tried to speak with him about them, he deftly changed the subject."

Jake was grateful for his father's hands-off approach on this deal. The Old Man was really letting him handle the project. "As well he should. This is my deal. He doesn't make the decisions, I do. Didn't I tell you that?"

She grimaced. "You did, but I didn't believe you."

"Thanks for nothing."

"Don't be insulted. I never figured Randolph Mason to be the hands-off type."

Jake knew his father's hands-off approach was because this project was so small, but he didn't dare tell Eleanor that. "Mason Publishing is a big enterprise. He can't have his hands in everything."

"I guess you're right. How do you feel having total control?"

"Responsible. I want to do the right thing, the best job, for all the concerned parties." He wanted to exceed beyond any and all expectations his father had or had ever dreamed.

She patted his knee. "Do what I tell you and you'll be fine."

He sucked in his breath. "That's the first time you've touched me since Friday night."

That kiss. She'd wondered which one of them would mention it first.

"No comment?"

"No comment." She glanced back at Megan and Carl. Seeing they were oblivious to the world, all cuddled in each other's arms, she spoke freely. "We've already decided the kiss was the beginning and the end."

"You decided."

She smiled coyly. "Unless you can do what you want by yourself, I guess that means I made the decision for both of us."

"You're a tough woman. You know that?"

"I thought you said I was soft," she said, then gasped, wishing she could take the words back.

"Hey," Carl interrupted. "What are you guys whispering about?"

Eleanor was relieved at the interruption. Jake

placed a hand on her knee, turned quickly to her, and mouthed, "Later."

"So you finally decided to come up for air?" Jake asked, glancing at them in his rearview mirror.

"If you want, Jake," Megan chimed in, "Carl and I can swap places and let you and Eleanor have the backseat for a while."

Eleanor turned around in her seat and glared at Megan. "I wouldn't trust you two. You'd probably try to sit in Carl's lap while he drove."

Carl captured Megan's lips for a quickie. "We'll have to try that, cupcake."

The look of pleasure and adoration on Megan's face was one Eleanor had never seen there before. After years of leading men around by the nose, her friend had finally been bitten by that old love bug. Eleanor was happy for her.

"Where did cupcake come from?" she asked.

Carl opened his mouth to answer, but Megan covered his mouth with her hand. "Don't you dare." Carl chuckled and Eleanor saw his tongue come out and caress Megan's hand.

Megan tore her gaze from him and looked to Eleanor. "I don't believe I almost let him get away."

Now Carl was the one who wore the satisfied look. Love looked as good on a man as it did on a woman.

Megan nudged Carl. "Tell her."

Carl frowned down at her. "I'll tell her later."

"Tell her now, sweetie. You know I can't keep a secret."

"Don't tell me you two got married?" Eleanor asked, shocked but at this point ready to believe about anything where these two were concerned.

They looked at each other and chuckled. "Well," Carl drawled. "There was this church."

Megan punched his arm. "Don't tease her." She turned to Eleanor. "No, we didn't get married."

Eleanor heard the unspoken "Yet." "What is it then?" she asked Carl.

"Megan and I have decided to take a vacation. Together. So I'm going to need some time off."

Eleanor relaxed. "You know that's no problem. You have enough vacation."

"Well, I was thinking about taking a month."

"A month? We can't do without you for a month. Not on this short notice. Who would fill in for you?"

Megan leaned forward. "We've already thought about this. Jake can cover for him."

"Jake?" Eleanor said, her voice high. She ignored Jake's quick glance at her.

"Yes, Jake," Carl said. "He took over sports. Now he can take over my assignments."

"But," she said, then stopped. She wanted to say, "But sports was easy." Looking at Jake, she decided to change her words. "Jake didn't come to Lamar to be a reporter. He has other things to do."

"You don't think I can do it, Eleanor?" Jake asked and she knew she'd insulted him.

She looked at him. "Of course you can do it. That's not the issue."

"It sure does sound like the issue to me," he said, his eyes focused on the road, his lips tight.

"Whoa, you two," Carl said. "You're beginning to sound like another couple I used to know. Now, if you don't calm down, I'm going to put you out at the next exit."

Megan giggled.

"Now be cool," Carl continued. "We'll talk about this when we get back to Lamar."

Eleanor turned around in her seat and looked at Jake. His jaw was set in a firm line and she knew he was upset. She hadn't meant to hurt his feelings. Why did she always say the wrong thing where he was concerned?

Megan collapsed on Carl's chest. "I've never been this happy before," she said when her breathing returned to normal.

"I know," Carl said, lazily brushing her short curls with his hand. "Me either."

Megan tightened her hold on Carl. She was so glad she'd found him. And now that she had, she couldn't imagine her life without him. When she thought about the time she'd wasted arguing with him, fighting her feelings for him, she experienced a deep regret.

"I love you, Megan," Carl said softly, his hand still in her hair. She loved his touch, whether it was in her hair like now or all over her body as they made love. "I suppose I've loved you since we were children, since you first moved to Lamar. I even suppose you're the reason I never left Lamar."

Overwhelming joy filled her entire being. Carl loved her. She buried her face in his chest and squeezed him even tighter, tears filling her eyes.

He lifted her head so he could see her face. "Don't cry, cupcake. Tell me you love me, too."

The tears flowed freely now. "I do. I do. I do,"

she said, dotting his face with kisses with each pro-nouncement. "You're the best thing that's ever hap-pened to me."

"I know," he said, and she heard the smile in his voice.

She looked up at him. "Don't get cocky with me." She pushed her pelvis against his. "I have my ways of getting satisfaction."

Carl groaned. "Don't I know it." He rolled over until she was under him, her beautiful face staring up at him. Everybody saw her beauty and he didn't mind, but he was glad he saw the woman inside where she was even more beautiful. And if possible, more desirable. He wanted to love her again so he lowered his head to kiss her.

"Not yet," she said, pushing at his chest with her arms. "I want to talk."

Carl groaned again and rolled to her side. Maybe this was part of being in love. She wanted to talk and he didn't mind. "Okay, cupcake, what do you want to talk about?"

Megan settled herself in Carl's arms, loving the cherished feeling he gave her. "Eleanor and Jake."

"Eleanor and Jake. Oh, no, I'm told the romance is over when your lady brings another couple to bed with you. That or she's into kinky." The smile was back in his voice.

"I'm serious," she said. "Don't you think they're perfect for each other?"

"Hmm . . ."

"The way I see it," Megan continued, "they're never going to find each other without our help."

"Oh, no," Carl began, feeling obliged to put up

some kind of resistance though he knew he'd go along with her plan. "I don't think they need us meddling around in their affair."

"I'm not talking about an affair. I'm talking about Eleanor and Jake finding what we've found." She laced her hand with his and brought it to her lips for a kiss. "I want them to be as happy as we are."

He couldn't argue with that kind of logic. "What is it you propose we do?"

"I don't know yet, but I'll think of something."

Carl rolled her over onto her back and poised himself above her. "Think about them later. Try thinking about me now."

"At least this plan of ours is not a total failure," Mathias mused.

"What do you mean by that?"

Mathias snorted. "We got Carl and Megan together."

"Damn," Randolph said. "I don't believe this. I really don't believe it. This is your fault."

"My fault?" Mathias raised his voice. "How is this my fault?"

"You were supposed to get Carl and Megan on that plane," he accused. "Maybe if you had, Eleanor and Jake would be a couple by now."

"Don't go blaming me, Randolph Mason. Some things never change," Mathias muttered. "It's never your fault. You haven't changed since we were kids."

"Okay, okay," Randolph gave in. "It's nobody's fault."

"I know it's not my fault," Mathias stated adamantly.

"Well, now that that's settled. What are we going to do about Jake and Eleanor?"

"Okay, Eleanor." Jake opened round two of their negotiations Monday morning when they returned to work. He hoped it wouldn't go the full fifteen. "Let's try this again. When I look at the list of projects you want Mason Publishing to fund, they fall into three categories: community support, infrastructure, and growth. Do you agree?"

He waited for her nod.

"Now, of those three items, only growth interests me."

"I sorta figured that," she muttered.

"But do you agree with me?"

Eleanor leaned forward and he thought again how attractive she looked with her hair down. He didn't trust himself even to think about her gorgeous legs in that hot pink miniskirt suit.

"To a degree," she said, "but the other items deserve discussion."

"In due time. Let's talk about the idea you have for this African-American family magazine." The more Jake dug into this project, the more apparent it became that his best angle was this magazine. The progressive concept filled a large void in the marketplace.

Eleanor stood up and framed an imaginary picture with her hands. "Picture this. The cover has a black-and-white silhouette of a man and woman in the foreground, and three children and two sets of grandparents in the background. The title, *Our Family,* is in bold black-and-gold letters across the top." She looked at Jake. "Are you with me so far?"

"So far. So good. I've got the cover. Now what's inside?"

"The purpose of the magazine is to foster and support the black family. So each issue would have that as its theme. With twelve issues each year, we could do three issues featuring kids; three on parenting; three on marital relationships; and three issues on dating relationships. Of course, there'd be something each month for all the groups."

"Where would issues related to elder care fall?" he asked, and her smile told him she was pleased with the question.

"I've thought about that and it can fall into one of the parenting issues or maybe kids or maybe even both. It's something we could work with. What's your first thought?"

He tapped his pencil on the table. "I like the idea of putting it in the kids issue. That way the focus won't be on age, but on the different roles we play in our lifetimes. From kid, to parent, to lover, to spouse. I like it."

"You do?" Eleanor asked, clearly pleased with his answer. "Oh, Jake, I've been thinking about this for so long and I couldn't see how we could make it work. We just didn't have the funds."

"Until Mason Publishing came along," he finished for her.

She nodded.

"Why didn't you take this idea to some venture

capitalists? I'm sure you would have gotten financing."

Eleanor shook her head. "That's not the way we do business. We use our own money or money we can borrow on our own terms."

"We're back to the control issue."

She nodded. "Right. That's one of the first lessons my father taught me."

"And you learned it well."

That sounded like an insult to Eleanor. Before she could comment on it, he asked another question. "How do you expect this magazine to pay for itself?"

Eleanor sat on the edge of the table and it took all of his willpower to keep from staring at her legs. "As with most publications, we'll only expect circulation to pay for paper and staff. Ads will pay for everything else."

"And you expect national circulation and thus national advertising?"

"Exactly. I figure we'll start small and branch out. Thus, the need for outside capital. It's probably too risky to go national immediately. By starting locally, expanding regionally, then nationally, I think we'll have the best chance for success."

"You've got this all planned out, haven't you?"

She nodded again.

"And how much cash do you think you'll need to get started?"

Jake whistled at the number she threw out.

"It's not that much, Jake," she argued. "At least, not for what we want to do. Once the magazine hits the marketplace, we'll have more advertisers coming to us than we can handle."

Jake showed no emotion, but he agreed whole-heartedly with her assessment. As the first magazine in its market, *Our Family* would be guaranteed a strong showing. It would take any copy-cat publication a while to match their numbers. "Are any infrastructure improvements included in that number?"

She didn't cower. "A few."

"I bet. I'm sure you have all this documented." Again, he waited for her nod. "I'd like to get a copy. I think we may be able to hinge the deal on this magazine idea."

She beamed. "That's great, Jake. Now what about the community projects and infrastructure? You've experienced our computer system. You've seen the press and the photo shop. You know we need updating. It'll mean a classier product. And it'll mean more work from our existing pool of employees."

"That brings up another issue," he said, ignoring her concerns. "What about staffing the new magazine?"

"That's another place we have to spend money. We need journalists, but we also need recognized authorities to discuss key issues and provide alternatives. We also need staff to manage the day-to-day operations of the magazine."

Jake had already considered those factors. "What role will you play in *Our Family*?"

"I'd love to be managing editor," she said immediately.

"What about your role as managing editor of the *Lamar Daily*? You'd do both?"

That's where Eleanor was torn. In her wildest dreams, she kept her role as managing editor of the

Lamar Daily in addition to being managing editor of *Our Family.* "I'd have to make a choice, I guess."

"Carl could probably take over as managing editor of the *Lamar Daily,*" he offered.

"No," she said quickly. "I want the paper to stay in the hands of the family. Not that Carl isn't a good man. If we have to use a nonfamily member, I'd rather that person be managing editor of *Our Family.* The *Lamar Daily* is family."

"You could really let someone else take over *Our Family,* your baby?"

She wasn't sure. She wanted them both. A part of her would willingly give up her role at the *Lamar Daily,* but another part, a stronger part, wanted to keep it. She didn't think too closely about why. She shrugged. "We do what we have to do. It would be a lot of fun, and not to mention challenging, to birth and nurture *Our Family* on a day-to-day basis, but I'll be happy to *see* it get done. I don't have to *do* it."

"I hear your words, Eleanor, but your heart's not in them."

"Maybe I'm getting like you, Jake. It's not about my heart. It's about business."

She knew he didn't buy it, but she was thankful he didn't pursue it.

"I don't think we can commit to the community projects you've talked about yet. We should focus on the magazine and the infrastructure needed to support it. We'll consider the community projects later."

Eleanor extended her hand. "Seems like we're working from the same page, Jake. We may be able to come up with a deal I can live with, after all."

Jake took her hand in his, and instead of shaking it, he caressed it. "We work well together."

She felt the sexual connotation of the statement all the way to her toes. She was as attracted to Jake as she'd always been. And if today's meeting was any indication, she had no reason to fear his plans for the paper. The roadblocks keeping them apart seemed to be disappearing. "The jury's still out on that, but it's looking pretty good."

"May I take that as a word of encouragement?"

She eased her hand out of his and strolled to the door. "You may," she said, opening the door of the conference room. "But just a little." She heard him chuckle as she closed the door.

Fourteen

"He'll be back," Eleanor said, tugging on Megan's arm to get her attention.

Megan reluctantly turned to her. "I miss him already."

"You've got it bad, don't you?"

Megan put her hands to her chest and whirled around. "I'm in love," she sang. "I'm in love."

Megan extended her hands to Eleanor. Eleanor took them and joined in her dance, a dance they had made up when they were kids. "Me-gan's in lo-ove," Eleanor joined in. "Me-gan's in lo-ove." Pretty soon they collapsed on Eleanor's bed in a fit of giggles.

"Remind you of one of our slumber parties?"

Eleanor nodded. "We always ended up laughing ourselves silly and Dad telling us to get some sleep."

Megan chuckled. "We almost drove Mr. S. crazy."

"That's why we had to alternate our sleepovers between your house and my house."

Megan rolled over on her stomach and propped her head on her hands. "You know, for a while I wished your dad and my mom would get together. Then we'd have been real sisters."

"We *are* real sisters," Eleanor said.

"But you know what I mean."

Eleanor nodded. "I never thought about my dad getting married again until I was much older. Maybe senior year. I know I thought about it a lot when I was in college."

"When you were dating Frank-lin?" Megan always exaggerated the syllables of his name.

"Why didn't you like him?"

"I did like him."

"You certainly didn't act like it."

"It could have been that he reminded me of Carl. They're a lot alike," she said, then added, "on the surface."

Eleanor considered Megan's observation. The only similarity between the two men was that they both were of the glasses and pen protector set. First-class nerds. But Franklin had changed a lot—become cosmopolitan—since she'd first known him. "At this point, Megan, everybody reminds you of Carl."

Megan rolled over on her back and pulled a pillow to her chest. "He's wonderful."

Eleanor shook her head and rolled her eyes. "You're beginning to repeat yourself."

Megan threw the pillow aside and faced Eleanor. "I want you to have what I have with Carl."

Eleanor wanted it, too. "One day. Maybe."

"Was it like this with Franklin?"

"What do you think?"

Megan pondered the question. "I don't think it was. At this point, I'd follow Carl anywhere if he married me. You wouldn't follow Franklin."

Eleanor nodded. "I loved Franklin. But I think it

was more a puppy love. He was the first guy who loved me and that by itself was intoxicating."

"I can't remember anyone before Carl," Megan said dreamily.

Eleanor threw a pillow at her. "Now I know you're exaggerating."

Megan retaliated with a pillow missile to Eleanor. "I'm not, and if you'd ever been in love, you wouldn't say that."

Eleanor took the pillow and held it in her lap. "If you say so."

"Come on, Eleanor. Loosen up. You and Jake seem to be getting a little closer. What do you think?"

Eleanor folded her hands and rested them on the pillow. "I have a confession to make," she said softly.

Megan raised up on her knees. "What is it? Are you pregnant?"

Eleanor's eyes shot up, but a burst of something akin to pleasure settled in her bosom at the thought of having Jake's baby. "Of course not. Are you crazy?"

"So what is it?" Megan asked as she sat back on her thighs.

"Jake and I were never a couple. We only pretended to be one to help get you and Carl together."

"What?" Megan asked, eyes wide.

"You heard me. We faked our relationship for you and Carl."

Megan's eyes filled with tears as Eleanor explained the plans she and Jake had made.

"You did that for us?"

Eleanor nodded and Megan pulled her into her

arms. "You're my best friend and my sister, all right. I'm so grateful for what you and Jake tried to do for me and Carl."

When Megan pulled away, Eleanor wiped at her own now-damp eyes. "We knew two people who argued as much as you two did belonged together."

"And I know you and Jake belong together. He's had you off your beat since he got here. Even Carl's noticed it."

"We're business associates," Eleanor stated emphatically.

"Understatement of the year. Did you sleep with him in your quest to get me and Carl together?"

Eleanor hit her with the pillow. "Of course not."

"But I bet you kissed him."

"Maybe."

Megan pushed her pillow away. "Maybe nothing. Come on, girl, tell me."

"Okay, I kissed him."

Megan jumped up and gave the high-five sign. "I knew it. I knew it. I told Carl . . ."

"You told Carl what?"

Megan settled back down. "Nothing. I didn't tell him anything."

"Yes, you did. Now tell me what it was."

"Don't bust your britches. Carl and I want you to be as happy as we are."

"And . . ."

"And we think Jake could be the guy for you."

She'd been having thoughts along that line herself. "Me and Jake?"

"Yes, you and Jake. You're perfect for each other."

"And why do you think that?"

Megan leaned back on the bed and smiled confidently. "Because he's the first man to make you get your panties in a snit."

"Want to go for a drink tonight?" Jake asked Carl after everybody had filed out of the conference room at the end of the weekly status meeting.

Carl grinned. "Not tonight. My lady's waiting for me."

Jake walked over and propped on the edge of the table in front of his friend. "You've got it bad. You know that, don't you?"

Carl whirled around in his chair. "If this is bad, I don't think I could handle good."

Jake laughed. "I knew there was something between you and Megan."

"Well, you knew more than I did. I'm glad you and Eleanor decided to make us come to our senses before it was too late. Thanks, man."

Jake slapped him on the back. "It was nothing. Eleanor and I did it for ourselves as much as we did it for you and Megan."

"What do you mean by that?"

"If we didn't get you two together, you would've killed us with your constant bickering."

Carl gave a smile, then quickly sobered. "I love her, man."

At that moment, Jake felt envy deep in his bones. Though he'd dated many women in his lifetime and he'd loved them all, he'd never been *in love* with any of them. When he saw Carl like this though, it made him wonder what he'd missed. "I'm happy for both of you."

"Thanks, man." Carl leaned back in his chair, linked his fingers and rested them on his stomach. "Megan tells me things are heating up with you and Eleanor."

That was news to Jake. He leaned closer. "What did Eleanor tell her?"

Carl shrugged. "She mentioned something about a kiss."

So, Jake thought, Eleanor couldn't get that kiss out of her mind either. "Well, that's about the extent of what's happened."

"Don't discount it, man. A kiss is a good thing. Maybe somewhere along the line your playacting became real."

Jake shook his head. "I doubt it. Eleanor's not interested in pursuing a relationship with the enemy."

Carl chuckled. "You're still the enemy?"

He thought about their last discussion of *Our Family*. "I'm gaining ground, but I still have a long way to go yet."

Carl shook his head. "What are you going to do about it?"

"What can I do?"

Carl studied him, before shaking his head. "If you don't know, man. I can't tell you."

"Yeah, yeah. When a brother falls in love, he wants every other man to be in love."

Carl grinned, but he didn't deny it. "It's great, man. You should try it."

"You mean, Megan's great."

"She is."

Those simple words expressed to Jake the love Carl felt for Megan even more than his earlier declaration of love. "You're a lucky man."

"You're telling me. Can you believe a woman like Megan waited for me?" Carl shook his head, then spoke without waiting for Jake's response. "She was a virgin, man," he said, his voice full of awe. "I was the first guy she was with. Do you know how that makes me feel?"

So he'd been right about Megan. He did know women. "Would it have made a difference if she wasn't?"

"Maybe to her," Carl said.

"What does that mean?"

Carl looked up at Jake. "I was inexperienced, too."

"What?" Jake exclaimed. "You've got to be kidding. You mean, you'd never . . ."

Carl shook his head. "Never."

Jake stood up and slipped his hands in his pockets. "I don't believe this. How old are you?"

Carl began gathering his papers. "I'm twenty-eight, the same age as Megan and Eleanor. And don't go making a big deal about this. I can't believe I told you anyway."

Jake sobered, then clapped Carl on the back. "I think it's great for you and Megan."

Carl nodded. "It makes me glad I waited." Carl grinned as if he'd remembered a funny joke.

"What?"

Carl's grin broadened. "Now I can't seem to get enough. Fortunately, neither can Megan."

"You lucky dog," Jake said in good humor.

"I'm not a dog," Carl replied with mock pique. He stood up and put his papers under his arm. "My cupcake says I'm a sweetie."

Jake laughed as Carl strutted out of the conference room.

On Thursday night of his seventh week in Lamar, Jake stared out the French doors of the Sanders living room wondering if he should go to Eleanor. She'd fled his presence as soon as possible after dinner with him and her father. He reached for the door latch for the fourth time. Should he go to her?

He dropped his hand. If she didn't want anything to happen between them, then he should respect her wishes. He placed his hand on the door latch again. On the other hand, her position was going to drive them both crazy before the summer was over, so he'd be doing them both a favor by forcing the issue.

He snatched the door open and stepped outside before he talked himself out of making the trek to her cottage. He strode past the pool and followed the lane to her front door.

He lifted his hand to rap on the door, then dropped it. Was he ready to face the consequences of sleeping with Eleanor? He knew she wasn't a woman he could casually make love to, then walk away from. But then he'd never done that. Every woman he'd been with had known the score. When he was with a woman, he was faithful. Yes, serial monogamy was his MO. But when he was ready to move on, he moved on. And since he'd made no commitments, he felt no guilt.

But what about Eleanor? Not only was she a *special* woman, she was his business associate and the daughter of his father's best friend. What the hell was he doing knocking on her door?

Before he could answer that question, Eleanor opened the door and peeked out. The answer to his question no longer mattered.

"What are you doing here, Jake?" she asked, her breath coming in short spurts. He wondered what she'd been doing.

"I want to talk to you," he lied.

Her eyes squinted and he knew she didn't believe him. "I saw you at dinner. You could have talked to me then."

He grinned. "I don't think you'd want your father to hear the things I have to say."

"Jake . . ." There was a plea in her voice.

He put his hand on the door in an attempt to push it open farther. "Fifteen minutes. Give me fifteen minutes."

He saw the indecision in her eyes.

"You must have it bad for me," he challenged, studying the hand that rested on the door as if he were indifferent to her answer, "if you don't trust yourself to be alone with me for fifteen minutes."

She grunted. "It's not me I don't trust, it's you."

He grinned again. "Scared?"

"You wish," she said, stepping back from the door and allowing him to push it open farther so he could enter. "I hope I don't regret this," she said when he was inside.

He couldn't form a response. Actually, he couldn't close his mouth. As he admired her form in the thigh-length fluffy white robe, he wondered if everything she owned was white. And skimpy.

His eyes traveled her full length, causing her to pull the collar of her robe closer. Unfortunately for her, the action only caused her breasts to be better outlined. Unfortunately for him, the puckered nipples caused a similar response in his groin.

"You wanted to talk," she said, turning around and walking to the overstuffed white couch.

He followed her, again admiring the sway of the lush hips atop her long, firm legs. "Yes," he said, stalling for time to clear his mind. He deliberately sat next to her on the couch and pretended to ignore the raised brow she directed at him because of the action.

"I'm waiting," she said, apparently eager for him to get on with it.

Jake wondered again if he was doing the right thing. He shuffled through the magazines on the table in front of him, then picked up *Family Focus*. "Studying the competition?"

That was the right thing to say, because Eleanor immediately relaxed, leaned forward, and picked up a copy of *Southern Families*. "Yes, if you can call it that. These magazines aren't directed at African-Americans, but they demonstrate the concept. Look at this one. The article on the fading nuclear family is the kind of story I'd like to do in *Our Family*."

Jake looked at her, about to comment, but the sight of the tops of her breasts peeking out from her robe made him forget what he was about to say.

"What do you think?" she asked, her eyes sparkling with excitement.

I think I'm in trouble, he said to himself. "Let me see." He briefly scanned the article, glad for a reason to take his eyes off her yet disappointed he couldn't look his fill. "Not bad."

"Not bad?" She took the magazine from him and scanned the article as if to make sure it was the one she was thinking about. "How can you say 'Not bad'? That's exactly the kind of article I want us to do in *Our Family.*"

Her eyes were shooting sparks now. He liked it. "I don't see anything unique about it."

She breathed deeply and he knew she was about to blow her stack.

"Maybe you don't know a good article when you see one," she said calmly.

He fought to keep from grinning. "Maybe." Pause. "Maybe not."

She threw the magazine down on the table and crossed her arms. "What did you want to talk about?"

He chuckled. "I liked the article, Eleanor."

She dropped her arms and rolled her eyes. "Then why didn't you say so?"

"Maybe I like to see you squirm."

Jake knew by the flash of passion in her eyes that the erotic picture his words painted in his mind was also painted in hers.

"I can't stop thinking about that kiss," he whispered.

"Jake . . ."

He reached for her hand and rubbed it between

the two of his. "I bet you've been thinking about it, too."

She attempted to remove her hand from his, but he wouldn't release it. Instead, he pulled it to his lips and kissed it. "Your skin's so soft," he murmured.

"Don't."

He looked up at her and knew the passion in her eyes was mirrored in his. "Don't what? Don't want you? That's impossible."

"But—"

"But you're afraid?" He released her hand. "What are you afraid of, Eleanor?"

She lowered her eyes, but she didn't answer.

He leaned closer and placed a soft kiss on her exposed neck. "Are you afraid of what you're feeling?" he whispered.

She inclined her head more and he began a row of kisses up and down her thin neck.

"Tell me what you're feeling," Jake whispered. "Tell me, Eleanor. I see it in your eyes when you look at me. I felt it in your kiss when you kissed me. Everything about you tells me we'd be good together. From the gentle sway of your hips when you walk, to your puckered nipples that greeted me at the door, to the way you chew the ends of your pens when you're working."

"Jake," she murmured, inching away from him.

He pulled back and lifted her chin so that she stared into his eyes. "Can't you see that I feel the same way?"

She shook her head, but she didn't say anything.

He took her hand and placed it on his crotch. "Can't you feel how much I want you?"

She stared at the bulge, then flashed her eyes to his and quickly removed her hand.

"I want to touch you," he said, then raised his hand to the top opening of her robe and touched her chest. His eyes never left hers. "May I touch you?" he asked, but he didn't wait for an answer. He slid his hand down to a warm breast and covered it. His eyes closed at the pleasure that shot through him.

"Jake," Eleanor pleaded in a thick voice. Her hand covered his own and he opened his eyes.

"Do you like that?" he asked, tweaking her erect nipple.

A rap sounded at the door before Eleanor could answer.

Fifteen

The interruption brought Eleanor to her senses and she finally had the strength and the desire to move away from Jake.

"Damn," Jake said when his hand fell away from her breast.

"Eleanor, it's me," Megan called from outside the door.

Jake dropped his head and muttered, "Talk about bad timing."

"I'd better get that," Eleanor said, straightening the collar of her robe.

She got up on wobbly legs, glared down at Jake, and headed for the door.

"What took you so long?" Megan asked as soon as Eleanor opened the door. "I've been knocking for five minutes."

Five minutes, Eleanor thought. Had she been so involved with Jake she'd missed five minutes of knocking?

Megan strode past her and stopped in her tracks as soon as she saw Jake.

He stood up. "Hi, Megan."

Megan, eyes dancing, turned around and faced

Eleanor. "I'm sorry, girl, I didn't know you had company."

Eleanor strode past her and took a seat in the overstuffed chair next to the couch. "It's not company. It's Jake."

Megan made a beeline for the couch. "Hope I didn't interrupt anything?" She sat down next to Jake. "Actually, I hope I did interrupt something."

Jake laughed and Eleanor rolled her eyes.

"Where's your shadow?" Jake asked, then stood up and stuffed his hands in his pockets.

That dreamy look of love came over Megan's face. "Carl stopped by the house to see you. It didn't occur to us you'd be here. I guess he'll be along in a minute or so."

"I'm sure he will," Eleanor muttered. "He doesn't let you out of his sight for more than ten minutes at a time."

Megan ignored Eleanor. "Why don't you sit down, Jake? There's no need to rush off. Carl and I won't stay long."

"He was leaving anyway," Eleanor said, but Jake contradicted her words when he sat back down on the couch.

Megan grinned. "I guess he changed his mind."

Eleanor chose to ignore that. "What brings you and Carl out?"

"Oh, we wondered if you and Jake wanted to see that new Robert Townsend movie with us."

"Not tonight," Jake and Eleanor said at the same time.

Megan looked from one to the other and grinned.

"No, I didn't think you'd be interested. Seems like you already have plans for the evening."

Carl's rap on the door saved Eleanor and Jake from having to respond.

"You'd better put on some clothes," Jake said to Eleanor, then stood up again. "I'll let Carl in."

Eleanor's mouth dropped open.

"Bossy, isn't he?" Megan said with a giggle. "But he has a point. Carl will probably be a little uncomfortable with you dressed like that."

Eleanor looked down at herself, remembering that she wore nothing underneath the skimpy robe. "I'll be back in a minute."

"I'll go with you." Megan got up and followed Eleanor to her bedroom. When the bedroom door closed, she dropped down on the bed and asked, "What was going on?"

"Nothing." Eleanor opened the sash on her robe and stepped into her closet. After slipping on a pair of satin bikini briefs, she pulled on a pair of jean shorts and one of her old high school T-shirts. First, she tucked the shirt into her shorts, then decided she best wear it out since her shorts were pretty short.

Megan grinned at her when she walked out of the closet. "I know it wasn't nothing. So tell me what happened."

"I don't want to talk about it now, Megan. Let's get back out there before Carl comes looking for you."

Megan got up from the bed. "Isn't he sweet?" she said in that dreamy voice.

"As syrup," Eleanor responded dryly.

"No need to be nasty, Eleanor. Just because you're having problems with Jake doesn't mean you have to be mean to my Carl."

Eleanor dropped down on the foot of the bed. "I'm sorry. I don't know what's wrong with me."

"I do, girl. You've got it bad." Megan moved to sit on the bed next to her. "You're falling for him, aren't you?"

All Eleanor could do was nod. In spite of all her efforts to stop him, Jake Mason had gotten under her skin. Deep. It was so stupid. Why did she have to fall for a man who was only going to be around for the summer, for about another five or six weeks to be exact. If she and Jake were different people, a long-distance relationship might have a chance. But they were who they were and she didn't see them in a long-distance relationship. Once he left Lamar, he'd forget her and her heart would break.

"Well," Megan said, in a sagelike voice, "the good news is he's fallen for you, too."

Eleanor stood up and slipped her hands in her rear pockets. "I'm not too sure about that."

"I am."

"What makes you so sure?"

Megan grabbed Eleanor by the shoulders and pushed her to the door. "A little bird named Jake has been talking to a little bird named Carl."

Eleanor stopped walking. "What did Jake say?"

"You know I can't tell you that. Carl thinks I can keep a secret. Now, let's get back out there. I miss my sweetie."

* * *

If Carl and Megan didn't leave in the next five minutes, Jake planned to throw them out. He took a quick glance at Eleanor. Damn! She was getting increasingly uptight with each one of Carl and Megan's not-so-subtle jabs.

Any other time with any other woman, he could have enjoyed the other couple's antics. But not with Eleanor. Not where they were in their relationship. If they even had a relationship.

And if he didn't get Larry and Moe out of there, they didn't stand a chance of becoming a couple.

"Are you two sure you don't want to check out this new flick?" Carl asked, mischief in his smile. "We'd love to have you come with us, wouldn't we, cupcake?"

Megan's smile was all butter. "We sure would. Especially since you two don't have anything better to do."

Eleanor refused to be baited. "Why don't you *all* leave?"

Carl gave Jake an understanding smile. "I think she wants you out, too, man. I hope we didn't ruin your evening."

Jake wanted to wrap his hands around Carl's neck. "See you later."

"I guess we'd better go, sweetie. They're both being rude." Megan giggled. "They must be frustrated."

Carl guffawed. "That must be it."

Jake stood. "That's it. You two are outta here." He walked to the door and opened it. "It's been real."

"We can take a hint," Megan said, moving to the

door. "I'll talk to you later, Eleanor." She giggled again. "Maybe I'll wait till tomorrow. You probably have a busy night planned."

Carl and Megan were still laughing when Jake slammed the door behind them.

Eleanor stood up. "You'd better go, too, Jake. It's getting late."

"That's not gonna cut it, Eleanor. We have to talk."

Eleanor didn't want to talk. She needed to think. "Not tonight, Jake. I can't handle it tonight."

Jake went to her and pulled her into his arms. "I'm sorry we were interrupted."

"I'm not."

He rubbed his hands up and down her arms. "Yes, you are."

She pulled back and looked up at him. "I don't like your bossy attitude. I know my own mind."

"Sure you do," he said, pressing her head back to his chest. This was his woman and he liked holding her. His woman. He'd never thought like that before, but he liked the sound of it.

He felt her relax in his arms. "What do you want from me, Jake? A summer fling?"

That question took him off guard. He didn't even like the sound of the word *fling* when thinking about Eleanor. But what did he want?

She pulled away from him. "You won't even admit that a fling is all you want?"

He wanted to tell her she was wrong, but he couldn't. This wasn't supposed to happen. He wasn't supposed to feel things for her. What had happened to his plans to work a deal that would make his father sit up and take notice? When had she become so important to him? "I want more than that."

The surprise in her eyes was clear for him to see. "Don't look so surprised."

She shook her head as if to clear her thoughts. "What do you want, Jake?"

He couldn't answer her because he didn't know. He hadn't thought much beyond his feelings for her *now*. He knew he cared about her. A lot. He knew a relationship with her would be different from any he'd had in the past. But he didn't know what that meant in practical terms. He didn't know where or how the relationship would progress. He was afraid even to think about it. He only knew he couldn't *not* be with her.

"I think you'd better go," she said finally.

"I don't want to go."

She smiled sadly. "I know, but you have to."

"But—"

She lifted a hand to stop his words. "Close the door on your way out. I'm going to lie down." She gave him a final look and left the room.

Jake stood rooted in place while she practically ran to her room and closed the door. *Damn! She was driving him crazy.*

Jake stared at her bedroom door for a couple of seconds, before taking the few steps that placed him only a door away from her. He lifted his hand to open the door, but he couldn't do it. He couldn't do it because he couldn't answer her questions. *Damn! Why did she have to make things so difficult?*

He turned slowly and walked out of her cottage, closing the door behind him. Maybe it was best, he told himself. He didn't need the complications that came along with Eleanor. No, he was much better off without her.

Maybe he could get Carl and Megan to introduce him to somebody else and he could keep his mind off Eleanor. Yes, that's exactly what he'd do.

Who was he kidding? he asked himself when he reached the French doors of the main house. There wasn't a woman alive who could keep his mind off Eleanor. He'd have to find a way to deal with her. And soon. God knows, he couldn't go through another night like tonight. Going unsatisfied was not a situation he found himself in often and he didn't like it. No, he didn't like it one bit. Thank God he hadn't had to resort to cold showers. Yet.

Eleanor released the breath she'd been holding as soon as she heard Jake's footsteps leave her bedroom door. She didn't know if she was glad or sad he hadn't opened the door and joined her in bed. Maybe she wished he had. Maybe that was why she'd stripped off her clothes and collapsed naked on the bed as soon as she'd closed her bedroom door.

It was all moot now that Jake was gone. At least, it was moot for the moment. Eleanor was mature enough to know that the feelings that raged between her and Jake wouldn't be denied forever. She and Jake would make love, and soon, as sure as the sun rose each day.

She rolled over on her stomach. Why was she delaying the inevitable? Maybe the wisest thing to do would be for them to go to bed, do the deed, and be done with it.

She eased up from the bed and headed for the shower. Yes, she and Jake needed to do the deed and get it over. There were only so many cold showers a woman could take.

Eleanor dragged into work the next morning after a nearly sleepless night. Thoughts of Jake and her own libido had kept her awake until early in the morning.

She grabbed a cup of coffee and hoped it would keep her alert enough to get out today's edition.

"Morning, Eleanor," Carl called. "Sleep well?"

Eleanor wanted to wipe that stupid grin off Carl's face. "Morning, Carl," she said and kept moving to her office.

She uttered a silent thanks that Jake wasn't at his desk. Hopefully, he'd be out all morning.

She dropped in her chair and began her morning ritual. Before long she was in her routine and her tiredness was forgotten.

"Morning, Eleanor."

The smooth silkiness of Jake's voice stopped the movement of her fingers. She glanced up at him. "Morning." She refocused on her screen and forced her fingers to move again.

She heard Jake settle himself at his desk and pick up his phone.

"So what do you think, Buddy?" she heard him ask.

Buddy? Who was Buddy? She didn't consider listening to his conversation as eavesdropping. No, they shared the same office and he talked loudly.

When his voice dropped to a whisper and she could no longer hear him, her fingers stopped their movement again and she leaned, ever so slightly, toward him.

"Do you want something, Eleanor?" Jake asked.

Busted, she sat up straight and resumed her keystrokes. "Oh, no."

"Look," she heard Jake say, "I'll talk to you a little later when I have some *privacy.*"

Eleanor heard the emphasis on the word *privacy* and knew it was for her. When she raised her eyes to him, he was staring at her, his eyes blazing with passion and something else she couldn't name. She gave a weak smile and returned her attention back to her keyboard.

She heard him hang up the phone then swagger over to stand behind her.

"You were eavesdropping," he whispered.

The spoken words couldn't have affected her more if he'd said *I want you.*

"I was not," she lied.

"You're lying," he said, so close his breath tickled the back of her neck.

She resisted the urge to swat him away. "I can't help it if you talk too loudly."

He moved away from her and sat on the edge of her desk. "You know what I like least about this office?"

"No," she said, turning around, "I don't."

"That damned window," he said, referring to the

window in the wall separating her office from the rest of the newsroom.

He sounded so sincere that laughter bubbled up in her and spilled out.

"I love your laugh," he murmured.

His passion sobered her and she looked through the window out into the newsroom to gather her wits. Carl, a knowing grin on his face, had the audacity to wave at her. Maybe she should consider getting rid of the window.

"Did you sleep well last night?" he asked.

Praying the passion she felt didn't show in her eyes, she glanced up at him and shook her head.

"Neither did I."

They were both silent for a while.

"Is this easy for you?"

She shook her head. If he thought this was easy for her, she must be one good actress.

"So what are we going to do?"

She smiled crookedly. "We could close the blinds and go for it right here."

He inhaled deeply. "Don't tempt me."

She stared up at him, wanting to tell him he wasn't the only one tempted. Instead, she got up out of her chair and walked to the window.

"What are you doing?" Jake asked, his eyes wide with banked passion.

She twisted the rod and the blinds closed. "I'm yielding to temptation." She started to walk back to him, but she turned around and twisted the lock on the door. "We don't want any interruptions, do we?"

Jake's mouth dropped open, but no words came out.

"What's wrong, Jake?" she asked as she sauntered toward him. "This is what you want, isn't it?"

"Eleanor . . ." Jake warned.

She walked into the middle of his spread legs and his thighs tightened against her. When he groaned, she placed a hand on either of his shoulders and stared into his passion-filled dark brown eyes. She'd known this man less than two months, but she knew the place he'd found in her heart was forever. She didn't kid herself the relationship was forever, though. Jake's stay in Lamar was limited. She knew that and she accepted it.

"Two can play this game," Jake said, unbuttoning her jacket and pushing it apart.

She leaned her face closer to his and rubbed her jaw against his. "What game?"

Jake reached inside her jacket, encircled her waist with his hands, and pulled her tight against him. "You feel so good."

"Umm, you don't feel so bad yourself." She relaxed in his arms and tightened her arms around his shoulders. She thought she could stay in his arms forever. There was something sure and right about it.

"I want to kiss you."

She leaned away from him and his eyes repeated his words. "I thought you'd never ask."

She closed her eyes when his lips captured hers. When his tongue slipped inside her mouth, she knew this moment was only the beginning for them.

When he pulled away, they were both breathing heavily.

"Do you want to come over tonight?" she asked when she could get her breath.

He pulled her back for another long kiss. "What time?" he asked.

"I'll be there all night."

"All night?" he repeated.

"All night."

He pushed her away from him and looked into her eyes. "Are you sure?"

Her confidence slipped a little and she wondered if her feelings were one-sided. She stepped out of the circle of his arms, went back to the window, and was about to open the blinds. Jake's hand stopped her.

He turned her around. "Make no mistake about it, Eleanor. I want you. I want you so bad now I hurt."

She relaxed and dropped her head against his chest. "I want you, too."

He grunted. "And you're going to have me."

Sixteen

Eleanor stripped out of her fifth outfit in the last twenty minutes. Why was Jake Mason making her so nervous? This wasn't her first date, nor was it her first time. Get a grip, she told herself. Jake is only a man.

"Right," she said, looking at the three piles of lingerie covering her bed. She never would have guessed she had this much lingerie. A piece here and a piece there over the years certainly added up. Her bedroom looked ready for a Victoria's Secret yard sale.

She opened the last drawer in her lingerie chest, praying the odds were with her. She pulled out garment after garment until there was nothing left in the drawer. And still she had found nothing to wear.

She pushed the piles of lingerie aside and dropped down on the bed. Maybe she should give up on clothes and greet him at the door in her birthday suit. She wondered what he would think of that.

She grabbed a pile of the lingerie in her hands and took it to the dresser. It didn't matter what Jake would think. She was going to be herself tonight. She stuffed the first pile in the dresser and went back to the bed for another. Finished, she propped her hands on her hips and stared at the third pile still on the bed.

Nodding her head, she pulled a white lace body-suit from the pile and held it up in front of her. "This is it. This is what I'll wear tonight."

Satisfied, she picked up the remaining items and placed them back in the dresser. When she turned to head for the bathroom, the phone rang.

"Are you nervous?"

Eleanor dropped down on the bed. "What are you talking about, Megan?"

Megan chuckled. "Carl told me about the closed blinds and locked door at the office today. When you canceled our date for tonight, I figured you must have had other plans."

She should have known Carl would say something. He'd been grinning at her all day. "I don't know what you're talking about," she lied.

Megan chuckled again. "Sure you don't. Anyway, have fun tonight. I'll call you tomorrow and see how things went."

Megan hung up before Eleanor could respond.

"Damn," she said, then scrambled into the shower.

Twenty minutes later, she was dressed in her body-suit, applying her makeup. Not too much, though, but she couldn't plan for a love scene without the proper look, could she?

She heard a knock at her front door as soon as she placed the cap on her lipstick. "Perfect timing," she said, grabbing her standard robe. "Let's make Mr. Mason wonder for a little while, at least."

Eleanor walked to the door, took a deep breath,

then opened the door. At the sight of Jake standing there in a pair of beige pants, a white open-collar dress shirt, and aviator sunglasses, her knees went weak and she tightened her hold on the doorknob to keep her balance.

"Hi," she said, praying her voice sounded normal since her pulse wasn't. It seemed her heart rate had doubled in the few seconds she'd been standing at the door.

Jake pulled off the aviator glasses and handed her a single white rose. "Hi, yourself," he said, his eyes shining with passion.

When she saw the burning passion in Jake's eyes, she immediately felt exposed. And this was a rare feeling for her. She was comfortable with her body and usually relished her nudity. But not now. Now she wished for a longer robe. Maybe even jeans and a T-shirt. She ran her hand through her hair, which fell in soft curls on her shoulders.

"Aren't you going to take it?"

The laughter in his voice alerted her to action and she reached for the rose. "Thank you," she said, stepping back into the room. "Come on in."

"Thought you'd never ask."

Eleanor walked to the couch, twisting the stem of the rose in her hand, very conscious of Jake behind her. She wished again that she'd chosen to wear more clothes. She sat on the couch and Jake sat next to her.

"Ouch," she said, and dropped the rose on the table in front of her.

Jake placed the aviator glasses next to the rose and reached for her hand. "Did you hurt yourself?"

She shook her head. "It's nothing. I pricked my finger."

Jake pulled the injured finger to his lips and his eyes met hers. "Let me kiss it and make it better."

"That won't be—"

Jake's tongue on her finger sent a shiver of desire through her and her words were forgotten. After he kissed the injured finger, he moved on to each finger of her hand. Eleanor felt warmer with each touch of his tongue.

"That better?" Jake asked, his eyes now glazed with passion.

She reluctantly pulled her hand away, wondering what had happened to her courage. Had she really expected to go through this evening in a mechanical fashion—wham, bam, thank-you, ma'am—and have it done with? What had she been thinking?

Jake shifted in his seat. He wondered if taking her finger in his mouth had been a wise move. He'd known his desire for Eleanor was great, but he hadn't anticipated his desire would work against him. But that's exactly what was happening.

He glanced at Eleanor and took small satisfaction in knowing she was as affected as he was. No, her eagerness could only enhance their union while his could ruin the evening for both of them. And he definitely didn't want that to happen. He needed to slow things down.

"Nervous?"

She looked at him with wide doe eyes and all he wanted to do was take her to bed. "Who, me?"

He chuckled. "No, the couch."

She gave him the laugh he wanted. Except the laugh was as enticing as if she'd stripped naked before him. He cleared his throat. "What do you want to do?"

She stared at him and he would have sworn he heard her mind speak, *Go to bed.* "Do?"

"Aw, hell," he said and pulled her into his arms.

"What—"

"Don't talk." His mouth covered hers and he felt his breath leave his body. What was it about this woman that affected him so? The opening of her mouth below his stopped any action of his brain to answer that question.

Eleanor leaned closer to Jake, needing to touch him all over. Her arms wound around his neck as his tongue entered into a mating ritual with hers. This wasn't the first time she'd been kissed, not even the first time he'd kissed her, but for the life of her, she couldn't remember any kiss except this one.

She took a quick breath when Jake groaned, but was grateful when he took up his assault again. The pressure of his eager lips against hers made her squirm against him, but it was the feel of his smooth hands against the bare skin of her chest that made her moan and want to touch him in return.

Why did he have on so many clothes? she wondered. Shouldn't he take off some of his clothes?

She grew impatient and dropped her hands from his neck to his shirt, still holding up her end of the kiss. As his hand slipped to her lace-covered breast, she undid the first few buttons of his shirt.

He lifted his mouth from hers and stared into her

eyes as his hand massaged her breast. She closed her eyes, not able to stand the intensity she saw in his coupled with the sensation his roving hands caused.

Jake stopped his massaging motion and she opened her eyes. Seeing the question in them, he gently pressed his lips to hers. When he pulled back, he brought the belt of her robe with him. "God," he said, pushing her robe off her shoulders onto the back of the couch.

The white lace that played peek-a-boo with the body he longed to possess mesmerized him. When he fingered the lace covering her right breast, she moaned again and her body lifted slightly from the couch.

Jake watched the play of emotions in her eyes and marveled that he could cause such abandon in her. When she closed her eyes again, he lowered his head to her right breast and lavished his tongue on its firm peak. The grainy sensation of her nipple against his tongue made his groin tighten. He was in trouble.

She didn't help his predicament any when she placed a hand to the back of his head and pulled him closer, all the while pressing her body more firmly against his. He groaned, then lifted a hand to tweak the nipple of her other breast. Now he wished he had another hand. Maybe even another mouth. There were so many things he wanted to do. With her. And to her.

He wanted to kiss her mouth again, but he didn't want to stop his attention to her breast. He opened his mouth and took in the nipple and felt he was actually being nurtured. He knew he'd die if he didn't get to sample the other breast.

When her hand fell limp from his head, he raised his head slowly from one breast and captured the other in both hands. He teased the extended nipple with his fingers before hungrily capturing its peak in his mouth. Yes, there was life in her breasts for him.

Eleanor's tongue slipped out of her mouth as spasms of desire shot through her body. With each movement of his tongue, each touch of his tongue, her body temperature rose and her need for him grew. She wanted to touch him, but she couldn't make her hand respond to her mind. It was as if her body was no longer under her control.

"Jake," she pleaded, wanting to touch him the way he was touching her.

He lifted his head and focused desire-glazed eyes on her while his hands continued to pull at her nipples. Somehow, she managed to mobilize her arms to pull him closer to her. "I want to touch you," she murmured.

She pushed his shirt off his shoulders. "Jake," she said again. "I can't get the shirt off."

He seemed to come out of his haze long enough to shrug out of the shirt and throw it on the hardwood floor.

Eleanor immediately leaned into him, splaying the fingers of both her hands across his broad, smooth chest. When he sucked in his breath, she gazed into his eyes and a feeling of pure desire swept over her at the knowledge that she could affect this man so.

"Oh, Jake," she cooed before lowering her head

to his nipple and loving it with her tongue. The twitching in his limbs encouraged her motions and she moved her hand to play with the other nipple much as his hand had played with hers.

Her satisfaction with herself increased with each involuntary movement of his body. She was becoming accustomed to the role of seductress until she felt his hands slip to her pubis.

Jake noticed the hesitation in her movements when his hands touched the lace covering her mound, but she quickly resumed her assault on his chest. The feel of her soft lips against his chest coupled with the feel of the wet flesh of her mound against his hand made him ache. He knew it wouldn't be long now.

"Eleanor," he murmured, moving both his hands to her head to stop her motions. The passion in her eyes when she looked up at him was almost his undoing and he forgot what he wanted to say as his mouth swooped over hers.

She gave herself to him completely, pressing her body so tight against him he could feel the imprint of every piece of lace that covered her.

They were both breathless when he broke the kiss. She rested her head against his chest while he stroked her jaw with his forefinger.

Eleanor heard his labored breathing and was hard-pressed to distinguish it from her own. She'd never felt as in tune with any human as she felt with Jake now. She knew he was as overcome with emotion as she was, and knowing they were equals in their feelings made her want him more.

Eleanor was ready when he moved his mouth to her ear and whispered, "Let's go to bed."

She kissed his forehead, placed her hand in his, then stood. She felt his eyes searing every inch of her as she led him to her bedroom and her bed.

She lay on her side on the bed and watched him remove his shoes and pants. When she saw his bikini briefs, she smiled. He definitely had the body for them—firm hips and thighs and everything in between.

An unbidden question as to the number of women who had thought that same thing entered her mind, and for the first time since he'd touched her, she became unsure of what she was doing.

"What's wrong?" he asked, his fingers in the waistband of his briefs.

"You've done this a lot, haven't you?"

He slipped the briefs past his hips and down his legs. Stepping out of them, he joined her on the bed and pulled her into his arms. "No you don't. There are only two of us in this room and I'm not letting you include some imaginary woman from my past." He kissed her lips lightly. "Understand?"

She forgot her question as he began his assault upon her senses again. He captured her gaze with his own while his hands eased under the straps of her bodysuit and pushed them down her arms.

When the lace covering her breasts fell away, his eyes darkened and she thought he was going to take the exposed flesh in his mouth again. Her disappointment when he didn't was acute.

He continued removing the lace from her body, his eyes getting darker and darker with each inch of revealed skin. By the time the lace covering her mound was removed, his eyes were practically black.

She licked her lips together as she lifted, first one leg, then the other, so he could remove the suit from her body entirely. When she was naked before him, his gaze left hers and roamed her body.

She burned with every touch of his glance. His gaze traveled her body leaving a trail of scorching flesh. A spot on her left shoulder burned especially hot and she wondered what he found so fascinating there.

Jake marveled at the beauty of her naked body. She was definitely the most beautiful woman he'd ever known. Her creamy brown skin drew him like magnets drew metal. There was no denying the hold she had on him.

He'd walked into this relationship with Eleanor knowing it was going to be different from other relationships he'd had, but he hadn't realized how different. He'd planned to leave Lamar when his job was finished and not look back. Now, he wasn't so sure he'd be able to. Hell, he wasn't sure he even wanted to.

Eleanor wondered what was happening between them. She knew as well as she knew her name she would never be the same after being with Jake. Her mind told her she should stop now, while she had a chance. Her body told her it was too late to stop and she didn't have a chance. Her body was right.

Eleanor couldn't stand it any longer. "Touch me," she said.

Jake honored her request by resting one hand on her stomach and using the other to pull her mouth to his. She sighed as they resumed the dance they had started in her living room.

Jake eased his body against hers. "I love the way your skin feels. So silky. So smooth. So soft. Oh, so soft."

His words made her feel as if her backbone had slid out of her body. His firm, warm skin felt as good to her, but she couldn't tell him. Her mouth's only purpose now was to kiss him. She moaned, her body a shivering mass of desire. She couldn't feel anything but her need for him.

And his raging need for her. Again, she was awed at the effect she had on him. She felt him, large and long, against her thigh and her body seemed to open up in anticipation of receiving him.

Jake wanted the evening to last longer, but he knew that was impossible. If he didn't have her now, he was sure he'd die.

"Eleanor," he whispered and slipped himself inside her warm, wet sheath.

"Jake . . ." she began.

He heard the awe in her voice and knew she experienced the same sense of rightness and oneness he felt. It was as though they were alone in the world, as if something bigger than the two of them was being set right by their union.

They moved together as if they'd made love thousands of times. She instinctively met his every thrust and anticipated his every desire. He found the most sensitive areas of her body with expert precision. They were one in every sense of the word.

Seventeen

When Eleanor opened her eyes the next morning with Jake's strong arm resting across her stomach and his head resting against her still-sensitive breasts, she knew her life would never be the same. She lifted her hand and rubbed it lightly across his head while memories of their night of passion saturated her mind.

She had guessed Jake was an accomplished lover, but she'd never guessed the heights to which his tenderness would take her. From his first touch, she'd been his to do with as he wanted and she hadn't been disappointed. She smiled a satisfied smile. Each of the four times their bodies had joined was perfect.

Yes, their night had been perfect. And though Jake's touch brought long-dormant emotions to life, she knew their relationship had no future. She understood Jake had only given himself for the night and she accepted it. She wasn't sure if she wanted more anyway. At least, not from him.

She'd needed Jake the previous night and she didn't regret being with him, but that night would be their first and last encounter. She didn't want to start thinking of a future with him.

Jake shifted his head and moved his hand to her breast. She sucked in her breath when his fingers began their massage. "Jake," she whispered.

"Good morning."

She felt his smile against her skin and his fingers increased their pressure. Though her senses were awakened and she was more than ready to make love with him again, she didn't think it was wise. She grabbed his hands and stopped the movement of his fingers. "Jake, we can't."

He raised his head and gazed into her eyes. "Why can't we?"

The sensuous smile curving his lips made her ask herself the same question. She shook her head and pushed the stray strands of hair from her face while she tried to remember why they couldn't.

He took advantage of her bemused state and kissed her. The kiss was a teasing kiss, one designed to make her want. And make her want it did. She pulled his head closer to her and gave herself up to the moment. Why fight it? She'd tell him later they couldn't do this anymore.

Uncontrolled strands of Eleanor's thick, nearly black hair tickled Jake's nose and he awakened to the sight of her beautiful, supple form sprawled across his body. Her nipples burned against his ribcage and he wanted her again.

He wanted her again, but he wasn't going to wake her. He grinned a satisfied masculine grin. No, he'd play the role of the gallant Southern gentleman and let her sleep for a while longer since he'd kept her up most of the night.

He shook his head when he thought of his first impression of Eleanor. He would never again apply the words *stern* and *prim* to her. She'd been everything but that with him last night. And this morning. He smiled again. Maybe he'd continue to use the word *mouthy*, though, but it would refer to the way she spoke when she kissed him. He'd never enjoyed kissing a woman as much as he'd enjoyed kissing her. He'd heard kisses described as soulful before, but it was only now that he thought he understood what a soulful kiss was.

He pressed his arms around her and closed his eyes. The restful contentment he felt was new to him. Normally, when the after-sleep sex was finished, he was ready to go home. But not this time. No, this morning he was content to hold Eleanor in his arms.

The next time he opened his eyes, Eleanor was moving out of the circle of his arms. He tightened his arms around her. "Don't go."

She struggled to lift her head and shift away from him a little. "I have to go to the bathroom."

"Oh," he said a little sheepishly and released her. "Hurry back."

He admired her naked body as she glided away from him. The swing in her hips caused his groin to tighten. He wanted her again and this time he wasn't going to play the Southern gentleman.

Eleanor quickly closed the bathroom door and leaned back against it, her legs weak. How could his looking at her do this to her? She knew why. Jake didn't *look* at her. He made love to her with his eyes. Though he hadn't touched her as she'd walked away, she'd felt his hands and his mouth all over her body. Her body was as taut as stretched wire and she knew only Jake could give her relief.

Eleanor moved away from the door and looked at herself in the mirror. She still looked the same, but she knew that was only because she looked on the outside. She knew if she could see the inside, she'd see the change in her. She knew her senses were heightened. The body she'd always been comfortable in was now foreign to her.

She touched her sensitive breasts. They were no longer breasts; they were fountains from which Jake had drank. Her shoulders were paths on which he had planted kisses. Her stomach, a wasteland he'd developed. Her navel would never again be just an inny.

She reluctantly touched her hand to her sticky mound and she knew that somehow Jake had marked this place as his own. She had no doubt that no man would ever claim her as Jake had done. And even though she knew that, she wasn't sad. No, she was happy. Happy to have had this special moment with Jake.

But now the moment was over and she had to tell him to go home. She ignored the dreaded ache that settled across her now-heavy heart at the thought.

Eleanor bumped into Jake's naked body when she walked out of the bathroom.

"I missed you," he murmured, gathering her in his arms.

She allowed herself a glorious second in his arms, before pulling free. "We have to talk."

He nibbled along her shoulder and she leaned her head to the side to give him better access. "I'm talking already. Do you hear what I'm saying?"

She forced herself to move away from him. "Jake!"

"God, I want you," he said, his eyes dark and piercing.

He lifted her in his arms, took her back to bed, and settled her against his chest. He kissed her while his hands explored the already familiar contours of her body.

Her traitorous body responded to his touch and she gave in to her desire. What was one more time?

Eleanor fanned at the annoying hand slapping against her rump. "Ouch, stop it." She turned over and was rewarded with Jake's smile.

"I'm hungry," he said, grinning.

"You can't be serious."

He laughed and kissed her briefly before getting out of bed. "We'll have to wait for more of that. Now, I need food."

Eleanor pulled the pillow over her head so Jake wouldn't see the rush of blood to her face and also to keep her eyes from his very masculine body. "Go eat then."

He pulled the pillow away. "Come with me."

Had he said those words to her during the night?

she wondered, then shook her head. She wasn't going to start looking for sexual innuendo in every statement he made. "I'm not hungry." Her traitorous stomach growled, making her a liar.

He laughed again. "Come with me. It's my treat."

"You don't have to do that." She wished he would hurry up and leave.

"Listen," he coaxed. "I'll even take you to Mel's."

A smile escaped when she thought of their first visit to the diner. "It's not open on Saturdays."

He pulled the covers away from her and made love to her with his eyes. "Well, if you won't go out with me, I guess I'll have to get my nourishment here."

Her nakedness worked against her. She hopped out of the bed. "Okay, let's go get something to eat."

He laughed at her. "Chicken."

"Is Jake still there?"

Eleanor brushed her hair back with her hand and looked over at Jake's sleeping form. After a late, late breakfast he'd coaxed her back to bed. She admitted that it hadn't taken much effort on his part.

"What do you want, Megan?"

Megan giggled. "I guess that means he's still there."

Eleanor heard Megan mumble something to someone in the background. It had to be Carl.

"Anyway," Megan said when she was back, "Carl and I were wondering if you two wanted to go dancing at the Farmhouse with us tonight."

Eleanor didn't want to go dancing. She wanted to be alone. She needed to think. One night with Jake had turned into almost two nights. She had to get him out of her cottage or they'd end up spending the entire weekend in bed. As if to confirm her prediction, Jake's hand reached for her in sleep and she knew then if they didn't go out with Carl and Megan they'd spend the rest of the night here in bed. "What time are you leaving?"

Megan mumbled something else to Carl, but Eleanor couldn't make out what it was. "Carl says we can wait for ya'll to get dressed."

"Megan . . ." Eleanor warned.

"Well, I'd understand if you two want to spend the rest of the evening in bed. I told Carl—"

"We'll go," Eleanor said, cutting her off.

"Good. Why don't you two drive over to my place when you get dressed?" She giggled again and hung up the phone.

"Megan has to stop giggling like some schoolgirl," Eleanor mumbled.

"What did you say?" Jake said, turning over to face her.

"Nothing."

He reached for her. "Well, come here."

Eleanor wondered how he could keep it up. Literally. "We can't, Jake. Megan and Carl have invited us to go dancing with them."

"I don't want to leave this bed."

She didn't either, but what she wanted didn't matter. This time she was going with her head instead of her body. "I want to go."

"We can dance here."

She rolled her eyes, knowing his kind of dancing

would not be done standing up. "We've been in this house for almost two days."

He grinned. "Are you complaining?"

He knew full well she wasn't complaining. At least, not about what they'd shared. "We need to get out. This room is no longer big enough for the three of us."

Jake looked down at his aroused penis. "Well, my man, now she counts you as another person. I guess that means you made a good showing."

Eleanor slapped him across the chest and got out of the bed. "I'm talking about your ego, idiot! Your ego is the third person."

"Now, you've hurt his feelings, Eleanor. He thinks you don't like him."

She glared at him. "I'm going dancing. You can sit here and talk to yourself all night, if you want." She stormed into the bathroom.

Jake looked down at his penis. "Well, my man, I guess you'll have to wait for your dance. It seems the legs get the next workout."

Eleanor and Megan had gone dancing at the Farmhouse many times on many Saturday nights. They'd always made it a rule never to dance with one guy more than once and to always come home together. They'd never broken that rule.

Until tonight. Carl and Megan were so wrapped up in each other they pretended each song was a slow dance and stood in the floor holding each other. Well, sometimes they did those face-swallowing kisses that made Eleanor wonder how they could breathe.

She and Jake were a little more circumspect. But barely. For the fast dances, she did force Jake to put a few inches between them. But the slow dances were torture.

"I must be losing my touch," Jake whispered in her ear, his breath on her skin adding to the erotic haze she now found herself in.

She didn't understand what his comment meant. How could he think he was losing his touch? Their bodies were pressed so close that neither of them were able to move a muscle without the other feeling the full effects of it.

"What are you thinking about?" he asked when she didn't respond.

She shook her head, too weary at her lack of self-restraint this entire weekend to even speak.

"Want me to tell you what I'm thinking?"

She grunted and pressed her face closer to his chest. "I can guess."

He chuckled. "But I want to tell you."

She gathered the material of his shirt in her hands. "Jake . . ."

"I want to see your eyes widen when I enter you," he murmured. "Did you know you did that?"

Eleanor swallowed. Hard. That warm feeling that had been with her since Jake had entered her cottage yesterday got warmer.

"Then I want to hear your whimpers of pleasure as I—"

"Don't," she pleaded, pulling away from him and running from the dance floor.

Jake rushed after her but she thwarted his efforts when she entered the ladies' room.

A couple of minutes later, Megan stormed in.

"What's wrong with you? Jake's hovering outside that door like he's going to break it down."

Eleanor buried her face in her hands and tried to shake off the emotions she was feeling. It didn't work. When she dropped her hands, the feelings were still there.

"What's wrong?" Megan asked again.

"Nothing. Everything." Eleanor dropped down on the plaid plastic settee.

"Did he say something to hurt your feelings?" Megan asked, her voice full of concern.

Eleanor shook her head slowly and extended her hand to her friend. How could she explain what Jake did to her?

Megan took her hand and sat next to her. "Want to talk about it?"

"There aren't enough hours in the day."

Megan settled back on the settee. "I've got nothing but time."

"What about Carl? I don't think you two have been apart for this long since you've been together."

"He's all right. Anyway, I think he has his hands full with Jake." She brushed a wayward strand of hair from Eleanor's face. "If I hadn't come up when I did, I'm sure he'd be in here by now."

"What's with him, Megan?" Eleanor asked, truly bewildered by her actions and his.

"He's falling in love."

"In lust, maybe," Eleanor muttered.

Megan shrugged. "If that's what you want to call it."

"That's what it is," Eleanor declared. "Strong, strong lust."

"And great, great sex," Megan finished for her.

Eleanor laughed and some of the weight she'd been carrying fell away. "Extraordinary sex."

"So, what's the problem?"

The problem was that Eleanor feared she was feeling something much more than lust. Much, much more.

Carl reached across the table and stopped the glass that Jake put to his lips. "Drinking is not going to help."

Jake shook off his hand. He needed something, and though he knew it wasn't a drink, a drink was all he had. "It might."

"I don't know, man. You might regret this drinking later on tonight, if you know what I mean."

Jake placed the glass on the table. "It probably won't matter."

"Then why did you put the glass down?"

Jake ran a finger around the top of his glass. "Why do women play with a man's mind? Just tell me that."

Carl chuckled and leaned back in his chair. "Is that women in general or one, stubborn, know-it-all woman, in particular?"

Those words made Jake smile. "One stubborn, know-it-all woman who's also the sexiest, most desirable, and most giving woman I've ever met."

"Uh-oh."

"What?"

"Sounds like you've got a bad case of—"

Jake lifted a hand. "Don't even say it. Don't even think it."

Carl ran a finger down the side of Jake's drink glass. "They say the denial stage is first."

"I'm not denying anything."

"If you say so."

"I do."

"Okay."

"You don't believe me?" Jake asked.

Carl leaned forward and rested his forearms and elbows on the table. "I've been there, man. You can run, but believe me, you cannot hide."

"Well, I'm not running and I'm definitely not looking to hide."

"Uh-huh," Carl said. "So what happened with Eleanor?"

Jake shrugged. If he knew the answer to that, he wouldn't be sitting at this table dying to take a drink he didn't even want. "You tell me. You're the expert with women."

"My guess is, you and she are suffering from the same problem."

Jake didn't have to ask what the problem was. The word *love* had crossed his mind more than a few times in the last thirty-six hours. Usually it was preceded by *making,* as in *making love.* But there were a couple of times the lone word formed itself in his mind. "You think so, huh?"

"I think so."

Eighteen

Jake took Eleanor's key and unlocked her door.

"You don't have to do this, Jake," she said, wishing he had allowed Carl and Megan to drive her home. She needed to get away from him. Their one night of do-it-and-get-it-over sex had turned into two days of glorious passion that would forever change her life. "I assure you I've been letting myself in for a while now."

He stared at her and pushed the door open. "Go in, Eleanor."

Eleanor sidestepped him and entered the house, stopping just across the threshold. "Well, thanks for a nice evening."

"A nice evening?" Jake practically yelled at her. "Is that all this was for you—a nice evening?"

No, it was much, much more than that to her, but she couldn't tell him that. He might want a summer affair, but she didn't. Her heart was already too involved. "There's no need to yell. I can hear."

"What's going on, Eleanor?" he asked, his voice a sensual whisper that caressed her skin as his hands had done earlier.

She grasped the doorknob tighter. "Nothing's going on. I'm tired and I want to get some sleep."

He shoved his hands in his pockets. "I don't want to leave."

Why was he making this so difficult? she wondered. Men with lesser egos would have taken a graceful exit at her sleep line, but not Jake. "Why do you want to stay?"

He leaned against the doorjamb. "I like being with you."

Heaven help her, her knees went weak. "You mean, you like sleeping with me."

"That, too."

She cleared her throat. She wasn't going to let him work his magic on her again. She knew it wouldn't take much for him to get back in her bed. She hated the weakness in her that made that true. "That's not enough."

He stood up straight and pulled his hands out of his pockets, all attempts at casualness gone. "What do you want from me?"

Everything. "Nothing."

He put his hands back in his pockets. "Nothing?"

"Look, Jake. We had a nice time. More than a nice time. But it's over. Let's not make more of it than it was. You wanted me. I wanted you. We both got what we wanted. Let's leave it at that."

"That's it?"

She nodded, then watched the play of emotions in his face. Anger and frustration reigned.

"Okay, then that's the way it'll be. See ya." He turned and made his way up the path to the main house.

Eleanor closed the door and leaned back against it. He was gone and she was glad. Nothing could become of them anyway. Jake was a big-city man with big-city plans. She was content in her small town working for her newspaper. She had been right to turn him away.

She dropped her purse on the couch and began shrugging out of her clothes. She was naked when she reached her bedroom and collapsed on the bed.

The feel of the fabric of the comforter against her naked skin sent shock waves through her. It was as if Jake had touched her skin. She jumped up from the bed and grabbed her robe, quickly sliding it on. She collapsed on the bed thinking about Jake. He'd invaded her body, her mind, and her life.

And he'd taken away her comfort in her own body.

Damn Jake Mason.

Jake made his way up the path and into the main house, all the while thinking about the thirty-six hours he'd spent in Eleanor's arms. He couldn't be angry with her, because he understood her. He'd known it would be different with her. And he'd been right. Though she hadn't said it, he knew she didn't want an affair; no, Eleanor wanted a relationship.

"Hi there, Jake," Mathias called when Jake reached the stairway leading up to his bedroom.

Jake turned and faced Mathias, who stood in the doorway of his office. "Hello, sir. How are you doing?"

"Fine. Fine. What have you been up to?"

For a split second, Jake thought Mathias knew exactly what he'd been up to. "Nothing much. Enjoying Lamar."

Mathias nodded. "So I see. You didn't come home last night."

Jake searched Mathias's eyes, but found no guile in them. "No, sir. I didn't. That's not a problem, is it?"

Mathias pulled off his glasses, took a white handkerchief from his jacket pocket, and wiped the lens. "No, that's not a problem. I was a little worried though."

Jake was immediately sorry for his suspicions. "I'm sorry about that, Mathias. I'm not used to having someone worry about me and my hours. You know, Eleanor may have been right. Maybe I need my own place."

"Nonsense," Mathias said quickly. He put his glasses back on. "That won't be necessary." He walked over and put an arm around Jake's shoulder. "I'm not going to put a cramp in your style."

Jake turned and allowed Mathias to lead him up the stairs. "That's not it, Mathias. I need some privacy."

Mathias dropped his arm. "Privacy, huh? I guess that means you've found yourself a lady friend."

Jake studied the older man's profile. He had the sneaking suspicion that Mathias *did* know about his evening with Eleanor. "Well, you could say that."

"Mind if I ask who the lucky young lady is?"

Jake was grateful they had reached the top of the stairs. Now, he needed to escape to his room. "I don't know if giving her name would be very chivalrous of me, Mathias," Jake answered, praying Mathias would let it rest.

Mathias nodded. "I see."

Jake sensed the older man wanted a response from

him, but he didn't have one to give him. "I guess I'll say good night."

"Good night," Mathias said, but he kept standing there as though he was waiting for Jake to say something more.

"Good night," Jake said again and reached for his doorknob.

As Jake stepped into his room, Mathias asked, "This woman. Do you have feelings for her, Jake?"

Jake turned around and met Mathias's stern gaze. The older man *did* know he had spent the last evening with Eleanor. "Yes, sir," he answered in earnest. "I care a lot about her."

Mathias nodded, apparently accepting the truth in Jake's words. "That's good, Jake. That's very good. I'll see you in the morning, son."

Jake watched Mathias travel down the hall to his bedroom and close the door, then he entered his own room.

Mathias knew Jake was sleeping with Eleanor. Jake was sure of it. And Mathias was upset about it. Jake was also sure of that. And he couldn't blame Mathias.

Jake cursed himself. He'd known when he moved in here that starting something with Eleanor would cause problems. He'd thought it wouldn't become an issue. But it had.

He had to make a decision. He had to move out of Mathias Sanders's house or he had to stop thinking about Eleanor. Jake leaned back on the bed. He'd start looking for a place tomorrow.

* * *

Mathias sat in the rocking chair in the corner of his room. He called the chair his thinking chair. The chair had been Barbara's idea. This was where either of them sat when they needed to sort out a serious problem or if they were trying to find a solution to a tough situation.

Well, he was in a tough situation tonight. He knew Jake and Eleanor had spent last night and most of today together. And he wasn't naive enough to think they'd been playing chess.

He got up from the chair, sat on the side of the bed, picked up his telephone, and dialed Eleanor's number.

"Hello," she mumbled.

"Hi, sweetheart. Were you asleep?"

"No, Daddy. I was just lying here."

He knew she was trying to mask the sadness in her voice, but he heard it and pain wrenched in his gut. "Are you feeling okay?"

"I'm fine," she said, her voice a little stronger. "How are you doing? I haven't seen you in a day or so."

"Fine. Fine."

He was silent.

"Did you want something special, Daddy?"

He wanted to make all her hurt go away as he had done when she was a child. That was his job as her father. But he couldn't do it this time. And what hurt most was that he had caused her pain. "No, I didn't want anything."

"Okay, I think I'll hang up then. I'm getting sleepy."

"Eleanor?" he asked.

"Yes."

"I love you."

He heard her smile.

"I know you do. I love you, too."

"Good night, daughter," he said and hung up the phone. He dropped his head in his hands. What have I done to my baby? he asked himself.

The phone rang and Mathias considered ignoring it, but he picked it up. It was Randolph.

"He had sex with her," Mathias declared.

"Great!" Randolph exclaimed. "Now we're getting somewhere."

"Have you lost your hearing, Randolph?" Mathias said in clipped tones. "I said your son had sex with my daughter."

"I heard what you said, Mat. But I don't know what your problem is."

"My problem is that your son had sex with my daughter," Mathias repeated, his voice rising. "Our plan was for them to get married."

"Aw, come off of it, Mat. That's the way things work these days. First, sex, then marriage."

"I haven't heard your son say anything about marriage."

"Give them time. Don't forget your daughter is twenty-eight, not thirteen."

"What's that supposed to mean?" Mat shouted.

"Calm down, Mat. I didn't mean anything by it."

"Then why did you say it?"

"You talk about them like they're teenagers. They're adults, Mat. Don't forget that."

Mathias wrapped the phone cord tight around his wrist. If he was a drinking man, he'd be drunk by now. "She's my baby, Randolph. And she's no match for a playboy like Jake."

"Are you saying Jake took advantage of her?"

"You said it. I didn't."

"Maybe you got it wrong and your little girl seduced my boy."

"Get serious, Randolph."

"I am serious."

Mathias took a deep breath. This discussion wasn't getting them anywhere. "Look, I don't want to talk about this now. My little girl is hurting and your son is to blame. You'd better hope this scheme of ours doesn't blow up in our faces. Because if it does, you and your son will have to deal with me."

Nineteen

"They can't do this," Eleanor exclaimed. "They can't do it."

Jake leaned back in his chair, determined not to be moved by the nervous motion of her tongue licking her lips. "They already did it."

"But how could they?"

Jake propped his legs on his desk and crossed his arms across his stomach. "Let's see. They probably made reservations. Drove to the airport. Got on the plane."

She rolled her eyes and sat on the edge of her desk facing him. "It's not funny. What am I going to do without Carl? You know he's our top reporter."

"If the loss of one man makes your paper fall apart, you've got more problems than Mason Publishing anticipated and we're going to have to reconsider our deal."

Eleanor smiled for the first time since she'd learned Carl and Megan had hopped a plane to the Caribbean for a couple of weeks. "Well, at least that would be one good thing to come out of this mess."

Jake dropped his legs from the desk. "There's no need to get nasty. Carl and Megan left. I'm still here."

I'm still here. The words repeated themselves over

and over in Eleanor's mind. *I'm still here.* "Does that mean you're going to take over Carl's assignments?"

"Carl and I talked about it."

Eleanor's eyes widened and she gave him an accusing stare. "You've talked to Carl?"

"Yes."

"When?" she said, her voice rising. He knew she wasn't going to like his answer.

"Now, don't get all upset—"

"When?" she demanded.

"I spoke with him yesterday."

"Yesterday?"

"Yesterday." Jake had spent a rainy Sunday hanging around Carl's apartment with him and Megan. They'd tried to con Eleanor into coming over but she'd rejected the invitation. Jake knew she was thinking about that now.

"And nobody thought I needed to know?"

Jake dropped his gaze to his hands, which were folded on his chest. "It came up suddenly. One minute we were talking and the next minute Megan was on the phone making reservations."

"She could have called me. This is so unlike Carl."

"The man's in love, Eleanor. He's entitled to be a bit adventurous."

"Adventurous? More like irresponsible," she muttered. "He's taking on all of Megan's negative traits."

Jake got up and stood in front of her. "And you're blowing this way out of proportion. Maybe you're frustrated about something else?"

"And what, pray tell, would that something be?"

Jake shrugged his shoulders slightly. "What makes a woman frustrated on Monday mornings?"

Eleanor got up and strode to the window facing the newsroom. "Her top reporter unexpectedly leaving town for two weeks with her best friend."

"It could be that or it could be an unfulfilled desire of some kind."

His words floated out to her and kissed her cheeks, causing her to turn back to him. "Don't start with me this morning, Jake. I'm not up for it. Carl is gone and we have a paper to get out. I suggest you get started. It's going to be a hell of a long two weeks."

In a way, Eleanor was thankful for the chaos that Carl's absence caused in the newsroom. It gave her an excuse to ignore any tension between herself and Jake. And she welcomed that.

"Is Carl's headline story ready?" she asked Jake, who was totally engrossed in the article he was editing. She had to admit he'd pitched right in there taking up the slack for Carl's absence.

Jake hit the Enter key on the computer. "It is now."

"Do you want the byline?"

Jake laughed, but shook his head. "Carl would kill me. It's his story. All I did was check some facts for him."

"If you're sure?"

"I'm sure. It's Carl's story. If tomorrow's story ends up the headline story, then I'll take the byline."

"Fair enough," she said and went back to her terminal.

Two hours later, the paper was sent to press.

"We did it," Eleanor said, brushing her hair back from her face.

"Did you doubt we would?" Jake asked, wanting to run his hand through her wayward curls. He definitely preferred her new style with the curls falling to her shoulders to the old bun. All in all, he approved of the changes she'd made, from the tinge of lipstick on her soft lips to the short skirts and jackets she wore each day.

A smile curved her lips. "Not really. I didn't realize how much I depended on Carl."

"Maybe you should tell him that when he gets back," Jake suggested.

She stared at him for a long second as she considered his words. "Maybe I should."

"I've moved into Carl's apartment," Jake added casually.

"When did this happen?"

"Yesterday."

"You had a busy day yesterday."

He captured her gaze. "It's not how I wanted to spend the day, but I got a lot accomplished."

"That's good," she said and flicked on her computer, dismissing him.

"I think your father knows about us."

Eleanor turned around. "Knows what?"

"I think he knows I spent the night at the cottage."

"How could he know? Did you tell him? Tell me you didn't tell him."

"Calm down. Of course I didn't tell him."

"Then how does he know?"

"I wasn't home all weekend." Jake asked softly,

"Does it bother you that he knows we slept together?"

His words slammed against her chest. "No more than it bothers any woman to know that her father is keeping track of her sex life."

Jake chuckled. "I wouldn't take it that far."

"That's because he's not your dad. How would you feel if your father knew?"

"That's why I moved out of your dad's house. What's between us is between us. I don't want to hide it from your dad or mine, but neither do I want to include them in our relationship."

She lifted a brow. "Relationship? I thought we slept together."

"I don't know about you, but one-night stands aren't my style. Is that all it was for you?"

After finishing her hundredth lap, Eleanor pulled up to the side of the pool and got out of the water. Unfortunately, her emotions were strung as tight now as they had been when she'd entered the water fifty minutes ago.

She grabbed her towel and marched back to her cottage knowing she'd have to hurry to get back to the paper for her dreaded 2 P.M. meeting with Jake.

"Need some help with that key?"

She jumped, then turned around at the sound of Jake's voice. "What are you doing here and why are you dressed for swimming?"

Jake gave a lazy grin. "Maxine told me you'd come home for a swim. I thought I'd join you, but I see I'm too late."

"Maxine talks too much," Eleanor said, turning away from him and opening the door.

He chuckled and the sound made her hands shake. "I don't think so."

She stepped across the threshold and turned to close the door, but she bumped into Jake's chest. "What—"

Jake took advantage of her surprise and gathered her to him for a kiss. "I've done nothing but think about you. I don't know how I made it this long without tasting you again."

She stopped her traitorous arms before they wrapped themselves around his waist. "Just what do you think you're doing?" she demanded, pulling away from him.

He stepped away from her and the glazed look of passion she expected to see in his eyes wasn't there. "That's my last invitation."

"Invitation to what?"

That lazy grin appeared again and the passion that had been missing in his eyes made its appearance. "Party. Carl's apartment."

"A welcome back party for Carl and Megan?" She didn't know why she'd asked. She wasn't going with him.

He shook his head. "This is a two-person party. I call it a 'More than a Summer Fling' party."

Understanding dawned and she leaned her head to the side slightly. "I don't think so."

Jake lifted her chin and kissed her again. She didn't try to pull away. "It's your decision." He stepped away from her. "I'll see you in the office at two," he said, then turned on his heels and left her standing in her doorway.

Eleanor touched her hand to her lips, which still throbbed from his kiss. What was Jake up to? she wondered.

Jake entered the conference room at exactly two o'clock, determined not to push Eleanor to make a decision about their relationship. He dropped down in the chair next to hers and placed a bulky manila envelope on the table. "Why do we meet in this room when we could talk in our office?"

"When the paper went from a weekly to a daily, Maxine decided we needed a conference room. Then she started bugging everybody to schedule meetings." She shrugged her shoulders. "It got to be a habit."

"This paper is really like a family, isn't it?" he said, more to himself.

She picked up her pencil and twirled it in her fingers. "Most small-town papers are. So what do you want to talk about?"

He wanted to say *Us*. Instead, he opened the bulky manila folder. "I've gotten some preliminary figures back from the guys in New York and I'd like to get your opinion on some things." He pushed a sheet of paper in her direction. "What do you think?"

Eleanor read the projections and cost estimates for *Our Family*. She looked up at Jake. "I guess my figures were slightly underestimated."

He raised a brow. "Slightly? I'd say *grossly* is a better word."

She focused on the spreadsheet again. "You're not cutting any corners. I had scaled back on some of my ideas to make the project more cost-effective."

"Are you complaining?"

She looked up at him again. "No way. As my father says, why look a gift horse in the mouth?"

Jake searched her face for guile and, seeing none, gave her a big grin. "Now Mason Publishing is a horse. Is that a step up from a gravy train?"

Eleanor laughed at his reference to an earlier conversation they'd had, and the tension in the room lessened. "I guess it is."

"Let's go over this line by line," Jake suggested.

Eleanor enjoyed every minute of their discussion. Jake shared her excitement about *Our Family*, and if he was able to get the support from Mason Publishing that he wanted, the magazine would be even better than she'd imagined.

"Oh, Jake," she began. "This is going to be great. I thought it would take us four years to get to where you want us to be in eighteen months. Do you really think we can pull it off?"

The joy in her eyes mesmerized him. "What do you think?"

She grinned from ear to ear. "With my brains and your money, we can't lose."

Eleanor drove around Carl's apartment building for the fifth time. She wanted to go in, but she didn't want to face the self-satisfied grin she was sure Jake would wear in greeting.

Yes, Jake had worn her down. Between his warm

eyes, and his interest and support for her plans for the paper and *Our Family*, he'd gotten to her more quickly than if he'd sent flowers and sang ballads to her every day.

On her sixth spin past the building, she pulled into the parking lot. She was a modern woman—if she wanted to visit a man she could, she told herself. Other women did it all the time.

By the time Eleanor reached Carl's door, she realized she was not "other women." But she was also not a coward. She rapped on the door and held her breath.

It seemed hours before Jake opened the door.

"Hi," he said, with no trace of a self-satisfied grin.

"Hi," she repeated, feeling awkward he hadn't yet invited her in.

Jake stared at her, wondering if she was really there or if she was an apparition brought forth by his wildest fantasies. He reached out and caressed her cheek to assure himself she was real.

Eleanor held his hand to her face and smiled at him with comforting eyes. "Is something wrong?"

He grinned at her. "Not now." He dropped his hand and stepped back so she could enter the apartment. "Make yourself at home."

She walked in, allowing her gaze to take in the whole room. A nondescript brown plaid sofa, love seat, and chair took up most of the room. They were accompanied by a solid oak coffee table and two end tables, all dotted with magazines.

"You've never been here before?"

She moved her eyes from the first edition print

hanging on the wall behind the sofa to Jake and shook her head. "I was never invited."

"Carl is not a wise man."

She smiled, accepting his compliment. "I don't know about that. He's always wanted Megan and now he has her. That sounds like wisdom to me."

"Or good luck."

She sat on the couch and crossed her legs. Jake didn't miss the expanse of thigh exposed when she did. "Do you really think it was luck?"

He couldn't think about much more than her warm brown thighs. "Maybe it was more than that."

Eleanor nodded. "He loves her. I like to think that it was destiny."

He sat on the coffee table in front of her. "I think a man makes his own destiny."

She uncrossed her legs and scooted back on the couch. "And what is your destiny, Jake?"

"You."

"Oh."

He leaned toward her and caressed her face with his eyes, before using his hands. "Yes, oh."

"Ah, but how long does your destiny last?"

He dropped his hand from her face. "As long as we want it to."

"Until you leave Lamar?"

He stood up, shoved his hands in the pockets of his khaki shorts, and turned away from her. "If that's all you want."

She sighed, then got up and stood behind him, wrapping her arms around his waist and resting her head on his back. "Why is it so hard to care about somebody, Jake? It's not supposed to be this hard."

He breathed deeply. "I don't know."

"I care," she said softly. "I didn't want to, but I do."

He felt her words attempt to penetrate the contours of his heart. "I care, too," he whispered.

She dropped her hands and moved to stand in front of him. "Say it again."

He cupped her face in his hands. "I care." He dipped his head to kiss her, and she opened her mouth to him. When he would have deepened this kiss, she pulled away.

"What's the matter?" he asked.

"Nothing." She kissed him lightly on the lips then took his hand and led him back to the couch. "I want to talk for a while."

He nuzzled her neck. "We can talk later."

"Do you really mean that?"

He pulled back and looked into her skeptical eyes. "Well, maybe not." He sat back, pulling her into his arms. "What do you want to talk about?"

"Us."

"I thought we'd already done that."

She locked her fingers with his. "We *started* to talk."

He raised their interlocked hands and kissed her fingers. "Okay, let's talk."

"While I was driving over here, I told myself I was only coming to get my itch scratched . . ." She peeked up at him from beneath half-lowered lashes. "If you know what I mean."

"Thank God I'm a good scratcher." He nuzzled her neck again.

She moved away from him. "I'm trying to be serious, Jake."

"So am I."

She shot him an accusing glare. "You're doing this on purpose, aren't you?"

He directed his attention to her neck again. "Doing what?"

"Seducing me to stop me from talking."

"You can talk."

"But you aren't listening," she accused.

He pulled away from her and she saw the sincerity in his eyes. "I told you I care. And I do. God help me, I care more than I'd planned to. I came here to do a job for my father. I had no intention of falling for you. But I did."

She touched her hands to his face, her heart so full of love for him that she thought it might burst with it. "Thank you for telling me that. Now, don't you want to know why I'm here?"

He grinned, then pulled her into his arms. "I know why you're here."

"You do, do you?"

"Sure." He pulled her into his arms and sank back into the couch. "You're here because somewhere in the back of your mind, I'm still that knight in shining armor you fell in love with when you were a little girl."

She laughed. "I always thought you were too modest for your own good."

"I believe in honesty over modesty." He kissed her again, this time pressing his hand against her breast. "Can we stop talking?"

Twenty

Eleanor heard Megan's giggles and raised her head from Jake's nipple. "Oh, shoot." She moved to get off him and out of the bathtub, but he pulled her back.

"Stop it, Megan," came Carl's voice from beyond the master bedroom door.

"They're going to find us, Jake," Eleanor said, frantically pulling away from him. "Let me up."

"Eleanor," Megan called. "Where are you?"

Eleanor felt the rumble of laughter in Jake's chest before she heard it.

"I can't believe you think this is funny." She pulled at his arms again. "Let me go."

"What are you going to do, honey? Walk out there in your birthday suit?"

Eleanor covered her mouth with her hands. "My clothes are in your bedroom."

Jake grinned. "That's right."

"You can't hide, Eleanor," Megan sang. "I know you're here. I saw your car outside."

"Leave them alone, Megan," she heard Carl say. "I knew as soon as we saw Eleanor's car we should have gone back to your place, but no, you wanted to come in."

Eleanor shot Jake a pleading look. "Any chance they'll leave?"

Jake shook his head. "Kiss me and I'll tell you my plan."

"How can you think about kissing at a time like this? Tell me the plan now."

Jake tightened his sudsy arms around her and shook his head. "Kiss me first."

"I don't believe you," Eleanor fumed.

"Maybe they're in the Jacuzzi," came Megan's voice.

Eleanor turned widened eyes to the bathroom door. She closed her eyes when she heard Megan enter the master bedroom.

"Eleanor," Megan sang. "I'm going to find you."

Eleanor slapped Jake on the shoulder. "Do something. The bathroom door isn't locked. What if she comes in here?"

"Kiss me first."

"Oh, you," Eleanor said, then kissed him. She'd planned on a short kiss, enough to pacify him, but he had other plans. He began a slow melody with her mouth that almost made her forget her friend on the other side of the door.

"I know you're in there, Eleanor," Megan said.

"Leave them alone," Carl pleaded. "Sometimes you can be a pain in the butt, Megan."

Jake released Eleanor from the kiss. "That's right, Megan," he yelled. "Leave us alone. We're busy."

"I'm dragging her out of here, Jake, don't worry," Carl said in an irritated voice. "Sorry about this, Eleanor."

"Sometimes you can be a stick-in-the-mud, sweetie," Megan said. "I was only teasing them."

Eleanor hit Jake again. "That was your plan. What kind of plan was that?"

"Well, they aren't in here, are they?"

Eleanor rolled her eyes and pushed at his arms again. "Let me go."

Jake released her, but his body was so slippery she almost fell backward in the tub. She shot an angry glance at him. "Are you trying to kill me or what?"

Jake laughed. "You said to let you go, so I let you go. I'll hold you again, if that's what you want." He reached for her again.

She scrambled out of the tub. "No way. Keep your hands to yourself."

Jake wiggled his brows at her. "What about my other body parts?"

"This is funny to you, isn't it?" Eleanor said, grabbing a towel and wrapping it around herself. "It's all one big joke."

Jake stood up in the tub and Eleanor admired his soapy body. Goodness, he was a well-built man. From his broad shoulders to his tapered waist to his tight buns and thighs.

"See something you like?"

Eleanor looked up into his grinning eyes. "Nothing I haven't seen before."

He stepped out of the tub and grabbed himself a towel. "Does this mean the thrill is gone?"

She looked down at his erection. "Apparently not for you."

He rolled up his towel and swatted her bare thighs. "Now, don't go hurting my man's feelings.

You ought to be proud of him, staying up through all this commotion."

"You know, Jake, sometimes I wonder what I see in you. You have the sensitivity of a door post."

Jake pulled her to him and let her feel him taut against her. "You talk too much, woman." He kissed her hard.

She gave herself to the kiss, admitting to herself it was somewhat erotic to think of her friends on the other side of the door while she and Jake made out.

Jake lifted his head. "Now that's more like it. Do you want to get back in the tub?"

Eleanor actually considered his proposal, but her more conservative self won out. She pointed to the door. "You first."

"Chicken," Jake said, tightening his towel around his waist. "Am I decent?"

"As decent as you're going to get," she said, pushing him toward the door.

Jake opened the door and peeked out, scanning the master bedroom. "The coast is clear. They must be in the living room."

Eleanor took a deep breath. "Lead the way then. Let's get this over."

She followed Jake through the bedroom, out into the hall, hoping her prayers would be answered and she'd be able to get to the guest room for her clothes before Megan saw her. It was not to be.

"You're looking good in that towel, girl," Megan said as soon as Jake and Eleanor walked out of the bedroom door.

"We're a matching set," Jake responded, and

Eleanor was glad he'd spoken. All she wanted to do was separate Megan from that silly grin she wore.

"So I see," Megan said, not taking her eyes off her friend.

Eleanor fingered her towel, then stepped away from Jake. "Well, I hate to disappoint you, but I'm going to change into something that covers a little bit more of my body."

Megan grinned. "I guess you'd better. I wouldn't want my Carl to get any ideas."

"Megan," Carl's voice came from down the hall. "Leave them alone."

Megan hunched up her shoulders and whispered, "I just love it when he goes Tarzan on me." With that, she turned and went down the hall to Carl.

Eleanor almost ran to the spare bedroom, a chuckling Jake in her wake. He grabbed her when her towel hit the floor.

"How about a quickie?"

She reluctantly pushed away from him. "You've really lost your mind. They could hear us."

He grabbed her again. "That's the point. A bit dangerous, a bit forbidden."

"No way." She pushed him away and quickly donned her black satin panties and a pair of white cutoffs. "Stop staring and get dressed," she ordered Jake, who stood studying her every move.

Jake looked as if he wasn't going to do as she suggested, then he tossed her bra to her. "Put this on so I can concentrate."

She quickly fastened the bra and slipped her T-shirt on over it. "Okay, slow poke, I'll see you when you're dressed." She dropped a kiss on his forehead as he riffled through his dresser looking for something to wear.

"You looked better in the towel," Megan said when Eleanor joined her and Carl in the living room.

"Thanks a lot." The sight of the two of them curled in each other's arms on the couch as if they'd been together forever caused a budding of envy to settle in Eleanor's stomach. "Why are you two back so soon? I thought you'd be away at least another day."

Megan pouted her red-glossed lips. "I wanted to stay, but Mr. Responsibility here started getting the guilts. He had to come back to the paper."

"Thanks, Carl," Eleanor said, then remembered a conversation she'd had with Jake about showing more appreciation for Carl. "We certainly missed you around the paper. It made me realize how much we count on you. I don't tell you often, but we really do appreciate what you do and we're glad to have you on our team."

The shock in Carl's eyes took Eleanor by surprise. "What?" she asked. "You don't believe me?"

Carl shook his head as if to clear his thoughts. "I never thought I'd hear you admit it."

"Well, even old dogs can learn new tricks."

Jake entered the room dressed in khaki shorts and a regulation New York Giants football jersey. "Who's an old dog?"

"Eleanor," Megan quickly chimed in.

Jake draped an arm around her shoulder. "I wouldn't call you a dog, honey. A tigress maybe, but definitely not a dog."

Eleanor colored, Megan laughed, and Carl grinned.

"What happened while we were away?" Carl asked.

Jake looked from him to Megan. "If you can't guess, it won't do me any good to tell you."

Megan giggled.

"Stop with the innuendo, Jake," Eleanor warned, slapping his wrists.

Jake dropped down on the couch and pulled Eleanor onto his lap, ignoring her discomfort in the company of Megan and Carl. In the almost two weeks Megan and Carl had been away, he'd gotten used to having her close. He wasn't going to give that up now. "Tell us about your trip," he said to Megan and Carl.

Carl and Megan told the story together, with Carl giving the highlights and Megan filling in the details.

After a few minutes of this, Jake whispered to a fidgety Eleanor, "You'd better stop wiggling before I embarrass us both."

Eleanor immediately stopped moving. Megan giggled, Jake groaned, and Carl resumed his story.

"Mat, you need to get away. You're worrying about them too much."

Mathias rested his chin on his hand propped on the desk. "I should never have let him move out."

"Come on, Mat. Jake is a grown man. There was no way you could make him stay at your house if he didn't want to."

Mathias leaned back in his chair and breathed deeply. "He's sleeping with her on a regular basis."

Randolph could barely contain his excitement. If Jake and Eleanor were sleeping together, maybe he'd have that grandchild a lot sooner than he expected. He didn't think it was wise to mention that to Mathias, though. No, Mathias wouldn't appreciate it. "Why don't you come up next weekend? I'm giving another party." When Mathias hesitated, Randolph urged, "Come on. It'll do you good."

"I don't know . . ."

"You're sounding like an old woman, Mat. You have to trust Eleanor. She's a grown woman. You need to treat her like one."

Mathias knew Randolph was right. His Eleanor was a good girl. And that was what had him worried. If Eleanor was sleeping with Jake, it meant she thought she was in love with him. He knew his daughter that well.

But Jake was the unknown. He knew Jake was a good man. But he was a man. And Mathias wasn't so old he didn't realize a man didn't have to be in love, or even in like, to have sex. Particularly good sex. "Do you think Jake cares about her, Randy?"

"I know he does," Randolph said without hesitation. "You should have seen them when they were here, Mat. Jake couldn't keep his eyes off her." Randolph chuckled at the thought. "The only person that kept his attention more was her date. Jake may not know it yet, but Eleanor is the one."

"I certainly hope so. I don't want my little girl's heart broken."

Randolph sighed. "I can't promise her heart won't

be broken, Mat. I loved Tammy, but there were times I thought my heart was going to split in half. I bet Barbara sent you through some rough times as well."

Mathias remembered with glad sadness the times he'd made Barbara cry and the times she'd driven him to beat his head against the wall. He shook his head. Why did love have to involve pain?

"You know I'm right, Mat," Randolph said, interrupting his thoughts. "Either one or both of them is going to feel like their heart is breaking before this is over."

"How can you be so calm about it? Aren't you worried about Jake?"

Randolph sighed. "He's my boy, Mat. Of course I worry about him. I worry about him growing old and alone. I worry about him looking back and regretting his carefree youth. I don't worry about him loving Eleanor. She's right for him. And when you first met Jake, you thought he was right for Eleanor."

"That was before he slept with her," Mat mumbled, not yet ready to give up his position.

"How about it, Mat?"

"How about what?"

"You coming to New York. It'll do you good."

"I'll think about it," Mathias hedged, not sure he wanted to leave town at this point. What if Eleanor needed him?

"You know, Mat, you and I have been the best fathers we knew how to be. But I think getting Jake and Eleanor together is the last thing we should do. They're grown. They need their own lives. And we need ours."

"What do you mean by that?"

Randolph cleared his throat. "Jake might not be the first Mason man to the altar."

Mathias straightened in his chair. "What are you saying, Mat?"

"Maybe I want to get married, too. Maybe I don't want to live out the rest of my days alone."

Mathias snorted. "You haven't exactly been alone."

"You know what I mean. I can't believe you haven't thought about it. Are you still seeing Maxie on the quiet?"

Jake grabbed the ringing phone on his way out of the office for lunch. Eleanor had already gone home for a swim and he thought he'd surprise her.

"Hello," he said, hoping this call would be short. He loved seeing Eleanor in her bathing suit.

"Jake, it's me, Buddy. Do you have a few minutes?"

Jake sighed. This was the second time he'd talked to his old college acquaintance, Broderick "Buddy" Hamilton, since he'd been in Lamar. "A couple. What do you want?"

"How about coming over to Welles for dinner? My old man wants to meet you."

Jake looked at Eleanor's chair. He'd done enough research on Hamilton News since his first conversation with Buddy to know Eleanor would consider his visit to the Hamiltons of Hamilton News Company a mistake. "What's this about?"

Buddy laughed. "Don't be paranoid. Consider it

one college pal being hospitable to another. That's
the benefit of a Yale degree. Networking. Contacts."

Jake leaned back in his chair. "So this is business."

"I won't lie to you, Jake. My dad and I have some
ideas for the *Lamar Daily* we'd like to toss at you."

Tell me something I don't know. "Why aren't you discussing these ideas with the Sanders? It's their paper,
after all."

"The word on the street is that Mason Publishing
is taking over."

"Not taking over. There'll be a merger, but control of the paper will remain with the Sanders family."

Buddy chuckled. "Maybe that's the way it'll start,
but you know as well as I do that the health of Mason
Publishing comes first. Maybe we can make a deal
that'll leave all parties happy."

"The question still remains: Why haven't you
come to Sanders with this deal if it's so reasonable?"

Buddy sighed. "Sanders and his daughter are un-
reasonable. They aren't moved by money. They
won't even listen to our plan."

"Maybe they have good reason."

"Look," Buddy defended. "What happened with
the *Gaines Weekly* was a one-time thing. That's not
the way Hamilton News normally does business."

Jake wasn't too sure. He'd become skeptical of
Hamilton News when he'd learned how they'd
bought the *Gaines Weekly* one day and dismantled it
a week later, deciding it was more cost-effective to
have the paper in a larger town nearby, which they
also owned, do weekly inserts for Gaines instead of

producing a weekly Gaines paper. "I'm not sure I believe that, Buddy."

"Come on, Jake. This discussion we want to have is bigger than any one newspaper, including the *Lamar Daily*. Much bigger. At least hear us out. If you don't like the deal, there is no deal. If you like it, then we can talk. No strings."

Jake looked at his watch. "I'll think about this, Buddy, and let you know. I have to go now."

Jake said his goodbyes, hung up, and rushed out of the office to meet Eleanor. His instincts told him to have the meeting with Buddy. Maybe he'd get some information that he could use to sweeten the Mason-Sanders merger.

Eleanor, dressed in his favorite white thong swimsuit, was already in the pool when he arrived.

"What took you so long?" she asked when he dived in after her.

"I'm a busy newspaperman. Emergencies come up all the time."

"Bah." She kicked water in his face and swam away from him.

"You're going to pay for that," he challenged, charging out after her.

After an hour or so of enjoying Jake's company, Eleanor swam to the side of the pool and hoisted herself out. "I'm tired."

Jake swam to her and grabbed both her legs in his arms. "I'm not," he said, eyes dancing.

"Oh, no, you don't," she said, knowing where his thoughts were. "We have to get back to work."

"You're the boss. You don't have to be anywhere."

She pulled away from him before she gave in to the temptation he posed. "Not today."

He lifted himself up and sat next to her. "What do you know about Hamilton News?" he asked casually, drying himself with a towel.

"They're scumbags as far as I'm concerned." She went on to repeat the story of the *Gaines Weekly*. "They come to us every year with some wacko idea or another. We don't even bother to listen." She paused. "Why the sudden interest?"

Jake stood up, extended his hand to her, and helped her to her feet. "I got a call from Broderick Hamilton."

She stared up at him, her fingers tightening on his hand. "What? Why is Broderick Hamilton calling you?"

"There's nothing to be excited about," he said, rubbing her hand with his thumb in an effort to calm her. "Buddy and I are old college acquaintances."

She released his hand and stepped back a few steps from him. "And?"

Jake picked up his towel and casually threw it across his shoulder. "And he wants to have dinner with me."

"Just dinner?" she questioned, her eyes sharp with skepticism.

He moved close to her and pulled her into his arms. "That's all. You're welcome to come along if you like."

Eleanor shook her head, then relaxed against him. "That's not necessary. You go if you want, but don't believe anything they tell you about the *Lamar*

Daily, Jake. They've wanted our paper for a long time, but they're never going to get a piece of it."

Jake thought about her words, and wondered, not for the first time, if Eleanor was too emotional about the paper. He believed the sense of responsibility she felt for the paper kept her from doing some of the things she really wanted to do. He knew how much she wanted to work on *Our Family*, but she was going to deny herself that joy because she couldn't see turning over control of the *Lamar Daily* to anyone else.

That didn't seem right to Jake. He could hardly wait to dive into the new magazine and he wanted her to share that joy with him. Somehow he knew that his future and Eleanor's was with *Our Family*, not the *Lamar Daily*.

He made up his mind then. He was going to have dinner with Buddy Hamilton. What harm could it be to listen to what the man had to say?

Jake spread the final sheet on the desk in front of Carl and ran his index finger down the last column. "So what do you think?"

"I think Eleanor is not going to understand."

"I didn't ask you that," Jake said, knowing Carl was right. Since his meeting with Buddy last week, he'd tried to think of a way to tell Eleanor of his revised plans for the merger without her discarding them out of hand. But he hadn't come up with one. Yet. "I asked what you thought about the idea. Let me worry about Eleanor."

"It's a great idea, you know that. But is it worth Eleanor?"

"I told you. I'll worry about Eleanor." And he was worried about her. When he'd agreed to meet with Buddy, he'd had no idea the Hamiltons would suggest such a viable venture. When he'd heard their proposal, he'd known immediately that it was the angle he'd been looking for to impress his father. So, even though he knew Eleanor didn't trust the Hamiltons and wanted no association with them, he'd considered their deal. And when he'd presented a counterproposal with conditions that safeguarded the *Lamar Daily* and Mason Publishing, he'd been surprised and elated the Hamiltons had accepted it.

"Why will you worry about me?" Eleanor asked as she entered the office she shared with Jake.

Jake stopped his musing and got up, covertly turning over the pages he'd been showing Carl. "What are you doing here?" He bussed her cheek. "I thought you were taking the afternoon off."

Eleanor glanced at Carl. "Is he trying to get rid of me?"

Carl raised both hands. "I'm not in this." He nodded to Jake. "See you later, man."

Eleanor watched Carl leave the room, then turned to Jake. "What was that all about?"

Jake shook his head and pulled her to him. "Nothing."

"Jake, we shouldn't."

He touched his lips to hers. "And why shouldn't we?"

She gave in to the kiss, then stepped away from

him. "We decided to keep our relationship out of the office. No kissing, no touching."

"But I like touching you," Jake said, walking toward her with a gleam of passion in his eyes. He reached behind her and closed the blinds. "I don't know why I didn't think of this before. We could reserve the conference room every day for about half an hour. I bet that would get Maxine going."

Jake backed Eleanor to the wall and placed his hands on either side of her head, effectively trapping her. She stared into his eyes and quickly dropped her glance. That look in Jake's eyes usually caused a similar one in her own.

"Look at me," he said, as if reading her thoughts.

She chose instead to duck under his arms and stand next to the door. "What were you and Carl talking about?"

Jake stopped in midstride. "I told you."

"No, you didn't," she said, shaking her head as the alarm that had been building in her stomach since Jake's dinner visit with Buddy Hamilton last week grew.

Jake walked to the desk and gathered up his papers. "I was telling him about my plans for the *Lamar Daily.*"

Eleanor stiffened her back. "Your plans? I thought they were *our* plans."

Jake didn't look up. He hated lying to Eleanor, but what choice did he have? "You're right. Our plans. I meant our plans."

"Is there something you're not telling me, Jake?" She prayed there wasn't.

Jake looked at her and considered telling her the

truth. "No," he said instead. He needed more time to plan what to say to her. "Come on, I'll take you to lunch."

Eleanor let Jake lead her out of their office. She tried to ignore the unsettling feeling in her stomach. Surely Jake wasn't keeping secrets from her about his plans for the paper. She had to believe that wasn't what he was doing.

Though she tried to ignore them, her suspicions grew during their lunch.

"Have you heard anything more from New York about your proposal for the magazine?" she asked when their plates were cleared.

Jake shook his head, but she noticed he didn't look her in the eye. "Don't worry. I'll let you know as soon as I know something."

Eleanor nodded, but she didn't believe him. She silently chastised herself for not grilling him after his dinner with Buddy. Against her better judgment, she'd allowed herself to trust him, to care for him. The uneasy feeling in her stomach told her that may have been a mistake. She prayed her feelings were wrong.

Twenty-one

When Jake pulled Eleanor into his arms later that evening, he knew he'd been wrong to keep secrets from her. He should have told her everything immediately after that meeting with Buddy so they could have mapped out a strategy together.

But he hadn't told her. And now she was suspicious. He knew he hadn't appeased her with that flimsy excuse he made for the conversation he was having with Carl. No, she hadn't bought it and he knew she hadn't bought it. And now he didn't know how to tell her what he'd done without making her upset with him. But he'd find a way. He just needed more time.

He pressed his mouth against her naked breast and gloried in the moan his touch drew from her. He didn't know what gave him more pleasure—the joy of touching her or the joy of knowing he pleased her.

She arched against him and he knew she wanted what he wanted. He lifted his mouth from her breast and moved it to her lips.

"I need you," Eleanor moaned into his mouth.

He needed her, too. He raised himself slightly, then lowered until he was buried within her.

He waited until she reached her pinnacle, loving the play of emotions that danced across her face, then he let go and took his own pleasure. When he'd emptied himself, he remained atop her, luxuriating in their connected bodies. Realizing he was much too heavy to stay atop her all night, he rolled to the side and tucked her into his arms.

"That was so good," she said softly then drifted off to sleep.

As he watched her sleep, he acknowledged this woman had stolen his heart. Somewhere along the line, he'd fallen in love with her.

"I love you, Eleanor," he whispered, then joined her in sleep.

Eleanor awoke with a start, surprised but relieved her quick movements hadn't awakened Jake. She slowly lifted his hand from her belly and eased herself away from him. She held her breath when he mumbled her name, then released it when he folded his hand under his head on the pillow they had been sharing.

She got up from the bed, rubbing her arms to ward off a chill caused by the thoughts that had troubled her sleep. Keeping her back to Jake, she scanned the room for the clothes she had so quickly discarded in her need to be with him.

After she'd found all the items, she quickly slipped into them. When she was dressed, she returned to the sleeping Jake. Her heart turned over at the satisfied and peaceful look on his face, so different from the anxiousness that had been there before

they'd made love. She'd responded to that anxiousness, hoping he'd tell her what was on his mind.
But he hadn't. He'd taken her in his arms and loved
her as if he'd never let her go. If she didn't know
better, she'd believe Jake was falling in love with her.

But she did know better. Jake hadn't made her
any promises. She'd known when she'd first gone to
bed with him that what they shared would be temporary. Yes, she'd known that with her head, but
somehow the message hadn't made it to her heart.

Her traitorous heart had done her in. She was in
love with Jake Mason. She'd probably fallen in love
with him the day he'd lost his article in the computer. She smiled at the memory. But her smile
quickly turned into a sorrowful frown. She was in
love with Jake, but she no longer trusted him.

If only he hadn't been so tight-lipped about his
conversation with Carl. It had been obvious they
were discussing something he didn't want her to
hear. He should have known she wouldn't be satisfied with his half-answers. Obviously, he hadn't.

If only he didn't need his father's approval so
much. Though Jake didn't talk much about it, she
knew this assignment meant more to him than he
let on. This assignment was his chance to show Randolph he could handle the responsibility of Mason
Publishing. She knew that about him and she re-
spected it because she understood it. In a lot of ways,
Jake's relationship with his father was similar to hers
with her father.

If only he'd told her the truth instead of lying to
her. That was what really bothered her. If he'd re-
spected her enough, cared about her enough to tell

her the truth, she'd feel much better about the whole situation. She could handle a man making a business decision. She could fight that, but she couldn't handle lies, because they signaled other deceits.

If only.

Well, she couldn't deal in if-only's. Now she had to deal in what-ifs. What if Jake was planning the demise of the *Lamar Daily*? What if he'd only been sleeping with her to gain her confidence so he could destroy her? Keep your friends close and your enemies closer, the old saying repeated itself in her mind. Was what she and Jake had shared his attempt to keep his enemies closer?

She closed her eyes. There was no way she could look at this man who made her body sing and her heart race and believe he'd betray her. He couldn't after what they'd shared. She opened her eyes and drank in her fill of him. Could he?

She placed a soft kiss on his forehead. Thankfully, he didn't stir. She pulled away and wiped at the tear that fell against her cheek. She loved him, but she couldn't let him ruin the paper that was so much a part of her life.

She closed the bedroom door quietly as she left, thankful Carl now spent most of his time at Megan's. She couldn't handle running into him on her way out. Spotting her purse and car keys on the end table nearest the front door, she quickly picked them up and left the apartment.

She wanted to trust Jake, but she couldn't. Too much was at stake. She'd had him investigated before, but this time she'd have to do the investigating herself.

Jake patted the bed next to him. "Eleanor," he mumbled, then opened his sleepy eyes. "Eleanor," he called again, staring at the indentation in the bed that marked the place her body had been. Where was she? he wondered. "Eleanor," he called yet again, this time louder.

He threw back the sheet and climbed out of bed, stretching to relieve his tired muscles. He grinned. Maybe he could get Eleanor to join him in a nice, warm shower. He padded to the bathroom with that plan in mind.

"Eleanor," he said again, opening the bathroom door without knocking. He quickly scanned the room. She wasn't there.

Worried, he hurried down the hall to the kitchen and living areas, calling her name. Still no answer. Where was she? he asked himself.

He went back to the bedroom, dread building in his chest. Her clothes were gone. He raced back to the living room, pulled back the curtains, and peeked out the window. Her car was gone. He dropped the curtain. Why had she left without waking him? She'd never done that before.

He went back to the bedroom and dressed in an old pair of shorts, hoping he'd find a note from her among the disarray in the room. No such luck. No note told him much more than any note could ever speak.

He'd taken a calculated risk tonight and he'd lost.

He'd hoped he could keep his plans from Eleanor until he had them finalized, but then she'd overheard that conversation with Carl earlier today. He pounded his fist on his knee. "Damn."

He stood up and went into the bathroom. He needed an aspirin for this headache that had come on like gangbusters. He caught a glimpse of his face in the mirror on the medicine cabinet as he opened its door, and he stopped his motion.

Who was this man? he asked himself.

He shrugged. He'd thought coming to Lamar would help him answer that question for himself and his father. And with the revised plan he had for the merger, he knew he'd carve out a place for himself in Mason Publishing that would make his dad proud. Then why did the face staring back at him in the mirror look so grim?

He closed the cabinet door without getting the aspirin. Aspirin wouldn't help this headache. He needed to talk to Eleanor. He needed her to understand where he was coming from. Business was business, he would tell her. But even as he said the words to himself, he knew Eleanor wouldn't understand.

She may have understood yesterday. She may have even understood before he'd made love to her. But she wouldn't understand now. He knew how her mind worked, and he knew if she learned of his plans, she'd think he'd used her.

But he hadn't. Actually, the opposite had happened. He loved her. He knew that now. He had known it when he'd taken her in his arms. Hell, maybe he'd even known it the first day he'd seen her by the pool. God knows, his life hadn't been the same since.

He smiled to himself. Beautiful Eleanor. Mouthy Eleanor. Smart Eleanor. Sexy Eleanor. His Eleanor.

His Eleanor. That was how he thought of her now. That was who she had become to him. She was his and he wasn't going to lose her. He'd lost too much in his life. He'd had no control over losing his mother, but he could have fought harder to remain a part of his father's life. He would fight this time. He would fight for his father's respect and he would fight for Eleanor's love. He wouldn't let her push him away. And he knew that's what she was doing by leaving in the middle of the night. And he wasn't going to let his father down with this deal. Somehow he'd come up with a plan that was acceptable to him, his father, and his woman. He had to.

The phone rang. Again. Eleanor stood by her bathroom door and listened for Jake's voice after the beep. She'd successfully avoided all his phone calls and she wasn't going to break that record now.

"Pick up, Eleanor," Megan's voice called after the beep. "I know you're there. You can pick up. Jake's not here."

Eleanor sighed. Jake had camped out on her doorstep for the better part of the morning, but she'd pretended she wasn't home. She should have known he'd go straight to Megan and Carl to find out where she was.

"I'm going to keep talking, Eleanor," Megan said. "So pick up the phone."

"All right, already," Eleanor said to the phone, then raced to pick it up.

"What do you want, Megan?" she asked in a tight voice. She wasn't going to discuss her relationship with Jake. She wasn't.

"What's up with you and Jake? The man is frantic. And he's got Carl frantic."

Eleanor tapped her feet impatiently as Megan droned on. When Megan stopped for air, she said, "I don't want to talk about him now, Megan."

"Oh, Eleanor," Megan said, and Eleanor heard the pity and concern in her voice. "Do you want me to come over?"

Eleanor dropped down on the side of the bed. This was why Megan was her best friend. She knew her and she cared about her. "That won't be necessary. I'm all right."

"No, you're not," Megan said quickly. "And neither is Jake. What's the problem? You'll feel better if you talk about it."

Eleanor wiped her free hand across her forehead and leaned back on her pillows. How she wished that were true. "Not this time, Megan."

"You're sure?"

"Not really," Eleanor confessed, disarmed by Megan's quick acquiescence. "But it's the best I can do right now."

"That bad, huh?"

Eleanor laughed lightly. "Not so bad I can't handle it."

"What are you going to do?"

Eleanor glanced over at the airline ticket on the dresser. "I'm taking a trip."

"Alone?"

"Very much alone."

"You need to think, huh? I can understand that."

Eleanor didn't bother to correct Megan since she *would* have time to think while on this trip. But the real reason for her trip was fact-finding. She needed to get the line on what Jake was up to. And she wanted to do it without Jake and her father looking over her shoulder. If things were as bad as she thought, she'd need the time alone to decide how to deal with them. If she was wrong, well, she didn't think she was.

"Where are you going?"

Eleanor's attention returned to Megan. "New York," she lied.

"Do you want me to go with you?"

"I appreciate the offer, but I need to be alone. Besides, I don't think I'd want you around me when you're going through withdrawal."

"Withdrawal? What are you talking about?"

Eleanor laughed again. "You'd miss too many Carl shots and you'd go into withdrawal. I can't handle that."

Megan laughed too and Eleanor heard her speak to someone in the room with her, someone she guessed was Carl. "Do you want us to come over tonight?" Megan asked when she came back on the line. "I could even come without Carl for a couple of hours. Withdrawal shouldn't set in that quickly."

"You're sweet to offer, Megan, but it's not necessary. I'm leaving for Atlanta tonight." That was true, and Eleanor immediately regretted telling Megan. She didn't want it to get back to Jake.

"I assume Jake doesn't know this," Megan said.

"You assume correctly."

"And you don't want him to know."

"Correct, again. Do you think Carl can keep a secret?"

"It won't be necessary," Megan said. "I guarantee you I'll keep Carl so busy tonight he won't have a chance to even think about Jake."

Memories of last night with Jake filled Eleanor's mind. She wished she could lose herself in him tonight. But that wouldn't work. She couldn't lose herself in the very person she was trying to get away from.

"She's not coming in today, man," Carl said Monday morning, flipping on his terminal. "We have to get the paper out without her. Think we can do it?"

"Where is she?" Jake asked, dismissing Carl's question.

Carl scanned the morning's AP stories. "Out of town."

"Out of town?" Jake flopped down in the chair next to Carl's desk. "When did she leave?"

"Yesterday morning," Carl said, his attention on the screen in front of him. "I think."

Jake grabbed the arm of Carl's chair and turned him around. "You think?"

Carl stared at Jake's hand on the arm of the chair, then glanced up at him. "I told you she wasn't going to like it."

Jake stood and rubbed his hand across his head. "She doesn't even know what I'm planning."

"Okay," Carl said, and turned around in his chair.

Jake turned the chair around again. "Okay, man, talk to me. What did she tell Megan?"

"What makes you think she told Megan anything?"

Jake stared at him. "I'm not in the mood for games, Carl. I've been up all night trying to figure out how to handle this situation with Eleanor and she's not here. Where is she?"

"You aren't going to like it . . ."

"Where is she?" Jake asked again.

"She went to New York."

"New York?" Jake repeated. Franklin was in New York. Had she gone to see Franklin? She couldn't have. Eleanor wasn't the type of woman to go from one man's bed to another's. He was sure of that.

"I knew you wouldn't like it."

"Why'd she go to New York?"

Carl shrugged his shoulders and turned back around to his screen.

Jake didn't even know why he'd asked the question. He knew why she'd left town. Oh, he might not know the specifics, but he knew part of the reason she'd left was to get away from him.

"Do you know how long she'll be gone?"

"Megan said a couple of days."

Jake considered joining her. They could use some time away from Lamar and the paper. Some time for the two of them. "Where is she staying?"

"I didn't ask."

"Maybe Megan knows," Jake said aloud, though he was really talking to himself. If he could find out where Eleanor was staying, he could join her and explain that this deal was good for everybody involved.

Carl turned around in his chair. "Leave Megan out of this, Jake. She's Eleanor's best friend. Don't put her in the middle."

Carl's strident tone surprised Jake. "But I need to see Eleanor. Who knows what she's cooking up in her mind?"

Carl stared directly in his eyes. "I don't think she could cook up anything worse than the reality of your plan, at least not in her eyes. Wouldn't you agree?"

Jake opened his mouth to say the situation wasn't that bad, but he knew it was. He knew what the paper meant to Eleanor. He'd rationalized his actions by saying *Our Family* was her future. Their future. But he knew that wasn't a decision he could make for her.

Eleanor wanted *Our Family*, but she was duty-bound to the *Lamar Daily*. She'd outgrown it, but she wouldn't or couldn't let go. He'd thought he could help her break free, but maybe all he'd done was make her dig her heels in deeper.

Yes, he'd been wrong to make the decision without her. He'd known it when he'd held her in his arms last night. He wiped his hand across his face. Hell, he'd known it was wrong all along. That's why he hadn't told her about it, why he hadn't allowed her to decide.

Twenty-two

"So what are you going to do about it?" Megan asked after Eleanor told her what she'd learned of Jake's deception.

"I'm going to stop him," she said matter-of-factly. "No way is Jake Mason going to partner us with Hamilton News." She'd converted all her feelings of hurt and betrayal into determined vengeance. Jake Mason would pay for trying to use her and her paper.

"How?"

Eleanor shrugged. "I'm not sure, but believe me I'll come up with something."

"I bet you will," Megan muttered.

"What's that supposed to mean? You can't be siding with Jake on this."

"No," Megan began, twisting the top on her soda. "I'm not siding with him. He was wrong to keep secrets from you and he needs to answer for that. But I love you and I don't think you're facing your real feelings."

Eleanor snorted. She'd faced her real feelings and it hadn't been a pretty sight. Now was the time to put feelings aside and turn to action. "I see Jake for what he really is. I'm glad I found out before I—"

"Before you what? Fell in love with him?"

Eleanor didn't answer. She'd been about to say that but she couldn't because she knew it would have been a lie. She had been fool enough to fall in love with him. "It doesn't matter."

Megan reached over and touched her friend's knee. "It does matter. It matters more than anything."

"How can it matter when it's obvious he cares nothing for me?"

"I don't see how you can say that. It's not obvious to me."

Eleanor stared at Megan and wondered if she'd heard a word of Jake's deception. "He used me, Megan. He used me."

Megan sat back. "It doesn't look that way to me."

Eleanor rolled her eyes. Megan had turned into a Pollyanna ever since she'd fallen head over heels for Carl. "And how does it look to you, Dear Abby?"

"I think you need to face your real fears. Are you upset with Jake because of his plan or are you using that as an excuse to keep from following your heart?"

"I don't know what you're talking about."

"Sure you don't."

Eleanor lifted her lip in a smirk. "And what's that supposed to mean?"

"It means Jake's the first guy to come along and make you question your safe and perfect little world here. You seemed not to mind until he touched your precious paper. Why did that set you off?"

"You don't understand. The paper is my business, my career. I can't let him take it."

"Eleanor," Megan said softly. "The paper is not your mother."

Eleanor jerked her eyes away from Megan. "I never said it was. Why would you even say that?"

"Because you treat that paper like it's sacred. It's not. Sometimes I think that paper has more of a hold on you than your father does."

Eleanor jumped up. "That's just not true. I can't believe you're saying these things."

Megan didn't move. "I'm your best friend and I love you like a sister, but you're wrong this time. I don't want to see you throw away what you and Jake have because of some business decision."

"You don't understand. It's more than that. It's about Jake respecting my wishes. It's about him including me in his decisions. He didn't do either."

"Have you told him this?"

Eleanor shook her head. She hadn't spoken to Jake since the night she'd left him alone in bed. There was nothing to say.

"Now that's real mature of you." Megan sighed. "You have to let him explain."

Eleanor shook her head again. "I can't let him know how much I know. If he knows, he may take action to keep me from stopping him. I can't take that risk."

"But you can risk losing the only man you've ever loved because of your pride?"

"That's not it."

Megan watched her for a long second. "If you say so." She sighed again. "Do you want to go over to Welles tonight? Victoria's is having another sale."

* * *

Jake answered the door after her first knock. When she saw him, her heartbeat increased and the attraction that had always been between them flared. Thoughts of his plans for her paper doused the flames. She studied this man she'd loved and been loved by and wondered how she could have so misjudged his character.

It hadn't taken her long to learn of his plans. If she hadn't been so taken by him, she wouldn't have let things get as far as they had. Thank goodness she'd overheard him talking to Carl.

"Eleanor," he said finally. "Where have you been? I've been worried sick."

She brushed past him, determined not to let the concern in his voice deter her. She'd remembered many times while she was in Atlanta that he was a trained actor.

He closed the door, then followed her back into the living room. She didn't bother to sit down. "Why'd you do it, Jake?" she asked, hating the hurt that came through in her voice. She'd planned to handle this in a professional manner.

He reached for her and she moved away from him. "Just answer the question. Why'd you do it?"

He didn't flinch. "It's business, Eleanor."

Each word was a shot to her already aching heart. "Was what we shared in bed business, too?" she asked, her voice a whisper.

He reached for her again and this time she let him hold her. "How can you even ask that?"

She jerked away from him, hating the weakness she exhibited. She had to maintain some measure of dignity. "Because from where I'm sitting it looks like you were sleeping with me to keep me from questioning your actions. That was certainly one way of gaining my trust."

He flinched at her words and she was glad she'd hit her target. "How can you think so little of me after what we've shared?" he asked.

She gave an empty laugh and wondered where the sound was coming from. "Now, that's royal. How can I *not* think little of you, Jake? You've taken everything we've shared and thrown it back in my face. How could *you* think so little of what we've shared?"

"I did it for us—" he began.

She slapped him before he could finish his thought. "Stop lying to me. You didn't do this for me. You did it for yourself. For your own ego. It had nothing whatsoever to do with me."

He rubbed his jaw. "You're wrong."

"I wish I were," she said, marching toward the door. She had to get out of this apartment, out of his presence. She put her hand on the knob then turned around. "It's not over, Jake. I'm going to fight you to the end. Your plans aren't going to make it off the paper you've written them on. There is no way the *Lamar Daily* will get in bed with Hamilton News. You have my word on that."

"This isn't about the paper, Eleanor. It's about us."

She laughed that laugh again. "There is no us, Jake. There never was. At least, not in your mind. If you had thought of us, we wouldn't be having this argument now." She turned and swung open the door.

"You can't run from me, Eleanor," he called after

her, repeating the words he'd told her early in their relationship.

She turned around and stared at him. "I never thought I'd need to, Jake, but I do. After all that we've shared, I don't know who you are."

Jake winced at the slamming of the door behind her. He was tempted to go after her, but he knew it was no use. What could he say? She'd said it all, and unfortunately, she'd been right on most counts.

Except for one. She'd been wrong about them. He'd never used her. He hadn't even planned to get involved with her. Lord knows, his life would be much simpler now if he hadn't gotten involved with her.

But he had. Against all reason, he'd fallen for his business associate and the daughter of his father's best friend. And now he couldn't let her go.

Eleanor bumped into Carl as she rushed out of his apartment.

"Hey, hey," he called, catching her by her arms to keep her from falling. "You'd better watch where you're going."

"Sorry, Carl," she mumbled and sidestepped him to continue to her car. She didn't want to talk now. Especially not to Carl. He'd probably been in on Jake's plans from the beginning. She'd talk to him tomorrow when she was calmer.

Carl grabbed her arm again. "Hey, what's the matter? You and lover boy have another fight?" He grinned. "You two fight as much as some other couple I used to know."

Eleanor couldn't smile with him. Her and Jake's relationship was nothing like the one he shared with Megan. "I can't talk about this now, Carl." She couldn't. She feared she'd cry if she did. And she wasn't going to give Jake Mason the satisfaction of making her cry.

"You love him, Eleanor, and he loves you."

His words were so confident that Eleanor met his gaze for the first time. "He told you that? Is that how he convinced you to betray me?"

Carl shook his head sadly. "I didn't betray you."

Eleanor was tired of lying men. "Are you saying you didn't know what Jake was planning for the paper?"

Carl had the decency to look away. "I knew, but only after he'd formed the plan. I told him you wouldn't go for it. I told him you wouldn't understand."

She believed him. "And what did he say?" she asked, but she knew. It was obvious. Jake didn't care what she wanted.

"He loves you, Eleanor," Carl said instead of answering her.

"Oh, Carl, come on. Don't use that line on me. Did he ever say those words to you?" She hated the hope that budded in her chest as she waited for his answer. She was still looking for some way to exonerate Jake.

"Well, not exactly."

Her hope died as quickly as it had bloomed. "Just like I thought. Good night, Carl."

He grabbed her arm again and made her face him. "Can you walk away from him, Eleanor? You know what moves him as well as I do. Maybe you don't love him after all."

"You don't have to use reverse psychology on me, Carl. I *do* love him. I've admitted that much to myself."

"Then you two can work this out."

She reached up and touched his face, her anger at him gone. He only wanted her and Jake to find what he and Megan had found together. "We don't have what you and Megan have. We never did. It wasn't meant to be for us."

He placed his hand atop hers. "If I'd given up on Megan, we wouldn't be together now."

Eleanor laughed and patted his jaw before dropping her hand. "You did give up on her, remember? You two could barely stand to be in the same room together."

"But I never gave up on her. Why do you think I stayed in Lamar all these years?"

She smiled. "I guess it wasn't the paper."

He shook his head, a look of wonder and amazement and love on his face. "I'm here because she's here. I don't think I could've left even if she'd married someone else."

"I envy what you have with Megan," she admitted. She'd thought she and Jake might have a chance at that but she now knew that had been a pipe dream.

Carl chuckled. "You envy us now, but I bet you didn't about two months ago."

"Good point."

"I'm not saying Jake didn't make a mistake, Eleanor. He did. But it's not one that the two of you can't get past." He touched his right hand to her cheek. "Take my advice. Don't make any decisions that can't be reversed and don't say anything you can't take back. Love is too precious to throw away."

Eleanor watched the clock, turning off the alarm before it went off at six o'clock. She hadn't needed to set it since she hadn't slept all night. She couldn't. Her mind was too full of thoughts. Thoughts of Jake. And her. In this bed. In his bed.

She threw back the sheet and slowly moved her pajama-clad legs to the floor. The room even felt different. But she knew it wasn't really the room. It was her. She wasn't the same woman she'd been before she met him. And she'd probably never be the same again.

She straightened her shoulders, got up from the bed, and made her way to the bathroom. In twenty minutes she was dressed and on her way to the main house for breakfast with her father.

He was seated at the kitchen table sipping coffee when she walked in. "Morning, Dad," she said and kissed his upturned forehead.

Mathias smiled at her, but she didn't miss the question in his eyes. "What a nice surprise! You haven't joined me for breakfast in quite a while. To what do I owe this pleasure?"

She turned her back to him and poured a cup of coffee from the coffeemaker. "Could it be that I wanted to have breakfast with you?" She turned back around and leaned against the counter.

Mathias pushed his plate away. "Out with it, Eleanor."

She reluctantly lifted herself from the counter and

sat down at the table in front of her father. It was quiet in the kitchen this morning. Too quiet. "It's about Jake," she said slowly, running her fingers down the sides of her coffee cup.

Mathias placed his hands over her fingers and stopped their motion. "What did he do to you?"

The alarm in his voice surprised her. She squeezed his fingers briefly, then removed her hand and brought her cup to her mouth, taking a long swallow before speaking. "It's not what he did to me," she said, though it wasn't really true. It *was* about what he did to her, but that was not her father's concern. "It's what he's planning to do with the paper."

Mathias sat back in his chair, and Eleanor could have sworn she saw relief in his eyes. "I thought you two had come to a working agreement about the future of the paper."

"So did I." She gave a weak smile. "But Jake was a little smarter than I gave him credit for. It seems he had other ideas."

Mathias looked at his watch then stood up. "I'm meeting with the mayor this morning. I'm sure you and Jake will work this out."

She looked up at him and her heart broke. How could her father be so trusting of men so undeserving of trust? "Not this time, Dad. Jake has approached Hamilton News."

Mathias's eyes widened and he sat back down at the table. Eleanor had known the name of the newspaper consortium would get his attention. Hamilton News approached them at least once a year with a deal of some kind, but Mathias never considered any of their offers. "Why would he contact them?"

She should have been glad for the suspicion she heard in her father's voice because it meant he was taking off the rose-colored glasses where Jake and his father were concerned. But she wasn't. No, she hurt because she knew her father's so-called best friend's betrayal would cause him considerable pain.

"Why did he contact them?" Mathias asked again.

She looked down at her coffee cup, then brought her eyes up to meet her father's. "Money."

"Money?" Mathias repeated. "Why would Jake want money from them?" Mathias snapped his fingers. "Mason Publishing could swallow them up like that."

Eleanor shrugged her shoulders. This entire conversation was suddenly making her tired. "Maybe it's power. Who knows what's going through Jake's mind?"

"Power?" Mathias nodded. "Now that I can understand."

Eleanor couldn't believe her ears. Her dad obviously had a blind spot as big as the state of Alabama where the Randolph men were concerned. "Well, in his plan he gets both. Not only is Jake arranging a merger between Mason Publishing and the *Lamar Daily*, he's also bringing Hamilton News into the deal."

Mathias leaned forward anxiously. "What are you talking about?"

Eleanor cleared her throat. She was only going to say this once. "Jake wants to create Mason News, a wholly owned subsidiary of Mason Publishing. Mason News will be the beginning of a conglomerate of small-town newspapers. Of course, Jake will be president and CEO, and Buddy Hamilton, of Hamilton News fame, will be his second-in-command. He and Buddy plan to gobble up every small-town paper in the Southeast within five years. The *Lamar Daily* is their first conquest." Eleanor winced as she spoke the words. The pain of Jake's betrayal ran deep.

Mathias sat back in his chair. "Well, the boy has guts. I can say that."

"That's all you've got to say?" Eleanor yelled, infuriated at the calm in her father's voice. Had he completely lost his mind? "Jake and his father are going back on the spirit of this whole deal. If they partner with Hamilton News, where will our autonomy go?"

"Calm down, Eleanor," her father said, standing up again. "You're going to give yourself a heart attack. This is bad, but it's not that bad. I'll speak to Randolph."

Eleanor grabbed his arm. "It won't do any good, Dad," she warned. "Randolph has given Jake a free hand with this project. There's nothing he can do now without going back on his word to his son. We have to handle this ourselves."

"What do you think we should do, Mat?" Randolph asked after Mathias had repeated Eleanor's news.

Mathias was surprised at the calm he still felt. Ever since Eleanor had told him the news, he'd waited for his anger to surface. But it hadn't. "I don't know that we should do anything. Maybe we've done enough."

"You're willing to let Jake go through with his plan?" Randolph asked, obviously not believing that.

Mathias rubbed the bridge of his nose. "Maybe it's for the best, Randy."

"I don't believe what I'm hearing. You love that paper."

"Maybe that's the problem. It's a paper. Maybe it was wrong to have so much emotion invested in something that can't feel."

"What's on your mind, Mat?" Randy asked, knowing his friend too well.

"I've been thinking a lot about Barbara and about Eleanor since this morning. Maybe it's time for Eleanor and me to move on."

"What do you mean?"

"Well, the paper has played a large role in our lives since Barbara's death. I've always wondered if it kept Eleanor tied to Lamar. And to me." He sighed. "Maybe it's time for her to make the break."

"How does she feel about this?"

Mathias sighed. He knew his Eleanor was feeling a lot of things these days. She was angry with Jake because of his plans, but she was also hurt by what she read as his betrayal. "She's hurting, Randy, but she won't go down without a fight. Jake's in for it."

Randolph chuckled softly. "In a way, I'm proud of him, Mat. No, this isn't what I wanted, what we wanted, but it's something of his own doing. I can understand him wanting his own business without my interference."

"I feel the same way. Your boy is turning out to be quite a man. I hope my Eleanor will see it that way."

"I think she will, Mat. I know it sounds strange for me to say, but I think Eleanor is going to find herself in this, too."

"I hope you're right." Mathias knew his daughter was in pain, but there was nothing he could do about it. He and Randolph could step in and effect some changes on the business front, but it was her personal life that caused the greatest wounds. He hoped she and Jake would work it out.

"So we're going to wait it out, see what they do?"

Mathias took a deep breath. "That's all we can do." He was silent for a couple of seconds. "Did you ever think it would come to this?"

"No," Randolph said quickly. "Do you regret what we've done?"

Mathias thought hard. "No, I don't. Sometimes change is necessary. We knew all we could do was bring them together. Now it's up to them."

Twenty-three

Jake met his father at the Atlanta airport at noon the next day.

"How're things going, Jake?" Randolph asked, stirring his vodka and tonic.

Jake observed his father, still wondering about this impromptu visit. He knew his father well enough to know there was a specific purpose for the meeting. He wondered what it was. He hoped his father wasn't checking up on him. "Moving right along," Jake said, trying not to give away too much. He'd wait for his father to reveal his hand first.

"Have you and Eleanor worked out the agreement?"

Jake met his father's gaze, trying to decide if there was more to the question than the obvious. Not seeing anything, he shrugged. "We're making progress. I think you'll like the proposal."

Randolph nodded and took another sip of his drink. "I'm sure I will."

They were both silent for a couple of minutes. Jake watched the red, white, and blue Delta jets through the windows while Randolph nursed his drink.

"I'm glad to have you working with me on this

deal, Jake," his father said. "I know I was a bit heavy-handed when I gave you the assignment, but I'm proud of what you're doing. I wished we could have worked together sooner."

A lump formed in Jake's chest. He hadn't expected this. He cleared his throat. "Well, it's been good for me, too."

Randolph nodded again. "I want you to run this business someday, you know." He grinned. "Not too soon, though. I still have a few good years left in me."

Jake grinned too and his shoulders straightened. "More than a few years, I hope."

"Yes, yes," Randolph said. "I'm sorry we didn't get started together sooner."

Jake ran his hand up and down his glass of water. "Why did it take so long, Dad?" Jake asked the question that had puzzled him for years. He held his breath while he waited for the answer.

"I don't really know." Randolph sighed. "After your mother died, I was lost. I didn't know what to do with a child. Your mother was the caretaker." A smile softened the older man's face and Jake wondered at the memory that triggered it. "Anyway, after she was gone, I did what I thought was best. I took you with me."

"There was nothing wrong with that. I loved being with you."

Randolph met his son's gaze. "I know you did, but that was no life for a growing boy."

"So you left me at home?" Jake couldn't keep the distaste out of his mouth.

Randolph winced. "I thought it was the right

thing at the time. Your mother and I always wanted you to have a better life than we did. We didn't want you to struggle like we did."

"So you made sure I had the best of everything?"

Randolph nodded. "I tried. I tried my best." He cleared his throat and Jake wondered if he was about to cry. "I've always loved you, Jake. I missed you and I wanted you with me, but it wasn't fair to you. I had to work and you needed a regular life."

"I needed a father," Jake said softly.

Randolph released a long breath. "I know that now. Aw, hell, I guess I figured it out over the years. But it was too late, the damage had been done. We'd grown so far apart I didn't know how to reach you."

Jake nodded. They had grown apart. Sure, they talked often and saw each other regularly, but they didn't share their lives. He couldn't remember when they had. "I used to sit at your desk in your office at the house and pretend I was you." He slowly rolled his shoulders back at the memory. "I'm not sure if I wanted to be you or if I wanted to be like you. Maybe if I was more like you, you'd want to spend time with me."

Randolph's eyes did mist then. "I'm so sorry, son. Do you think you can forgive your old man?"

When Jake looked at his father, he knew the older man wasn't sure what his answer would be. "There's nothing to forgive."

"Yes, there is. I want you to forgive me for giving you things when I should have given you myself. I want you to forgive me for ignoring your interest in the business, our business, when you were younger. I should have encouraged that. I know that now."

Jake nodded. "Is that why you gave me the assignment in Lamar?"

Randolph raised his brow. "You didn't seem to be interested in the business anymore. I had to find a way to get you involved." He paused. "Why'd you take the assignment? You didn't have to, you know."

The memory of his father ordering him to take the assignment made him smile. "That's not exactly how I remember it."

Randolph laughed a rich, full laugh and his eyes cleared of their mist. "I was a bit forceful, but that's never stopped you from ignoring my wishes in the past. Why this time?"

Jake shifted in his seat. "I thought it was some kind of test and I wanted to prove to you I could do it."

"It was never a test, Jake. I had no doubts about your ability. Your will, maybe, but never your ability."

Jake examined his father's eyes and saw only his sincerity. He lips curved in a smile. "I wish I had been as sure."

"You're doing a good job. Hell, a great job."

Jake's chest puffed out at his father's words. "Thanks. It means a lot to hear you say that."

Randolph cleared his throat. "Well, you'd better remember it because it may be the last time."

"Somehow I already knew that," Jake said with a grin.

"So," Randolph began. "How's it really going here? I got a call from Mathias."

Jake's shoulders stiffened. So, his father had come to check up on him.

"Don't get all ruffled on me. This is still your deal. I'm here if you need me. I want you to know that."

Jake relaxed. "What did Mathias say?"

Jake nodded when Randolph finished telling him of the concerns Eleanor had expressed to Mathias.

"So she's right?" Randolph concluded.

"She figured out most of it," Jake said, then told his father the details of his plan.

"Whew, that's some deal you've worked. How did you get Hamilton News to agree to your terms?"

Jake leaned forward, warming to the topic. "This is all verbal. Nothing has been done contractually, as you know. Hamilton News has been trying to do this for a while. They saw the *Lamar Daily* as their first step. When we got involved with the *Lamar Daily*, they thought they could work a deal with us to get a piece of it." He shrugged his shoulders. "I countered. I hate to admit it, but I was surprised when they went for it."

Randolph was quick in his response. "Hell, that's the way it is with most big deals. You study, you plan, you make your pitch, and you hope like hell they go for it. How do you think I built this business?"

Jake grinned. "I thought you were a shrewd businessman, smarter than all your competition."

"That, too. But big business takes guts. And you've got them. Not everybody does."

"Well, some of the credit goes to Buddy Hamilton. He's stepped into his father's shoes and he's determined to make a new name for Hamilton News."

"Aha," Randolph said, after taking a sip from his glass. "I ought to call the older Hamilton for a drink to celebrate."

"You know, this isn't the response I expected from you."

"What did you expect?"

"For you to think I'd betrayed you by trying to carve out something of my own."

Randolph shook his head. "Never. You remind me of me when I was younger. I wanted to build something of my own. I understand those feelings in you. It's part of being a man."

Those were exactly Jake's feelings. He was relieved his father understood. Why couldn't Eleanor? "Too bad everybody doesn't understand that."

"Eleanor?"

Jake lifted his gaze in surprise. "How'd you guess?"

"I saw the way you two looked at each other when you were in New York. I'm not so old I've forgotten what desire looks like. Do you care about her, son?"

Jake nodded. "It's a difficult relationship. Hell, it may not even be a relationship anymore."

"She's that upset?"

"She doesn't trust Hamilton News and refuses to even consider our plans as a valid business decision. One that will benefit all of us. The paper is like family to her and she wants things to stay as they are."

"So you've talked to her about it?"

Jake shook his head slowly. "Not in any detail. She's not talking to me much these days."

"What are you going to do about that?"

Jake stared at him. "What can I do? She doesn't understand how important this is to me."

"And you don't understand how important the paper is to her?"

"That's not it. You don't understand—"

Randolph held up his hands. "I *do* understand. But now you're facing the decision I had to face with you. Do you make the best business decision or the best personal decision?"

Eleanor tucked her pen in her mouth and scrawled her options on the sheet in front of her. Option 1: Shoot Jake. Option 2: Run over Jake. Option 3: Strangle Jake.

She dropped her pen on the table, folded her hands across her stomach, and wished Randolph's flight would hurry up and arrive. She'd been waiting over two hours now and she was getting cabin fever.

She looked over at the bar and her gaze met that of a rather handsome, dark-skinned brother with a mustache. Any other time she might have smiled at him, but not today. Today she gave him a haughty glare that said she was unavailable and uninterested. Unfortunately, the man must have been dense for he hopped off the bar stool and made his way toward her table. Oh, no, she thought.

"Eleanor," she heard a voice call from behind her.

"Randolph," she said, relieved he was here. She stood and rose up on her toes and bussed his cheek. "Sorry," she whispered, "but that guy over there was about to make a move on me."

Randolph hugged her to him and chuckled. "At least the young man has great taste."

Eleanor moved away from the older man and returned to her chair. A cheerful feeling bubbled up in her as she remembered the last time she'd seen him. "You're too much, Randolph."

Randolph pulled out the chair next to her and took a seat. "So what's happening with you and Jake?"

"You don't waste any time, do you?"

Randolph signaled the waiter for a drink. "Time's too precious to waste. When you're my age you'll appreciate that."

"You and Dad certainly use your age to your advantage, but I don't see either one of you slowing down."

Randolph grinned at her. "Won't work, young lady. This conversation is about you and Jake, not about me and your father."

Eleanor met his gaze. "I think the issue is your relationship with my father. He entered into a good faith agreement with you, and your son has reneged on it. What are you going to do about it?"

The waiter delivered Randolph's drink and he took a sip before answering her. "I can see why Jake fell in love with you."

Eleanor swallowed hard. She hadn't expected that. "Let's keep this professional, Randolph," she said calmly. "Are you going to keep your word to my father?"

Randolph sighed. "Technically, Jake has adhered to the *law* of the agreement. And as for the *spirit* of that agreement, well, I've already spoken with your father about that. We've reached an understanding."

An understanding. That didn't sound good. "Exactly what kind of understanding are you talking about?" she asked slowly.

Randolph leaned forward and pulled one of her hands into his bigger ones. They were warm to the touch and she was somehow comforted by them. "Mathias understands this is Jake's project. My hands are tied."

Eleanor snatched her hand out of his. "Why are you doing this to us?" she asked. "My father thinks you're his best friend."

Randolph leaned back in his chair and brought his glass to his lips. "I am his best friend."

She snorted. "You sure have a funny way of showing it. Is that how you built Mason Publishing—by taking advantage of all your friends?" Randolph visibly recoiled at her words, but she didn't feel any triumph that her jab had hit. She stood and gathered her belongings from the table. "Yes, I know about the ruthless Randolph Mason, building his empire with no regard for anything or anyone but himself. My father was never in your league."

"You—"

Eleanor waved her hand in dismissal. "Forget it, Mr. Mason. I thought Jake was a bastard, but maybe I was wrong. Maybe he's just his father's son."

Eleanor turned on shaky legs, head held high, shoulders straight, and walked away from Randolph Mason.

"Eleanor," he called after her.

She stopped but she didn't turn around.

"Be angry with me. Be angry with your dad. Hell, be angry with Jake, but don't give up on him. He loves you and he needs you."

She stiffened at his words, wishing they were true. But they weren't. She swallowed deeply and continued out of the restaurant. She had work to do if she was going to keep her newspaper.

Twenty-four

Eleanor jumped when the smooth hand touched her shoulder and the keys to her cottage fell to her feet.

"I'm sorry," Jake said, bending over to pick up her keys. "I didn't mean to frighten you." He handed her the keys.

"What do you want, Jake?" she asked, trying to calm her shaking fingers so she could insert the key in the door.

"We need to talk."

He stood so close she felt his breath on her neck. "It's a little late for that now, isn't it?" She breathed a relieved sigh when she finally got the door open and slipped inside.

"You should have talked to me, Eleanor."

She turned around and faced him. "I should have talked to you?" she said, her voice rising. "You have some nerve, Jake Mason." She moved to close the door in his face, but he inserted a loafer-shod foot in the opening.

"We have to talk," he said. "Please."

The softness of his plea made her heart warm to him, but she couldn't give in to it. She couldn't let him use her again. "It won't do any good. I don't trust you, Jake. We should have talked before you made plans to sell out my newspaper."

He blinked rapidly and she wondered if his eyes were wet. They couldn't be, could they?

"I care about you, Eleanor. We can't end like this."

"You care about me? You care about me? Well, you have a funny damn way of showing it." She pushed the door against his foot, hoping the pain would make him move it. It didn't.

"I'm not leaving until we talk."

She could tell from the firm line of his lips he was telling the truth. She could let him in for a few minutes or she could stand there all night. She released her hold on the door and walked into her cottage.

Jake followed her. When he was seated on the couch, he began, "I know I should have told you about my plan . . ."

She wiped her hands across her face. She was so tired. "You didn't make any commitments to me, Jake. We both knew this was a business deal. I was a fool to trust you."

He winced at her words, then reached for her. She pulled back. "You weren't a fool."

She shook her head slowly. "Yes, I was. Every time I made love to you, I was a fool." She smiled a sad smile. "Did you get a kick out of it, Jake?"

"It wasn't like that."

She lifted a brow. "What was it like then?"

He didn't answer immediately. He wanted to tell her that he loved her and wanted a future with her, but he knew her anger would force her to throw the words back at him. He wanted to tell her that his actions were not premeditated, that his relationship with her hadn't been part of some diabolical scheme.

She stood up. "Just like I thought. I think you should go now."

Jake felt they had played this scene before. Eleanor asks how he feels and he holds back. Not this time. "I'm not through yet."

"I think you are," she countered, impatiently tapping her foot on the hardwood floor.

He looked down at his folded hands then raised his gaze to her. "I met with my father a couple of days ago," he began.

"This doesn't interest me, Jake," she said, but it did interest her.

"Anyway," he continued, as if she hadn't spoken, "we talked like we hadn't talked in a long time. He understands what I'm doing, Eleanor. Why can't you understand? Why does this have to come between us?"

She strode to the door and grabbed the knob. "Oh, I understand, all right. I understand that proving something to your father is more important than keeping your word to me. That's what I understand."

He shook his head. "I haven't lied to you, Eleanor. My only sin was keeping you out of my discussions with Buddy Hamilton."

"Don't forget selling out my newspaper," she added, her eyes full of anger and hurt. The anger he could handle, but it almost killed him to see the hurt. And to know that he had put it there.

"I haven't sold out your paper," he said calmly. "Buddy Hamilton—"

"I don't want to hear about Buddy Hamilton. You knew how I felt about Hamilton News and you still went behind my back and made plans to align my newspaper with them. Don't tell me you didn't think that would make me angry."

"I thought I could make you understand," he said, but he knew his words fell on deaf ears. Eleanor wasn't ready to listen to him. Yet. "I wasn't trying to hurt you. I was trying to help myself. And us. My plan can benefit both of us."

She dropped her hand from the doorknob and propped it on her hip. "The paper is everything to me, Jake. I've told you over and over that I want complete control. Why did you even consider a deal with Hamilton News? They're control freaks."

"It's not as bad as you think. They were willing to deal on a lot of issues."

Eleanor shook her head. "I don't want to hear it. This paper belongs to the Sanders family. I don't want anyone else involved in it."

"You were willing to let Mason Publishing become involved," he noted carefully.

"That's because I let you deceive me. Like a fool, I thought caring feelings were associated with your erotic touches. I was wrong." She eyed him. "What was I, Jake? A summer fling, after all?"

Jake stood up and went to her. "It wasn't like that. How many times do I have to tell you?"

She reached for the door and opened it. "You don't have to tell me anything again. Get out."

He touched her cheek with the back of his hand

and she moved her head away. "I'm going to prove to you it was more than that for me."

He stepped out of the door and she slammed it behind him.

Eleanor settled back on her bed with the latest Evelyn Coleman mystery, hoping to take her mind off her troubles for at least a short time. Making that call to Hamilton News was the hardest thing she'd ever done. But she'd had to do it. If Jake had made a deal with the devil, she had to know the details of it before she could fight it. And at this point, she didn't trust Jake enough to believe his statement of the facts.

The sound of her doorbell startled her. She quickly jumped up from the bed, tightened the belt on her robe, and ran to the door. A part of her wondered if it was Jake. "Who is it?"

"It's me, Eleanor," her father's voice answered.

Eleanor sighed, not sure if she was happy or sad it wasn't Jake, then opened the door. Her father stood there still dressed from his day at the office. "Is something wrong, Dad?"

Mathias shook his head. "I wanted to talk to you. I haven't seen you much around the paper."

Eleanor stood back so he could enter the cottage. "Carl and Jake are taking care of everything, aren't they?"

Mathias entered the cottage and eased onto the couch. "Of course, but I still miss you. I've been worried about you."

Eleanor leaned against the mantel in front of him.

"There's no need to worry. I'm taking care of business."

"That's what I'm worried about," Mathias muttered. He patted the space next to him. "Come over here and sit down."

She moved over to him. "What's wrong?"

He took her hand in his. "I don't want you to fight Jake on this."

"What?" She tried to pull her hand away but his hold tightened.

"You heard me. I don't want you to fight Jake on this."

"Why not?" she asked, wondering what Jake or his father had said to her father to make him give up so easily.

"Because we need a change around here."

"What did Randolph say to you, Dad? How did he convince you to go along with Jake?"

Mathias shook his head slowly. "Randolph didn't have to say anything. This is my decision."

She jerked on her hand again, but still he wouldn't release it. "I bet this is your idea. Just like it was your idea to bring Mason Publishing into our business. Why are you letting those people use us?"

"Is that what you think I'm doing?"

The tinge of sadness in his voice almost stopped her words. "That's what it looks like. First, you bring them here against everything you've ever taught me and now you're willing to let them throw our paper willy-nilly at Hamilton News. What's happening to you?"

Mathias patted his daughter's knee. "You're a good child, Eleanor. You always have been."

Eleanor wondered where all this was coming from, but she didn't have time to ask.

"I did my best to raise you after your mother died, but sometimes I wonder if I didn't do the wrong thing by bringing you into the paper so early."

She shook her head and tried to keep a lid on the anxiousness that was building in her. "You raised me right. And you did the right thing by bringing me into the paper. I loved you and I loved the paper. I still do. Don't you know that?"

"Maybe I do. But haven't you ever wondered what your life would've been like if you'd stretched your wings beyond Lamar? I've held you back, Eleanor. You were meant for greater things than a small-town paper."

Her heart rebelled at the words. "That's not so, Dad. I love working at the *Lamar Daily*. I love Lamar."

He rubbed his thumb across the back of her hand. "I know you're frustrated a lot, Eleanor."

"No more than any other newspaper managing editor," she said, dismissing his concern.

"I don't think other editors have to deal with reporters and columnists who've known them since they were kids and still treat them that way."

She smiled at his observation. "It's not that bad."

"And what about your idea for the magazine? Haven't you ever thought about dropping your duties with the *Lamar Daily* and pursuing that dream?"

Yes, she'd thought about it. More than once. But she'd never been able to do it. The magazine was a dream. The *Lamar Daily* was reality. It was her heritage. "The *Lamar Daily* is more than a paper."

He smiled sadly. "No, it's not. That's the problem. To us it's become more than a paper."

She looked toward the mantel, not liking the direction this conversation was taking. "And that's bad?"

"Not in and of itself. But when you look at the big picture, it takes on a different spin."

"And what's the big picture?" she asked, not sure she wanted to hear his answer.

He tightened his hold on her hand, and she turned to him. "The big picture is a grieving husband and his motherless daughter seeking refuge in the family business."

Tears quickly filled her eyes. "And what's wrong with that? At least we had some place to seek refuge."

"There's nothing wrong with it, but we sought refuge too long. Pretty soon we started hiding."

She wiggled her hands free of his and wiped at her eyes. What could she say? She'd never thought of it that way. She'd told Jake as much. "I don't think we're hiding."

"Then what are we doing? I'm a fifty-five-year-old man and I've been sneaking around with Maxie for almost fifteen years."

Eleanor's eyes widened. "You and Maxine? Fifteen years?"

Mathias nodded. "Me and Maxie. Fifteen years. I call that hiding."

Eleanor felt as if the wind had been kicked out of her. How could she have missed a fifteen-year relationship? "I knew Maxie had a crush on you, but I never knew you returned her feelings."

"That's because I didn't want you to know. I didn't want you to think I was cheating on your mother."

"But Mom was dead. How could you cheat on her? You could have told me. I would've understood and I would've been happy for you."

"Maybe."

"You don't think I would've been happy for you?"

"I don't know."

She leaned into him. "Oh, Dad. I'm so sorry you had to sneak around."

He patted her knee. "Don't worry about me and Maxie. We'll be okay. As a matter of fact, we're coming out of the closet."

"You're getting married?" she asked, not sure how she would feel if he said he was.

He chuckled. "I asked her, but she likes the status quo. Maybe when things change at the paper, she'll change her mind."

"So you have personal reasons for going along with Jake's plans?"

He nodded. "I used the paper for a lot of years to hinder my personal life. I think it's only fitting that now I use it to further my personal life."

Eleanor chuckled. "You and Maxie. I don't believe it."

"It's good to hear your laughter. I haven't heard much of it lately."

She sobered. "There hasn't been a lot to laugh about."

"Nobody ever said love was easy."

"Love?"

"That's what this is really about, isn't it, Eleanor? You love him, don't you?"

* * *

Carl opened the door as Jake was about to insert his key. "Hey," Carl said. "It's about time you got home."

"I'm glad I caught you before you left," Jake said, rushing into the apartment. "I need to talk to you. Can you give me a few minutes?"

Carl checked his watch. "I guess I can spare a couple of minutes. We have dinner reservations for eight."

Jake hung his jacket on the back of one of the kitchen chairs and sat down. "Come over here."

"What is it?" Carl asked, making his way to the table.

"I've been talking to Buddy Hamilton."

Carl whistled. "Don't I know it. Megan is practically spitting fire. I told you Eleanor wasn't gonna like it."

"Sit down. Sit down."

"Hold your horses, I'm sitting down. What do you want to show me?"

Jake pulled a legal pad out of his briefcase. "Here's the latest deal." He'd gone over the highlights with Buddy on the phone. He wanted one more meeting with him before presenting the plan to Eleanor.

Carl picked up the pad and began reading. Jake felt hope spring up in him when a smile slowly spread across Carl's face.

"So, what do you think?"

Carl clapped him on the back. "I think you should've come up with this deal first."

Jake wished he had. He'd almost lost the most important thing to him in his macho quest to impress his father. "What do you think Eleanor will say about this one?"

"She'll go for it."

"I hope so," Jake said, knowing she had to go for it. He couldn't go through his life without her.

"You finally realized what was important."

Jake gave a wry smile. "It took me long enough." His father's words about making the best business decision or the best personal decision had stuck with him and he'd been able to come up with a third alternative—a decision that satisfied both his business and his personal needs.

"I hate to say this . . ."

Jake grinned. "Go ahead and say it."

"I told you so."

Jake clapped Carl on the back. "Thanks for that, friend. The next time you give me advice about my woman, slap me if I don't listen."

Carl rubbed his hands together. "Can I get that in writing?"

Jake laughed.

Carl looked at his watch, then stood. "So when are you going to tell Eleanor?"

"As soon as I get a formal okay from Buddy."

"And when are you going to ask her to marry you?"

Jake's heart hammered in his chest. "As soon as I think she'll give me the answer I want. I'm willing to wait."

"Take my advice. Don't wait. She's in love with you."

The hope that Eleanor still loved him kept Jake going. "From your mouth to God's ears. I can't live without her, Carl."

"Welcome to the club." He grinned. "Ain't love grand?"

As Eleanor closed the blinds in her living room in preparation for going to bed, she acknowledged the effect Jake Mason still had on her life. Her closing blinds? She couldn't remember the last time she'd had her blinds open. Since she'd walked around her house nude most of the time, it served her better to keep the blinds closed. That was before Jake Mason.

Tonight was an after-Jake Mason night and she was closing blinds that she'd had open all day. As a matter of fact, her blinds had been open every day since she'd gotten back from her fateful fact-finding trip. No use keeping them closed since she no longer walked around nude.

And Jake Mason was the reason she no longer walked around nude. She couldn't do it anymore. She couldn't bear her naked body without thinking of him and how he'd made love to her, so she kept herself covered. She sighed. She'd given too much of herself to him before she found out that he was undeserving.

After the blinds were all closed, she checked the lock on the front door and headed for the shower. She slipped out of her pink terry cloth sweatsuit and threw it in the hamper. She glimpsed her naked form when she walked by the bathroom mirror, but she quickly averted her eyes so as not to see herself.

It was still too painful. She couldn't look at her breasts, her body, without feeling the caress of his hands, his mouth.

She stepped into the shower and let the warm water work its magic. In here, alone, she could relax. In here, for a short while at least, she could forget her problems.

When she was sufficiently relaxed, she turned off the shower, stepped out onto the cool tiled floor, and grabbed a towel to dry herself. Once she was dry, she slipped on her gown, then left the bathroom and climbed into her bed.

She closed her eyes, but sleep wouldn't come. That was not unusual in her post-Jake Mason world. She couldn't go to sleep without thinking about him, what she'd felt for him, and what she'd experienced with him.

Tonight her father's comments joined her regular thoughts. "You love him, don't you?" her father had asked.

She hadn't answered him, but she knew the answer. Yes, she loved Jake. She'd probably always love him. But she wasn't sure if love was enough. What was a relationship without trust?

She didn't trust Jake. He'd betrayed her as surely as if he'd slept with another woman. She shuddered at the thought, then shook her head. No, his betrayal hadn't reached that depth.

She turned restlessly toward the clock. Her mother's clock. How she wished her mother were here now! Relationships were almost too difficult for a woman to handle without an advocate. And her

mom would have been her advocate. She was sure
of it.

When she turned away from the clock and closed
her eyes, she saw Jake the last night they'd made
love. In his eyes, she saw love. Love for her.

She'd seen that same look in his eyes the day she'd
confronted him in his apartment. And it had still
been there when he'd confronted her at her apartment.

"I want you to love somebody so much it hurts,"
Franklin had told her. "You know it's real when it
hurts, when you've given all you think you have and
you still have to give more. You know it's love when
you're willing to dig deep to find the extra strength
it takes to make the relationship work."

Eleanor loved Jake. And though he hadn't spoken
the words, she believed he loved her. She'd walked
away once from a man who loved her; could she do
it again when she loved him back?

Eleanor arrived at the newspaper early the next
morning. Again, she wanted to beat Jake in. She col-
lected the papers from the stoop, tucked them under her arm, and let herself in. She smelled Jake's
cologne as soon as she entered their office. A feeling
of contentment washed over her and she could
hardly wait to see him. After a night of soul-searching, she'd decided to put the past in the past and
move forward with the future. A future that included
Jake. It was a decision she believed her mother
would commend.

She'd thought about going over to Carl's, but she

decided it was more appropriate they meet on the grounds of the battle. Taking a seat at her desk, she flicked on her computer and pulled up the AP stories. It was good to be back in her routine again.

"Morning, Eleanor."

Jake's voice floated over her skin. She turned around and drank in the sight of him. "Morning, yourself," she said, noting that he looked tired. "What's wrong?"

He placed his briefcase on his desk and leaned back on its edge. "I should be asking you that."

She stood and sat on the edge of her desk facing him. Their knees touched, but she didn't pull away. "Why didn't you tell me?" she asked, no venom or anger in her voice.

He shrugged. "I didn't think you would understand." He moved his knee away. "And I was right."

She shook her head slowly. "I didn't understand your lying to me and your keeping secrets from me. You'll never know whether I would have understood the reasons for your plans."

He twisted around, pulled open his briefcase, pulled out a legal pad, and handed it to her. "Here's the deal. What there is of it."

She took the pad, never taking her eyes from his. "Why are you showing it to me now?"

"Read it." He ignored her question.

She handed the pad back to him. "I don't need to read it."

He stared at her hand for a long second then took the pad. "You're not going to give me chance to explain, are you?"

She heard the frustrated defeat in his voice.

"There's nothing to explain. I've done a lot of soul-searching, Jake. And I know what I want." She walked over to the window. "You asked me once to trust you. Well, I'm going to trust you now." She twisted the cord and the blinds closed. His mouth dropped open.

"What are you up to, Eleanor?"

She sauntered back to him and draped her arms around his neck. "Do you love me, Jake?" She hoped her uncertainty didn't sound in her voice.

He clasped his arms around her waist and pulled her tight against him. "I've missed you so much."

"But you didn't answer my question." She pulled back from him and stared into his dark, inviting eyes. "Do you love me?"

He lifted his hand and traced a line down her jaw. "I didn't think I could love anybody the way I love you."

She bit her lip to keep back her tears of joy and fell back in his embrace. "I love you, too."

She reveled in the massaging motion of his hands along her back. When his hand moved around to caress her breast, she moaned.

He pushed her slightly away from him and captured her mouth in a life-giving kiss. They were both out of breath when he pulled away.

He touched his fingers to her lips softly, as if he were touching something precious. "Your lips are so soft. You can't know how it feels to touch them after having been apart from you."

She kissed his fingertip and captured his hand in hers. "Oh, yes I can. I've missed you more than you can know."

He stared into her eyes and she wondered what he was looking for.

"You don't mind about my plans for the paper?"

She kissed him softly on the lips. "This paper has been a part of my life for as long as I can remember. In some ways it filled the void left by my mother's death. So, I do care about your plans."

He rubbed his finger along her bottom lip. "Then why are you here with me now? Are you trying to torture me?"

She chuckled at the distress in his voice. "No, I'm not trying to torture you."

He pulled away from her and stood up. "What do you want from me, Eleanor?"

"All I want is your love." She rested her head against his back and wrapped her arms around his waist.

He turned in her embrace and looked at her with hard eyes. "And you want me to stop my plans. Is that what this is? Blackmail? I get you if I give up my plans."

Her heart filled with pain at the anguish in his voice. "I wasn't sure enough of your love to come up with a plan like that."

He buried his head in her shoulder. "You should have known."

"I'm not psychic, Jake. You should have told me."

"I did," he whispered against her skin.

She pulled back. "No, you didn't. Believe me, I would remember something like that."

"You were asleep."

"When was this?"

He kissed her lips. "The night you skipped out on me."

"I'm sorry about that."

"It doesn't matter," he said, but she knew it did.

"It does. I shouldn't have left like that, but I was afraid. You'd made such sweet love to me. I could almost feel your love. Yet I knew you were keeping something from me. I wondered if I was falling for an act." She smiled. "You do have acting training, you know."

"There was never any acting between us, Eleanor. Every time I've touched you, I've loved you." He slapped her bottom. "Don't you think we'd better open the blinds?"

"Do we have to?"

He pushed her away. "We still have a paper to get out."

She walked to the window and opened the blinds. "Oh no," she said, covering her mouth with her hands.

Twenty-five

Jake turned and saw the smiling faces of Carl and Megan. "Damn!"

Eleanor dropped her hand from her face. "My sentiments exactly. Brace yourself, they're coming in."

"And what have you guys been doing in here?" Megan asked, wagging her finger at them. "We've been waiting for the blinds to open for the last hour."

Eleanor rolled her eyes. "Now that was an exaggeration of an exaggeration."

Jake looped an arm around Eleanor's waist. "To what do we owe the pleasure of your visit this morning?" He winked at Carl. "Maybe I should say, Who?"

"We have an announcement," Carl said, pulling the blinds closed again.

"You're getting married!" Eleanor practically screamed.

Megan flashed the three-carat diamond on her left hand. "Yes, yes, yes."

Eleanor stepped away from Jake and enveloped her friend in a hug and soon both women were crying happy tears.

Jake extended a hand to Carl. "Congratulations, man."

"Thanks," Carl said, pulling Megan back to him. He kissed her forehead. "I couldn't let her get away."

"I had to drag him to the jewelry store," she said. "I thought he didn't want to marry me."

Carl shook his head. "That wasn't it. I wanted to pick out the ring myself. I wanted it to be a surprise."

She kissed him. "I love you, Carl Winters."

Jake caught the joyous look on Eleanor's face as she watched the engaged couple. She saw him looking at her and gave him a smile between her tears. He pulled her to him. "I love you, Eleanor Sanders," he whispered.

"Oh, Jake," she said.

Jake pressed a kiss on her forehead, cleared his throat, and said, "Come on, everybody. Let's stop with the crying. Eleanor and I want to take you two to dinner tonight to celebrate."

"Sounds like a good idea to me," Megan said. "I think we have a lot to celebrate. Do you two have an announcement to make?"

Jake grinned down at Eleanor. "Let's say we've called a truce. We'll keep you posted on any other developments."

Eleanor looked at her watch. "Sorry to break this up, guys, but we have a paper to get out."

"I told you she was a slave driver," Carl said to Megan as he led her out of the office.

Jake opened the blinds again. "The staff will be talking about us. Do you think we should say something to them?"

Eleanor shook her head. "I don't think we'll have to say anything." She pointed to the newsroom, where Megan and Carl had a group of people surrounding them. "They'll be too busy talking about Carl and Megan's engagement."

Jake grinned. "I wish this were the end of the day instead of the beginning."

Her eyes took on a glazed look and his groin tightened. "So do I," she said.

Jake cleared his throat again. It was going to be a long day. "I'd better get to work."

Eleanor didn't release his gaze. "Maybe you should."

Jake moved from one foot to another. "You'd better stop looking at me like that or they're going to have to get this paper out without us."

Eleanor grinned. "Is that a threat or a promise?"

"Eleanor," Jake warned, his gaze traveling from her feet to her head before settling on her lips.

Eleanor released her breath. "Okay, I get your message."

"You don't," Jake said with intensity. "But you will. I promise you that."

Jake went through the day in a state of sexual anticipation. He tried to keep his mind off Eleanor, but he couldn't do it. Her presence surrounded him and filled his every thought.

By lunchtime, he was exhausted.

"How about a swim for lunch?" Eleanor asked, a gleam in her eyes, and Jake understood the invitation was for more than a swim.

He licked his lips. "You certainly know how to hurt a man."

"What do you mean?" she asked, her eyes bright and inviting. "I only asked if you wanted to go for a swim."

"I can't," he said softly. "I'm really sorry, but I have a business meeting."

Her smile dimmed. "Oh."

"No, oh." He got up, walked to her desk, and sat on its edge facing her, his back to the newsroom. "I have a meeting with Buddy Hamilton."

"Oh," she said again, and he knew she was wondering at the wisdom of giving him her trust.

"I love you, Eleanor."

"I know," she said finally.

"And don't forget it. I'm going to make this right for us. Do you believe me?"

She wore a grave look as she considered his question. When the corners of her mouth turned up in a smile, though slight, he knew they were going to be all right.

Jake held Eleanor's hand for the entire drive from the restaurant where they'd had an enjoyable dinner with Carl and Megan to Eleanor's cottage. They didn't talk much, because there was nothing more to be said. He'd gotten a verbal okay from the Hamiltons today and he'd had to force himself to wait until they were alone to tell Eleanor the details.

He glanced over at her. She faced straight ahead and he wondered where her thoughts were. He knew she'd been taken aback by his lunch meeting with the Hamiltons, but she hadn't said anything. She'd given him her trust and she wasn't going to take it back. Her trust and confidence in him made him feel strong and capable. With a woman like her by his side, he knew he'd always take the high road.

She glanced over at him and smiled when he pulled up into her drive. He placed a soft kiss on her hand, then got out of the car and opened her door. He smiled at the memory of the first time he'd taken her out when she hadn't bothered to wait for him to do the task. He was glad she'd waited tonight.

When she grasped his hand to lift herself out of the car, he pulled and she fell into his arms. He crushed her to him, then pushed her back slightly so he could see her face. He lowered his head to kiss her and she closed her eyes in anticipation. He groaned, then rested his chin against the top of her head.

"What is it?" she asked softly.

"I can't kiss you now," he forced out.

"Why not?"

He gazed down into her questioning eyes. "Because if I kiss you now, we may not make it to the house."

Passion blazed in her eyes. "I see."

He turned up the corners of his mouth. "You don't, but you will."

He took her hand in his and led her into her house. It seemed to take forever to get the door unlocked, but finally they were in the house. As soon as the door closed behind them, he pulled her into his arms.

"It's been too long, Eleanor," he murmured. "I've missed you so much."

She wrapped her arms around his neck. "Oh, Jake."

The pressure of her breast against his chest made him moan. "I want to go slowly, and make this beautiful for you, but I don't know if I'll be able to. I need you so much."

She pressed a series of kisses along his neck. "Who wants to go slow? I need you too, Jake."

That was all he needed. He lifted her off her feet and carried her to the bedroom. His knees almost buckled when he reached the bed and she nipped at his ear. "Eleanor, you're going to make me come too soon if you don't stop."

"I can't stop," she said sluggishly. "I want you. Now."

He deposited her on the bed and would have pulled back to discard his clothes, but she wouldn't release the hold she had on his neck.

"No," she said. "Don't leave me. Please don't leave me."

He sank down against her. "I won't leave you. I couldn't leave you. You're my heart. Don't you know that?"

She lifted her head and pressed her mouth against his in answer. Jake lost all rational thought. Eleanor's passion consumed him.

Soon they were pulling at each other's clothes. She was as impatient to feel his naked body against hers as he was to feel hers.

When they were both finally naked, he was so taut he entered her with haste. "Did I hurt you?" he asked when she moaned loudly.

She rolled her head back and forth on the pillow

and lifted her hips in rhythm with his. His thrusts were hard and fast, but he could do it no other way. He was glad when she reached her climax, because he knew he couldn't wait for her.

Eleanor awoke contented, but feeling a bit decadent. Blood rushed to her face when she thought about their earlier coupling. It had been wild and primitive. A necessity, not a desire.

She twisted in Jake's arms until she could see his face. Her heart turned over at the contented smile he wore even in his sleep. She knew exactly how he felt because she felt the same way.

Tonight had been different. Tonight there had been no pretense between them. With the confession of their love, they'd removed all barriers to the perfect expression of that love. They hadn't verbally spoken of a future together, but tonight she'd made that commitment as surely as if she'd accepted his marriage proposal.

Not that he'd made a marriage proposal. He hadn't, but she believed he would. Soon. And she'd be Eleanor Mason. Mrs. Jake Mason.

"What are you smiling about?" Jake's sleepy voice asked.

She kissed the tip of his nose, glad he was awake. "A girl has to have some secrets."

"Secrets? I thought we got rid of all those earlier tonight."

So she'd been right. He'd felt it, too.

"It was good with us before," he continued, his finger tracing a line along her lips, "but tonight was phenomenal. I now know what it means to be *one* with somebody. Do you understand what I'm saying?"

She nodded, not trusting her voice to speak. His words touched a chord in her heart and she knew theirs was a forever kind of love.

"I love you more than I thought I could love anybody. There's nothing I wouldn't do for you. Nothing."

"Oh, Jake," she moaned. The intensity of his words made her body warm with the need to be close to him.

He folded her into his arms. "I won't let you go. You know that, don't you?"

"I know," she whispered, feeling safe and cherished in his arms.

"Nothing will ever come between us again. I promise."

"I know that, Jake. You don't have to say it."

He brushed her hair back from her face. "Yes, I do. I want us to be like we were tonight forever. I don't ever want anything to come between us again. Not even our work."

"It won't, Jake. We'll make the right decisions for the right reasons."

He kissed her again, needing to touch her more. When the phone rang, his first impulse was to ignore it, but the singsong voices of Megan and Carl on the answering machine caught his attention.

"We'll understand if you two are busy and can't answer the phone," they began, then interrupted themselves with giggles. "We wanted to make sure you two knew you were the best man and maid of honor at our wedding." More giggles. "Or that could be matron of honor if you make it to the chapel before we do." More giggles. "Since you two haven't picked up, I guess we'll hang up and let you get back to what you're doing." More giggles and then dial tone.

Jake dropped his head in the space between Eleanor's neck and her shoulder. "They're outrageous."

Eleanor chuckled. "But they're perfect for each other."

He pulled back and looked at her. "And we're perfect for each other."

"Prove it," she challenged, a sensual gleam in her eyes.

"There's nothing I'd rather do," he responded and began to show her all the ways they were perfectly matched.

Twenty-six

Jake's face was the first thing she saw the next time she woke up. She wanted to wake up to that face every day of her life. "Good morning," she said, reading the love in his eyes.

He kissed the tip of her nose. "I love you, Eleanor Sanders."

A contented feeling settled in her stomach. She wanted to experience that feeling every day of her life. "And I love you, Jake Mason."

"Sit up. I want you to see something." He turned to the nightstand and brought out a legal pad like the one he'd handed her earlier when they were in the office.

She handed the pad back, then raised her eyes to him. "Why don't you tell me what it says."

"It's a new deal."

She smiled. "I kinda thought that."

"With Hamilton News."

"Oh."

He kissed her quickly on her lips. "No, oh. I didn't make the decision this time. We'll make it together."

She smiled, knowing that he wasn't talking about only this decision, but every decision they'd ever make. "Okay, what are our options?"

He kissed her again, lingeringly. "We can go with the original deal the two of us had mapped out. You stay at the helm at the *Lamar Daily,* and I take the helm of *Our Family.*"

She touched her lips to his again. "What's the next option?"

"Okay," Jake said, barely able to form a rational thought. He wanted her again. "We merge the *Lamar Daily* and Hamilton News and begin to build the largest consortium of small-town papers in the country."

"Hmm," she said, nibbling on his lips. "And who's in charge of this new consortium?"

"You and Buddy run the consortium, and I run *Our Family* as a separate entity."

She reflected on this possibility, the queasy feeling in her stomach about Buddy's involvement replaced by a cautious acceptance of the need for change. "Any more options?"

He couldn't resist one more kiss. "Same as the last. We merge with the Hamiltons. But Buddy and your dad run the consortium, while you and I build *Our Family* together."

She leaned into him, pressing her breasts tight against his chest. "I like the sound of that."

He pulled back, wanting to make sure he'd heard her correctly. "What?"

"You and I building our family together. I like the sound of that."

His heartbeat raced. "Does that mean what I think it means?"

She smiled at him. "Depends on what you think it means."

He pulled her into his arms and tilted her face up so he could see her. "Are you going to marry me, Eleanor?"

"I think that's what I said."

He crushed her to him, relief flooding his body. He and Eleanor had a future. After a few seconds of holding her close, he asked, "So which option do you want for the paper?"

"Which one do you want?"

"It doesn't matter. As long as I have you, it doesn't matter."

She pulled back and looked up at him. "What about your father? Which option will impress him most?"

He looked deep into her eyes and knew he was a changed man because of her. He'd come to Lamar to impress his father with a megabusiness deal. But somewhere along the line he'd fallen in love with a mouthy Southern miss who'd showed him what was really important. "I think Dad wants me to be happy. As long as my decision keeps you in my life and in my bed, he'll be impressed." He paused. "So, the choice is yours. I'm yours."

She squeezed him to her. "You and me and *Our Family.*"

He looked down at her. "Are you sure this is what you want?"

She nodded. "I want a future with you, Jake. I want us to build something together. My father and my mother built the *Lamar Daily* and it'll always be my legacy, the legacy of our children. But I also want to give them something from us. A legacy started by you and me."

His eyes darkened and he kissed her again. When he lifted his head, he said, "I guess we have a deal."

She grinned. "Though I was never too high on the idea of a Mason-Sanders merger, I now think this alliance could be the best thing that's ever happened to me."

Epilogue

"Twins?" Mathias propped his feet up on the table in front of the couch in Randolph's library and stuck an unlit cigar in his mouth. "Can you believe they're going to have twins?"

Randolph lit Mathias's cigar, then got one for himself. He'd ordered four cases as soon as he'd heard Eleanor was pregnant. A second order for four more cases followed when he'd learned she was having twins. Not one to stand on tradition, he'd already started giving them away. "My great-grandmother's sister had twins. It's those strong Mason genes."

Mathias harrumphed, then tapped his cigar on the ashtray in front of him. "We did it, didn't we, Randy?"

Randolph pulled the cigar from his mouth and blew a circle of smoke. "I never doubted it, Mat. I never doubted it."

"Neither did I, Randy. Neither did I."

Angela Benson

When Angela Benson sold her first book, **BANDS OF GOLD,** to Pinnacle Books, it was a dream come true. Since then, Angela has continued to dream. And she's seeing those dreams come true. Reviewers proclaimed her second novel, **FOR ALL TIME,** a book "all women should read." December 1995 brought her short story, "Friend and Lover," in the Arabesque Holiday Anthology, **HOLIDAY CHEER.** Her next book, **THE WAY HOME,** is scheduled for release in March 1997.

A graduate of Spelman College and Georgia Tech in Atlanta, Angela is a retired engineer who now writes full-time while she works on her second graduate degree. She uses her professional training and experience to provide realistic characterization and motivation for her strong and independent, yet vulnerable, heroines.

A native of Alabama, Angela currently resides in the Atlanta suburb of Decatur. When she's not weaving her own tales of romance, Angela can be found curled up on her couch reading her favorite romance authors.

Angela loves to hear from readers. Write to her at P.O. Box 360571, Decatur, GA 30036.

Look for these upcoming Arabesque titles:

June 1996
SUDDENLY by Sandra Kitt
HOME SWEET HOME by Rochelle Alers
AFTER HOURS by Anna Larence

July 1996
DECEPTION by Donna Hill
INDISCRETION by Margie Walker
AFFAIR OF THE HEART by Janice Sims

August 1996
WHITE DIAMONDS by Shirley Hailstock
SEDUCTION by Felicia Mason
AT FIRST SIGHT by Cheryl Faye

SENSUAL AND HEARTWARMING
ARABESQUE ROMANCES FEATURE
AFRICAN-AMERICAN CHARACTERS!

BEGUILED   (0046, $4.99)
by Eboni Snoe
After Raquel agrees to impersonate a missing heiress for just one
night, a daring abduction makes her the captive of seductive Nate
Bowman. Across the exotic Caribbean seas to the perilous wilds of
Central America . . . and into the savage heart of desire, Nate and
Raquel play a dangerous game. But soon the masquerade will be
over. And will they then lose the one thing that matters most . . .
their love?

WHISPERS OF LOVE   (0055, $4.99)
by Shirley Hailstock
Robyn Richards had to fake her own death, change her identity, and
forever forsake her husband, Grant, after testifying against a crime
syndicate. But, five years later, the daughter born after her disappear-
ance is in need of help only Grant can give. Can Robyn maintain
her disguise from the ever present threat of the syndicate—and can
she keep herself from falling in love all over again?

HAPPILY EVER AFTER   (0064, $4.99)
by Rochelle Alers
In a week's time, Lauren Taylor fell madly in love with famed author
Cal Samuels and impulsively agreed to be his wife. But when she
abruptly left him, it was for reasons she dared not express. Five years
later, Cal is back, and the flames of desire are as hot as ever, but,
can they start over again and make it work this time?

*Available wherever paperbacks are sold, or order direct from the
Publisher. Send cover price plus 50¢ per copy for mailing and
handling to Penguin USA, P.O. Box 999, c/o Dept. 17109, Bergenfield, NJ 07621. Residents of New York and Tennessee must
include sales tax. DO NOT SEND CASH.*

PUT SOME FANTASY IN YOUR LIFE—
FANTASTIC ROMANCES FROM PINNACLE

TIME STORM (728, $4.99)
by Rosalyn Alsobrook

Modern-day Pennsylvanian physician JoAnn Griffin only believed what she could feel with her five senses. But when, during a freak storm, a blinding flash of lightning sent her back in time to 1889, JoAnn realized she had somehow crossed the threshold into another century and was now gazing into the smoldering eyes of a startlingly handsome stranger. JoAnn had stumbled through a rip in time . . . and into a love affair so intense, it carried her to a point of no return!

SEA TREASURE (790, $4.50)
by Johanna Hailey

When Michael, a dashing sea captain, is rescued from drowning by a beautiful sea siren—he does not know yet that she's actually a mermaid. But her breathtaking beauty stirred irresistible yearnings in Michael. And soon fate would drive them across the treacherous Caribbean, tossing them on surging tides of passion that transcended two worlds!

ONCE UPON FOREVER (883, $4.99)
by Becky Lee Weyrich

A moonstone necklace and a mysterious diary written over a century ago were Clair Summerland's only clued to her true identity. Two men loved her— one, a dashing civil war hero . . . the other, a daring jet pilot. Now Clair must risk her past and future for a passion that spans two worlds—and a love that is stronger than time itself.

SHADOWS IN TIME (892, $4.50)
by Cherlyn Jac

Driving through the sultry New Orleans night, one moment Tori's car spins our of control; the next she is in a horse-drawn carriage with the handsomest man she has ever seen—who calls her wife—but whose eyes blaze with fury. Sent back in time one hundred years, Tori is falling in love with the man she is apparently trying to kill. Now she must race against time to change the tragic past and claim her future with the man she will love through all eternity!

Available wherever paperbacks are sold, or order direct from the Publisher. Send cover price plus 50¢ per copy for mailing and handling to Penguin USA, P.O. Box 999, c/o Dept. 17109, Bergenfield, NJ 07621. Residents of New York and Tennessee must include sales tax. DO NOT SEND CASH.

FOR THE VERY BEST IN ROMANCE—
DENISE LITTLE PRESENTS!

AMBER, SING SOFTLY (0038, $4.99)
by Joan Elliott Pickart
Astonished to find a wounded gun-slinger on her doorstep, Amber Prescott can't decide whether to take him in or put him out of his misery. Since this lonely frontierswoman can't deny her longing to have a man of her own, who nurses him back to health, while savoring the glorious possibilities of the situation. But what Amber doesn't realize is that this strong, handsome man is full of surprises!

A DEEPER MAGIC (0039, $4.99)
by Jillian Hunter
From the moment wealthy Margaret Rose and struggling physician Ian MacNeill meet, they are swept away in an adventure that takes them from the haunted land of Aberdeen to a primitive, faraway island—and into a world of danger and irresistible desire. Amid the clash of ancient magic and new science Margaret and Ian find themselves falling helplessly in love.

SWEET AMY JANE (0050, $4.99)
by Anna Eberhardt
Her horoscope warned her she'd be dealing with the wrong sort of man. And private eye Amy Jane Chadwick was used to dealing with the wrong kind of man, due to her profession. But nothing prepared her for the gorgeously handsome Max, a former professional athlete who is being stalked by an obsessive fan. And from the moment they meet, sparks fly and danger follows!

MORE THAN MAGIC (0049, $4.99)
by Olga Bicos
This classic romance is a thrilling tale of two adventurers who set out for the wilds of the Arizona territory in the year 1878. Seeking treasure, an archaeologist and an astronomer find the greatest prize of all—love.

Available wherever paperbacks are sold, or order direct from the Publisher. Send cover price plus 50¢ per copy for mailing and handling Penguin USA, P.O. Box 999, c/o Dept. 17109, Bergenfield, NJ 07621. Residents of New York and Tennessee must include sales tax. DO NOT SEND CASH.

IF ROMANCE BE THE FRUIT OF LIFE—
READ ON—
BREATH-QUICKENING HISTORICALS FROM PINNACLE

WILDCAT   (722, $4.99)
by Rochelle Wayne
No man alive could break Diana Preston's fiery spirit . . . until seductive
Vince Gannon galloped onto Diana's sprawling family ranch. Vince, a
man with dark secrets, would sweep her into his world of danger and
desire. And Diana couldn't deny the powerful yearnings that branded
her as his own, for all time!

THE HIGHWAY MAN   (765, $4.50)
by Nadine Crenshaw
When a trumped-up murder charge forced beautiful Jane Fitzpatrick to
flee her home, she was found and sheltered by the highwayman—a man
as dark and dangerous as the secrets that haunted him. As their hiding
place became a place of shared dreams—and soaring desires—Jane
knew she'd found the love she'd been yearning for!

SILKEN SPURS   (756, $4.99)
by Jane Archer
Beautiful Harmony Harper, leader of a notorious outlaw gang, rode the
desert plains of New Mexico in search of justice and vengeance. Now
she has captured powerful and privileged Thor Clarke-Jargon, who is
everything Harmony has ever hated—and all she will ever want. And
after Harmony has taken the handsome adventurer hostage, she herself
has become a captive—of her own desires!

WYOMING ECSTASY   (740, $4.50)
by Gina Robins
Feisty criminal investigator, July MacKenzie, solicits the partnership of
the legendary half-breed gunslinger-detective Nacona Blue. After being
turned down, July—never one to accept the meaning of the word no—
finds a way to convince Nacona to be her partner . . . first in business—
then in passion. Across the wilds of Wyoming, and always one step
ahead of trouble, July surrenders to passion's searing demands!

*Available wherever paperbacks are sold, or order direct from the
Publisher. Send cover price plus 50¢ per copy for mailing and
handling to Penguin USA, P.O. Box 999, c/o Dept. 17109, Bergenfield, NJ 07621. Residents of New York and Tennessee must
include sales tax. DO NOT SEND CASH.*

DENISE LITTLE PRESENTS
ROMANCES THAT YOU'LL WANT TO READ
OVER AND OVER AGAIN!

LAWLESS (0017, $4.99)
by Alexandra Thorne
Determined to save her ranch, Caitlan must confront former lover Comanche Killian. But the minute they lock eyes, she longs for his kiss. Frustrated by her feelings, she exchanges hard-hitting words with the rugged foreman; but underneath the anger lie two hearts in need of love. Beset by crooked Texas bankers, dishonest politicians, and greedy Japanese bankers, they fight for their heritage and each other.

DANGEROUS ILLUSIONS (0018, $4.99)
by Amanda Scott
After the bloody battle of Waterloo, Lord Gideon Deverill visits Lady Daintry Tarrett to break the news of the death of her fiance. His duty to his friend becomes a pleasure when lovely Lady Daintry turns to him for comfort.

TO SPITE THE DEVIL (0030, $4.99)
by Paula Jonas
Patience Hendley is having it rough. Her English nobleman husband has abandoned her after one month of marriage. Her father is a Tory, her brother is a patriot, and her handsome bondservant Tom, an outright rebel! And now she is torn between her loyalist upbringing and the revolution sweeping the American colonies. Her only salvation is the forbidden love that she shares with Tom, which frees her from the shackles of the past!

GLORY (0031, $4.99)
by Anna Hudson
When Faith, a beautiful "country mouse", goes to St. Louis to claim her inheritance, she comes face to face with the Seatons, a wealthy big city family. As Faith tries to turn these stuffed shirts around, the Seatons are trying to change her as well. Young Jason Seaton is sure he can civilize Faith, who is a threat to the family fortune. Then after many hilarious misunderstandings Jason and Faith fall madly in love, and she manages to thaw even the stuffiest Seaton!

Available wherever paperbacks are sold, or order direct from the Publisher. Send cover price plus 50¢ per copy for mailing and handling to Penguin USA, P.O. Box 999, c/o Dept. 17109, Bergenfield, NJ 07621. Residents of New York and Tennessee must include sales tax. DO NOT SEND CASH.